Zoe stood beside a crib.

She looked at the baby, the fierce love etched on her face stopping Mitch from moving. He'd always thought Zoe was pretty, but now she took his breath away. Becoming a mother had transformed her. She was no longer just his high school sweetheart. Before him stood a full-grown woman, a mother, who had become more beautiful in the time he'd been away.

"Come see your son."

Leaning on the cane, he made his legs move forward. When he came to the side of the crib and gazed down at the sleeping boy, with one thumb brushing his lips, his breath caught.

A longing, unlike any he'd ever experienced before, pummeled him. This was his son. His flesh and blood. A mira

Dear Reader,

It's summertime in Cypress Pointe. Finally, you get to be a guest at the weddings you've been waiting for since the Business of Weddings series started. I've loved spending time in this beach community, loved visiting old friends and new, so wrapping up stories from previous books has been gratifying and a tad bittersweet.

His One and Only Bride features Zoe and Mitch Simmons. High school sweethearts, they thought their lives would be filled with days of happiness and a household full of children. Fate wasn't so kind, and as the two ponder the state of their marriage, they learn the true meaning of love.

I had so much fun writing baby Leo. Children have a tendency to steal scenes in a book, and after all the angst and heartache it took for Zoe and Mitch to finally get this little bundle of joy, he was worth every moment. He brought me back to those early days of motherhood, remembering the ups and downs of parenting with fond memories and joy.

I hope you've enjoyed the adventures in Cypress Pointe. What started out as a book about brides turned into a series about wedding professionals that I have loved from start to finish. I look forward to moving on with a new series full of strong heroines, daring men and lots of adventure. Until then, enjoy reading Zoe and Mitch's story.

Happy reading!

Tara

HEARTWARMING

His One and Only Bride

___

USA TODAY Bestselling Author

Tara Randel

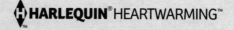

ISBN-13: 978-1-335-63346-0

His One and Only Bride

HARLEQUIN®
www.Harlequin.com

Printed in U.S.A.

Tara Randel is an award-winning, *USA TODAY* bestselling author of fifteen novels. Family values, a bit of mystery and, of course, love and romance are her favorite themes, because she believes love is the greatest gift of all. Tara lives on the West Coast of Florida, where gorgeous sunsets and beautiful weather inspire the creation of heartwarming stories. This is her sixth book for Harlequin Heartwarming. Visit Tara at www.tararandel.com. Like her on Facebook at Tara Randel Books.

Books by Tara Randel

Harlequin Heartwarming

The Wedding March
The Bridal Bouquet
Honeysuckle Bride
Magnolia Bride
Orange Blossom Brides

To Mark, Sarah and baby Leo. Thanks for your friendship and letting me hang out with your son. Mark, thanks for always answering my questions.

CHAPTER ONE

"By the virtue of the authority vested in me under the laws of the state of Florida, I now pronounce you husband and wife. You may kiss the bride."

Zoe Simmons took a big step back as the groom hauled his bride in for an enthusiastic smooch. The bride wrapped her arms around her new husband's neck while the guests clapped and hooted their congratulations.

Once the couple disengaged, with wide grins meant only for each other, Zoe peered around them to say, "It is with great pleasure that I introduce to you for the first time, Lilli and Max Sanders."

Lilli sent Zoe a grateful smile, and Max winked before tucking his bride's hand securely into the crook of his arm as they turned toward the happy faces before them. Linked in the promise of a new life together, the newlyweds strode down the aisle.

With a bittersweet sigh, Zoe watched them walk away.

When she'd agreed to officiate this marriage—a privilege she'd never considered as part of her duties as the mayor of Cypress Pointe, but then soon learned it was a tradition—she'd had good intentions. Lilli had been her friend for years and even though standing here stirred up a bittersweet web of emotions, Zoe wanted to be part of her friend's special day. In the past few years, Zoe had generally avoided weddings, especially since…

Don't go there.

The guests filed out of the pews, chatting and greeting friends and family. The mother of the bride, artfully dressed in a jade-colored designer dress and shoes, wiped her eyes with a lacy handkerchief. The bride's father, tall and distinguished, spoke into her ear. The woman broke out into a wobbly laugh.

Never having known her own father, Zoe had walked down the aisle alone at her small wedding ten years ago. She tried to deny the slight hint of jealously at Lilli's good fortune, then decided to be honest with herself. This wedding had been a million times different than her own.

"Zoe. Are you coming?"

Shaking off the direction of her thoughts, Zoe nodded, briskly placing her regrets where they belonged, buried deep down in her heart. Today was about Lilli and Max, not the what-ifs and could-have-beens shadowing her own life. There would be plenty of time later, when she was alone, to mull over the events that had led to her current state of affairs.

"I'll be right there," she told her date.

Date. It still sounded strange. She'd been out with Tim three times now. He was fun, smart and good-looking. *What's not to like, right?* When he'd first approached her, it had been at a fund-raiser they'd both attended. After spending the entire evening talking, he'd asked her out. It had seemed like a good idea at the time. Hadn't she just decided to put herself out there? See what could happen? The initial date, dinner at an Italian restaurant, had been awkward but soon they'd eased into a companionable friendship. He made her laugh and went out of his way to take care of her. You couldn't ask for more. So why did she hold back? Was she afraid to put her heart on the line? She hadn't totally recovered from the fallout of her marriage, which probably said it all.

Gathering the binder containing the wedding script and her small clutch, she watched the scene playing out at the back of the church. The maid of honor fussed with the bride's veil. One of the groomsmen slapped the groom on the back and made some comment they both laughed over. The flower girl, darling in a pretty pink dress, chased the ring bearer, who tugged at the bow tie circling his neck.

Zoe moved down the center aisle, savoring the sweet herb-scented fragrance of lavender bunches, tied together with twine ribbon, at the end of each pew. Wide swaths of lace were draped between the rows. The ceremony had been simple, along with the rustic decorations. Lovely flower arrangements of white, purple and yellow wildflowers spilled from dark brown rectangular baskets, adorning the platform in the front of the church. In the back, additional woven handbaskets of daisies complemented the bright bouquets carried by the bride and her attendants. The early June weather had been perfect. Not a humid Florida day, as had been predicted. Instead, a light breeze and sunny sky created a picturesque wedding tableau.

She reached the vestibule to find Tim waiting for her. He smiled as she joined him.

"I want to give my regards to Lilli before we leave."

"I'm right here with you," he replied.

Honestly, snagging Tim as her date had been the talk of the town. A handsome firefighter, dressed in a navy suit, they'd clicked despite his knowing her history. Her friends had been after her to start dating again. *Mitch, your husband, has been gone for almost two years*, they'd said. *You're young. You deserve a second chance at happiness*, they'd insisted.

So why did she feel like she was cheating on a ghost? A ghost she was still angry with.

They had tried putting the pieces back together before his last assignment, taking a short trip to rekindle their marriage. But the reality was, she and Mitch had grown apart and there hadn't seemed any possible way back to the love they'd once shared. He'd left her, after the last in a long line of arguments over a career he'd increasingly placed more and more value on than their relationship. Things had ended up with Mitch taking an assignment overseas where he'd gone missing and was presumed dead. They'd never located his body. Could that be the reason she was having a hard time moving forward?

Zoe stopped before the bride, beautifully attired in a frothy cream-colored gown. Lilli reached over to grab her hands. Max, handsome in his fitted tuxedo, stood beside her as if never wanting to let Lilli out of his sight. They were so ridiculously happy looking they could have posed as cake toppers.

"Congratulations."

"Thanks so much for being here," Lilli said in way of greeting. "You were right. The vows you picked out for us were perfect. Max was never going to write his own, and to be honest, I probably would have been crying too hard to speak my own words if we'd gone that way."

"I'm honored you asked me to officiate. Although, I'm surprised your mother didn't insist on the pastor presiding over the wedding."

"My mother is just so delighted I'm finally married. She never once staged a takeover. Well, not much of one, anyway."

They both laughed. Lilli's mother, Celeste, was a force of nature. No one said no to the woman— not about her fund-raising events and especially not about her superb taste in...everything else.

"I was as surprised as anyone when she actually let me plan my own wedding. I never thought she'd let me get away with barn chic, but I have to say, her input was invaluable. And we grew close during the planning."

Zoe forced a smile. A mother who was invested in her daughter's life. Imagine that.

"What more could I ask for?"

"White cowboy boots instead of sparkly sandals?" Zoe threw out.

"That would have been pushing it."

"I wouldn't have complained," Max added, eavesdropping on the conversation.

Lilli playfully slapped his arm. "When Mom suggested we hold the reception at the Grand Cypress Hotel, I didn't fight her. I knew Nealy would continue to carry out my vision over there."

"And peace reigned." Max glanced at Zoe. "I hate to rush you two, but the photographer is ready for us."

Glancing around the foyer, Zoe noticed she was the last guest to give her congratulations to the couple. The attendants and relatives were mingling and the photographer politely hovered, waiting to take church shots with the entire wedding party and family.

"Looks like all you have to do is smile and look pretty for the camera." Zoe hugged her friend. "I'll see you at the reception."

Max took Lilli's hand, drawing it to his lips for a tender kiss. "After you, my wife."

Lilli giggled.

The sight made Zoe grin as well: rough-and-tumble Private Investigator Max indulging feminine, soft-spoken Lilli. She'd put off the wedding date from the moment they'd gotten engaged, then had slowly dragged Max through the process of the engagement party and the ongoing myriad selection of flowers, music and so on that weddings required. He'd gamely participated when he would have been just as content getting hitched at city hall.

Another friend, Maid of Honor Nealy Grainger, hurried by in a gorgeous pale pink off-the-shoulder, full-skirted dress. "Come on people, we have a schedule to keep."

A consummate event planner, she'd patiently walked the couple through the entire process, just as excited as everyone else in town to see the two finally married.

"Great job," Zoe called out after her.

Nealy grinned and waved, the diamond on her left hand glittering in the overhead lighting. Zoe supposed she'd be invited to another wedding soon. It seemed all her friends were getting married lately. Could she handle all the happiness?

"Do you want to head over to the reception?"

Zoe glanced up at Tim. Taller than her, although most people were, his dark hair was neatly cut, his blue eyes lighting up when she met his gaze.

"Sure." She opened her clutch and pulled out her cell phone. "I'm just going to call my mom and check on Leo."

"I'll get the truck and bring it around front."

Standing on the sidewalk in front of the church, Zoe hit speed dial. Her mother answered on the third ring.

"Hi, Mom. How are things going?"

"Leo didn't sleep much this afternoon. I'm getting ready to feed him now, then put him down for a nap."

In the background, she could hear her son, Leo, rambling in his nonsensical baby language. Unable to hold back a smile, she chuckled at the sound of his voice, in awe of how quickly he'd become the light of her life. She'd always wanted to be a mother, but she'd had no idea how much this little bundle of joy would grab and hold on to her heartstrings. After several miscarriages, and almost losing hope that she would ever have a child of her own, he had been her miracle baby. Just a year old, he had her wrapped around his tiny finger. And Zoe's mother? Let's just say Samantha Collins was way more of an attentive grandmother than she'd ever been a mother when Zoe was growing up. Still, Zoe was eternally thankful for her mom's help. She'd stepped up when Zoe had needed her most. Raising a child alone was not easy.

Nor was getting over the death of a husband.

Mitch had started his photojournalist career documenting local and regional current events. As his reputation grew, he covered noteworthy national news subjects, like elections and natural disasters, eventually moving on to photograph world-famous events and celebrities.

But on his last trip, he'd insisted on a different assignment than what he'd normally taken, traveling to a refugee camp to photograph and document its conditions. While there, he'd been killed. She didn't have many details, only that there had been an explosion.

She closed her eyes and a picture of Leo popped into her mind's eye. Chubby and healthy, his light fuzzy hair standing on end. The ready smile with a few teeth coming in and rosy cheeks that took her breath away. Hot tears stung her lids. Already at this young age, Leo had that cocky grin Zoe had loved on Mitch. If she'd found out she was pregnant before he'd left, would his knowing he'd be a father have changed things? Would it have kept Mitch from willingly plunging headfirst into danger?

She supposed she'd never know.

"He's not a big fan of the peas I introduced this week."

"That's why he's getting scrambled eggs. And bananas. Aren't you, big boy?" her mother cooed. "You should see him holding his spoon. You'd think he could really manipulate it instead of pushing his food to the floor."

"He thrives on messes."

"He does, but who cares. His cuteness out-weighs the cleanup."

Zoe's heart squeezed. She hated being away from him, especially since he'd experienced separation anxiety in the last couple of weeks. He loved his grandmother, though, and Samantha adored him, so Zoe had been able to leave the house today without the inevitable crying.

Leo's and hers.

"I shouldn't be late. Maybe I'll be home in time to put him to bed."

"Honey, enjoy yourself. Leo is fine. Stay out and have fun."

Her admonition to enjoy herself took Zoe by surprise. Samantha had been Mitch's biggest supporter and his death had deeply affected her. She hadn't been thrilled about Zoe taking the plunge into the dating world. Since she'd favored Mitch so much, in her mother's eyes, no man could replace him.

Zoe had held back for as long as she could, until the thought of spending the rest of her life alone began to depress her. She'd told her mother and Samantha had apparently gotten onboard.

"I know. It's just—"

"Zoe?"

"Yes, Mom?"

"I have everything under control here."

Zoe bit her lip. Growing up, her mother had never been big on responsibility, schedules or running a household. A budding artist, she'd get caught up in her newest project for days, immersed in paint and canvas and flourishes of ideas, forgetting she had to feed a daughter. Or bills to pay. At a young age, Zoe had taken over the mothering role. Old habits died hard, even more so when it came to her son's welfare.

She blew out a breath. "I appreciate it." Tim's truck pulled up to the curb. "Call me if you need me."

"I will."

Tapping the end button, Zoe walked the few steps to open the door, but Tim beat her to it.

"Have I told you how nice you look today?" he asked as, always a gentleman, he helped her into the cab.

For the wedding today, she'd found a pretty floral sleeveless dress with a flared skirt and strappy silver sandals to wear, in addition to getting her shoulder-length wispy-cut hairstyle trimmed and actually put on makeup. Very different from her stay-at-home uniform of mom jeans and baggy tops or the more professional wardrobe she used for her mayoral duties. It felt good to dress up for a change and, in a way, she'd wanted to please Tim.

She sent him a genuine smile. "Thanks. You look pretty spiffy yourself."

Tim closed the door and jogged around the front of the truck. She tried to ignore the jitters that quaked over her at the thought of socializing at the reception. People still gave her *the look*, the one reserved for a wife who'd lost her husband early in life. Actually, Mitch had been lost to her a few years prior, but no one knew the miserable details. Placing her hands over her stomach, she told herself to calm down. She knew most of the people who would be at the party. Really, she could think of this as another one of her town events. Even though this party had more to do with hearts and arrows than a function benefiting Cypress Pointe.

Tim jumped back in the cab and placed the truck in gear. "I'm glad you decided to come with me today."

"Thanks for asking. I was already scheduled to do the ceremony, but it's nice to have your company," she said, determined not to let reminders of the past ruin her present.

"Look, Zoe, I understand that I'm the first guy you've gone out with since Mitch…um…passed away. I know this decision wasn't easy." He paused. "You got this watery look in your eyes when you were reading the vows. I thought you might not make it through the ceremony."

Yeah, she'd had a moment of self-pity. She'd hoped it hadn't been that obvious. "Maybe we should talk about something else."

"I want you to know I admire you," he soldiered on. "Having a baby and finding out Mitch wasn't coming home? I can't even imagine the pain you must have gone through. And then performing this wedding today? You're one tough cookie."

In the past two years, she'd had to be. "Thanks. I think."

"I just mean you'll move on with your life."

He turned his head in her direction. The surety in his gaze made her squirm. "Someday, you'll find another man."

Tim continued extolling the virtues that were *Zoe Simmons* while her stomach churned. She really wanted to make a go of it with Tim. Stop holding him at arm's length. Let the relationship advance naturally. Grow closer. Maybe if he kissed her, she'd be able to open up to him and get past the reservations about the way her marriage had ended.

Before long, they pulled into the hotel parking lot scattered with crushed white shells. The charming southern plantation facade of the building greeted guests like long lost friends finally coming home. After Tim pulled into an empty space, Zoe grabbed hold of the handle and opened the door without waiting for him to do the honors. She slid out of the cab, shaking off her misgivings. She could do this.

Her feet hit the shells and she made her way to the wide veranda of the Grand Cypress Hotel. The porch was stocked with cozy rocking chairs situated in front of the wide windows with thick plantation shutters.

"Hey, Zoe. Wait up."

She was being prickly, and she knew it. He'd

made her sound like a saint and she was far from one. If she'd been a better person, she wouldn't have been filing for a divorce after making one last-ditch effort to fix her marriage. Wouldn't have screamed, *I never want to see you again*, the final time her husband walked out the door because her heart was breaking and she'd had enough.

Yes, she'd picked up the pieces after Mitch's death. Grieved the man, as well as the marriage that had been collateral damage when his career had carried him to every corner of the world. If there was the hint of a government coup, political upheaval or celebrity scandal, Mitch was there with his camera. But the idea of a new man, Tim or anyone else for that matter, took some getting used to. One day, she would be totally one hundred percent over Mitch. Today was now or never.

Stopping by the glass-etched main entrance, she faced Tim when he caught up to her. "Please go inside," she told him. "I'll be there in a few minutes."

For the first time he looked unsure of himself. "Was it something I said?"

"I need to gather my thoughts." She tilted her head toward the building. "I'll be in soon."

"If you say so."

A blast of air conditioning drifted over Zoe as Tim went inside. Heaving a breath, she lowered herself onto a rocking chair a few feet away and smoothed the cotton skirt of her dress with shaky fingers.

Mitch still had the power to reduce her to uncertainty. It hadn't always been that way. When they'd met in high school, then married young, he'd always made her laugh. Given her hope.

But once he'd become Mr. Hotshot Photojournalist, things had begun to change. Subtly at first. He was a thrill seeker from the get-go; she shouldn't have been surprised when he thrived at his job. She, on the other hand, had always been leery about walking into the unknown. She had been wounded as an innocent bystander in a bank robbery, and the helplessness she'd felt then had never left her. It had, in fact, spurred on her commitment to the town and the people of Cypress Pointe. Mitch, meanwhile, had craved the action and on the way to success, her concerns hadn't seemed to matter to him.

Can't blame him. You had your part in the breakup.

It was true, but she'd hoped Mitch would put their failing marriage first. When he didn't, she'd become even more civic-minded, throwing her energy into projects bettering the lives of her friends and neighbors. But what if she'd tried harder? Maybe battled her fears? Gone with him a time or two to show her support? If she'd known then what she knew now, she might have made a different choice.

A couple headed in her direction, dressed up for the wedding-reception revelry inside.

"Good afternoon, Mayor."

She waved. It still felt odd answering to that title. She'd always been Zoe. Just plain Zoe. Mitch Simmons's wife. Leo's mother. Samantha's daughter. Now she had a responsibility to the good people of Cypress Pointe. She wasn't completely sure how that had happened. One day she was busy with her latest community project, a food bank, when her best friend suggested she'd make an awesome mayor. Next thing she knew, she was running an election and won.

Now she ran a town, dealt with a town council, worked closely with the police and fire chiefs, along with other officials, and found herself thriving. Her ideas were accepted and embraced, and best of all, successful. Her passionate goal of keeping Cypress Pointe safe for current and future generations was falling into place.

"Are you going inside?" the man asked as he held open the door.

Not wanting to appear rude, she stood and joined the couple as they ventured inside. Following them into the cool, spacious lobby, her heels echoed on the marble floor leading to the assigned banquet room. As she entered, voices carried over the soft music flowing from hidden speakers. Waiters moved about the room with trays of hors d'oeuvres and flutes of champagne. The yummy aroma of a loaded baked potato made her stomach growl. She took a small plate and helped herself to the potato and a BLT on a cracker. She'd forgotten to eat lunch in her rush to get ready and had to stop herself from swallowing the comfort food too quickly. Taking a bite of the potato, she closed her eyes and savored the gooey melted cheese spiced with bits of bacon.

"Whoever came up with these hors d'oeuvres is a genius," a familiar voice said beside her.

Zoe's eyes flew open. "Bethany. I missed you at the rehearsal party last night."

"My flight got delayed. I came in too late."

"I knew you wouldn't miss the wedding."

"After hearing all your stories about Lilli

making Max crazy by dragging out the wedding plans, I had to see the ceremony with my own eyes."

Depositing her plate on the tray of a passing waiter, Zoe threw her arms around her best friend and squeezed. "I'm glad you're here."

Bethany squeezed back. "Me, too."

Zoe pulled away to scrutinize her friend. Bethany's shoulder-length brunette hair gleamed under the subtle banquet room lighting and her mocha eyes sparkled. "I see the road agrees with you."

"What can I say? I love my job. Even if it does keep me away from Cypress Pointe."

Zoe hugged her again. "Which is more often than I like. But now you're here. That's all that matters."

"Just for the weekend. I fly out Sunday."

Tomorrow? Pushing away the pinch of dejection, Zoe smiled. "Great. We can catch up. Leo would love to see his godmother."

"And I'm dying to see him. Half of my suitcase is filled with toys and adorable little outfits I couldn't resist buying."

Bethany might be busy, but she always had time to dote on Leo.

"Stop by in the morning."

"I will." She sized up Zoe. "You okay with all this lovey-dovey, happy couple stuff?"

Zoe laughed. Bethany was not a believer in happily-ever-after.

"I'm fine."

"You're sure? I thought I saw you tear up during the ceremony."

Good grief. "Did everyone notice?"

"I suppose only people paying attention. I'd say the majority were focused on the bride and groom."

Which, hopefully, meant only Bethany and Tim saw the moment of weakness.

"No matter. I'm good. Better than good." She scanned the room. "I even have a date roaming around here somewhere."

"So you've stuck to your moving-on plan?"

"Absolutely."

"I guess Tim is a good choice…" Bethany's voice trailed off.

"But?"

"He's a firefighter. Why do you pick guys who run to danger?"

Why, indeed?

"Forget I said anything. If you like him, that's good enough for me."

"I do," Zoe insisted. "He's a nice guy."

"But he doesn't get your pulse racing?"

"Been there. Had the broken marriage to prove it. Next time, I'm going for solid and steady."

Bethany snorted. "Good luck with that."

Yeah, Zoe had a thing for thrill-seekers. Could it be because she lived vicariously through them? *How's that working out for you?*

Not well.

Bethany frowned. "My folks are sending me the stink eye. Gotta run."

It took everything in Zoe not to turn toward Mr. and Mrs. Donahue. Since the ill-fated robbery when Zoe and Bethany were young teens, they hadn't wanted much to do with her. Unconsciously, she rubbed her arm, her fingers brushing over the raised scar.

Growing up, she'd based the idea of what a family should look like by the Donahues' example. Bethany's parents had normal jobs, normal hours and normal relationships, while Zoe had cooked her own meals and basically ran her mother's life. Even today, she missed the security of their home, the comfort of their friendship, a life she'd been a part of for too short a period of time.

A waiter passed by again. The zesty scent of mac and cheese, served in little porcelain ramekin bowls, drew her from her thoughts.

She wandered around the room, admiring the wildflower theme carried over from the wedding. Each table resembled a picnic table with yellow gingham cloths covered with burlap and lace runners. The centerpiece consisted of a small galvanized bucket with overflowing greens and wildflowers, surrounded by candles flickering in mason jars. Fat water goblets and white plates with yellow napkins circled by a wooden holder adorned each place setting. Simple and inviting. Very Lilli.

A riser had been assembled at the far end of the room for Luke Hastings's band to set up their instruments to play after dinner. The opposite wall boasted a large window overlooking the hotel pool. From there, the hotel lawn swept down to the beach. There was a wooden outdoor deck on the far side of the building with an amazing view of the sand and water beyond. Truth be told, the private deck was her favorite place at the hotel. With today's temperate weather, Zoe imagined the party would eventually spill outside.

"There you are." Tim came up beside her, handing her a glass. She took a sip of the sparkling wine, suddenly at a loss for conversation.

Guilt itched over her. She shouldn't be thinking about the past when she was on a date. "Sorry about before."

"No need to explain."

There was, but she kept quiet.

"Pretty room," Tim said.

"Yes. Nealy did a stellar job as usual. Between her event planning company and her boyfriend owning this hotel, they're a real power couple."

Silence fell between them and she took another sip.

"When do you think the wedding party will get here?"

"Soon, I would imagine."

Tim shook his head, gazing around the room.

Yeah, this had turned awkward.

"The only thing that would top this day is if I get called out to a fire. A real date-killer."

Zoe laughed. She knew Tim wasn't on duty, but appreciated his attempt at levity. If he could try, she would, too.

"Or I could get called into an impromptu late Saturday afternoon town council meeting, because we all know council people have nothing better to do than call weekend meetings."

He chuckled and sent her a warm smile.

Should she take his hand in hers to reassure

him they were fine, or was that rushing things? It had been so long since she'd dated; she was definitely rusty. *Just take the plunge.* She could do this.

"Ah, the life we live as public servants," he said.

Actually, a public life hadn't turned out all that bad. She gave to the town and her work brought a sense of satisfaction. She was keeping Cypress Pointe a good place to live, work and raise a family, ensuring that nothing threatened this quiet community she treasured. She didn't imagine her motivation would ever be swayed.

As she looked around for a place to set down her glass, deciding to take his hand and finally show Tim she wanted their relationship to move to the next level, the volume level in the room rose. Guests shifted to the open doorway.

"Must be the happy couple now," Tim commented.

Her timing stunk. To cover her disappointment, she said, "Now we can get this party started. Have I told you I like to dance?"

"I believe you have."

Thankful to get this date back on an even keel, Zoe joined in the clapping as the bride and groom made their grand entrance. Toasts were offered. The meal was just about to be served when she noticed a new face appear in the crowd. Wyatt Hamilton, Mitch's best friend, searched the crowd until his gaze landed on her. With a determined air about him, he worked his way across the room. What on earth could he want? She'd noticed him at the church earlier, but he'd left through the backdoor before the ceremony started, talking on his cell phone. Then Zoe had gotten busy and hadn't given his exit a second thought. At the time, she figured he was talking to his girlfriend, Jenna, the caterer for this reception. From his serious expression and focused stride, a note of worry scurried over her.

"Zoe, I've been trying to get ahold of you."

She reached for her phone and came up empty-handed, which was highly unusual since she always kept her phone nearby when Leo was with a sitter. "I must have left my bag in the truck."

He nodded at her explanation. "I need to borrow you."

Tim stepped closer. "Right now?"

Wyatt sent him a dark look. "It's important."

Zoe grabbed Wyatt's sleeve. "Is it Leo? Is something wrong?"

His expression gentled. "No. Not at all. I'm sure Leo is fine."

Zoe let out a breath, then met Wyatt's gaze. "What's up?"

"Come with me."

Beyond curious, Zoe turned to Tim. "I'll be back as soon as this mystery is solved."

Frustration crossed Tim's face. "I'll be waiting."

"Thanks, Tim." Zoe glanced at Wyatt again. Something was off and she wanted to find out what was bothering him.

Wyatt cocked his head toward the door leading to the backyard outdoor area. Zoe passed by him and then he fell into step beside her as they approached the pool, the chlorine heavy and pungent. A few folks lingered at the open-air cafe, but most guests were inside enjoying the party.

"Care to give me a heads-up?" she said once they were out of hearing distance from the crowd.

"You'll understand in a moment."

Tendrils of unease trickled down her spine. "You're making me nervous."

His quick smile put her marginally at ease. "It'll be worth it."

"Really? Does Jenna know what you're up to?"

"Yes. And she's with me on this."

"Okay. Lead on."

They continued walking. Once they reached the arch exiting to the cement pathway that led to the far deck, he stopped. "Go on out there."

"What?" She crossed her arms over her chest. "You got me this far and now I'm on my own?"

"It's not my place."

She stood her ground.

"It's important."

Disconcerted by this clandestine mission, she reluctantly made her way along the path. Tall sea oats swayed in the gentle breeze. A seagull squawked before diving for its prey. Out here, briny seawater tinted the air. As she grew closer, she noticed a tall figure standing on the far side of the deck, his back to her as he looked over the natural vista spreading out before him. She hesitated as fear gripped her. Surely, Wyatt wouldn't have brought her here if it weren't safe.

The solitary man remained still. Zoe's heart began to pound. She didn't have it in her to stop, as if an invisible force shoved her closer to her destination.

The man turned around.

She slowed her steps, wary now.

When he removed his aviator-shaped sunglasses, she gasped, her knees nearly buckling beneath her.

"Hello, Zoe," the stranger standing before her said.

She blinked. It couldn't be, could it? *How* could it be?

"Mitch?" she whispered past the obstruction in her taut throat.

"Yes. It's me."

The husband she'd thought was dead stood before her, very much alive.

CHAPTER TWO

MITCH HAD EXPECTED his wife's surprise. After all, to her, he'd risen from the dead.

His hand gripped the cane that had become his lifeline. He wanted to heave it over the railing, but that meant lifting an arm that still needed rehab to function properly. Instead of cataloguing his injuries, he focused on his shell-shocked wife.

"I don't understand. We were told… I thought you were…"

"Dead?"

She reached out to place her palms on the deck railing.

"The report was mistaken."

"But… How… Why?"

"I was injured in a truck accident while leaving a refugee camp."

She visibly pulled herself together. Took a step toward him, faltered and stopped. "Pretty soon I'm going to have a ton of questions, but right now… I don't know what to say."

"How about 'welcome home'?"

He watched her struggle with this major surprise. "When did you get here?"

"About fifteen minutes ago."

"How?" Her gaze took in his appearance and he knew what she saw. A guy who'd lost weight, whose complexion had turned pasty after weeks in the hospital. Not the image of the healthy husband who'd walked out of her life nearly two years ago.

"Wyatt. I called him to tell him I was heading home. He picked me up at the airport."

A flush of red crept up her neck. "You didn't think to call your wife?"

"I did, but considering how we ended our last conversation, I thought it would be better if I talked to you in person."

She ran a hand through her shoulder-length black hair. What had happened to the long straight strands that had reached to her mid-back? In the hospital, he'd dreamed of running his fingers through it. Had dreamed of her easy smile, which was nowhere to be found right now. Had he expected her to jump into his arms when she saw him again despite the circumstances? Expect that old feelings would rush over her again? Disappointment swamped him. She looked like the same Zoe, yet there was something different about her. He couldn't put his finger on it.

"I'm sorry, you didn't want to call me? Despite everything, didn't you think I'd have wanted to know you were at least okay?"

He shifted as the weight on his weak leg grew uncomfortable. "I should have called, but after the accident and long recovery, I just wanted to get back to Cypress Pointe."

She opened her mouth, then slammed it shut. His excuse probably echoed false, like so many of the ones he'd tossed her way in the past.

"Zoe, I realize this is a shock."

"Really? A shock?" Her voice cracked. "We thought you were dead!"

"I get it—"

"Do you? We went for weeks not knowing where you were. I tried every number I could think of. Your assistant, Maria, got ahold of a few contacts who pointed us in the direction of Jordan. And then the only information she could find was that you were somewhere along the Syrian border. I hoped…prayed…"

He took a halting step forward to stand closer to his wife. Her familiar scent of vanilla mixed with a hint of floral enveloped him. All he wanted was to cup her sweet face and stare into her blue eyes. Instead, he met her gaze, which had finally moved from shock to anger.

The headache knocking at the back of his skull leaped to a full-blown hammer. He closed his eyes. Took measured breaths.

A soft touch landed on his tender arm and the muscles seized.

"Mitch. Are you okay?"

He slowly opened his eyes. "Pain. In my head."

"Do you want to go inside? Get out of the sun?"

The old Mitch rebelled at her suggestion. He'd been cooped up for too long. Yeah, the bright light wasn't helping the throbbing in his head, but he needed to feel the warmth on his skin, savor the earthy scent of sea and sand, listen to the waves rush upon the shore and ebb back into the blue water he'd dreamed of while gone.

"In a few minutes."

The current Mitch tried to be more level-headed, to take the advice of the doctors to not overdo. He hadn't exactly been a model patient.

"At least sit down."

He shook his head and immediately regretted it. "It feels good to stand."

"Okay. Can I get you water?"

"Not right now. I just want to enjoy being here."

A shadow crossed her face. He hadn't known what to expect in terms of a homecoming. Confusion? No doubt. Awkwardness? Sure. Anger? Most definitely. Now that the conversation had stalled, he wasn't sure which direction to steer it.

Zoe ran a shaky hand over her forehead. "So much has happened. Changed, since you've been gone."

"I imagine. I know it'll take a while to catch up."

"Why did it take so long for you to contact… Wyatt?"

"I lost my memory after the crash. Only recently was I able to fit the pieces of my life together."

The color washed out of her cheeks. "It was that bad?"

"Apparently. I remember driving down a dirt road, then waking up in the hospital. They told me I was unconscious for a week."

"Why didn't the hospital contact your family?"

"It was in a pretty remote area. I didn't have my press credentials with me and my ID got lost in the confusion."

Her brow wrinkled. "We got word that you were dead a year ago. What happened?"

"I kind of went rogue. After I left last time, with all that went down between us, I started traveling, working on my own and didn't bother to report in to Maria. I don't know how the rumor of my death started, other than I was near an explosion site early on, so I guess since I hadn't spoken with anyone, they assumed the worst. The accident happened later."

"But before, I tried to find you. I called different publications you'd worked with to see if you were on assignment and no one could get ahold of you."

"I was off the grid."

"Why would you do that?"

"It's a long story. And since we'd decided to separate, I didn't think it mattered."

"This is overwhelming." Zoe's gaze swept over him again. Taking inventory of his shortcomings? He pushed himself to stand taller, even with the pain screaming in his leg. "I need to sit down." She moved to a nearby wrough iron patio chair and dropped into the seat.

He followed, making sure she wasn't looking before taking a bracing breath and lowering himself into a chair beside her. There was no way he'd admit how bad his injuries were. At least not until he got a handle on how things stood between them after his sudden reappearance. To his dismay, tears were rolling down Zoe's cheeks. She brushed them away and said, after a bitter laugh, "When I got up this morning, I never expected to find out my husband is alive and back in Cypress Pointe."

"I'm sorry, Zoe."

She glanced at her clasped hands, then back at him. "You should have called me, Mitch. I would have come to get you. You are my husband."

"Am I? Or was I?"

Her gaze slid away.

To be honest, he hadn't been sure she'd come to his rescue. Sure, he'd never stopped believing, hoping, that her love for him would be bigger than their problems. Enough to push her out of her comfort zone and into his arms. But as his career took off, her connection to the people of Cypress Pointe had grown. Her loyalty to a town had been one of the sticking points in their relationship, so he'd decided to take the easy way out and call his friend instead of his wife.

"I wasn't too sure about the husband part."

She'd threatened to file for a divorce before

he left. Had she followed through? He hadn't signed any papers, but that didn't mean she hadn't had them drawn up. Is that why she'd tried to find him? To end the marriage for good?

"Yes," she said in a quiet voice. "We're still married."

Question answered.

"I had the papers, but when we thought you were dead, I put them aside."

The abbreviated relief evaporated. She'd made good on her promise. He hadn't thought she'd carry through, but he had been wrong. About a lot of things.

He stretched out his leg to relieve the cramp twisting his calf.

"Everyone will be happy to see you."

"Are you?"

"How can you ask me that?" Indignation laced her tone. "Of course, I'm glad you're okay."

"Glad he was okay" and "happy to see him" were two different answers. They'd had their share of epic arguments in the past but at her core, Zoe wasn't mean-spirited enough to wish he'd stayed dead and gone.

She glanced at his cane. "So you'll need more recovery time?"

He'd been told as much. Physical therapy. Probably someone to talk to about his memory loss. Figure out if there was any way to get back the life he'd lived before the accident.

Traveling for two days had sapped his energy. Layovers. Uncomfortable seats on long flights. Not to mention the unsettling sensation of being watched when he'd flown out of Queen Alia International Airport in Jordan. Did he need to add paranoia to his list of injuries?

A cough sounded from the steps. Zoe jumped and looked over her shoulder.

"I'll be right back," she said, guilt washing over her features.

She hurried over to a guy dressed in a suit and they spoke in low tones. Who was he? Why was Zoe so concerned about this other guy? He sent Mitch an I'm-watching-you signal and backed away. Ah. A new guy in her life? The territorial scowl explained it. Mitch wasn't sure he liked the idea of his wife seeing another guy but, under the circumstances, he had no right to object. He'd made the decision to check out of her life a long time ago.

Zoe returned but didn't take a seat. "Sorry. I needed to…um…"

"Let me guess. Your date to the wedding?"

Her face flushed. "Yes. I've only—"

He held up a hand. "You don't have to explain," he said even with his mind crying, *Of course, she does!* "You didn't think I was alive. You never would have dreamed I'd show up here today."

"Mitch, we have a lot to talk about."

Yeah. They did. He rubbed the jackhammer tempo pounding his temples. "Maybe later?"

She looked like she was going to argue, then thought better of it.

"Where are you staying?"

He'd thought with her. *Guess not.*

"I'll bunk at Wyatt's place."

"I'll drop by later. I've got to let Mom and—" she stopped abruptly "—others know you're alive."

He dropped his hand to his knee. "Fine."

"Mitch?"

He squinted up at her.

"I am happy you're alive."

He merely nodded. Relieved that she still had some kind of feelings for him, he watched her turn on her heel and hurry off, taking the arm of the man who was waiting for her before disappearing into the hotel.

So. This was what jealously felt like. He'd

never experienced it concerning Zoe before. Didn't much care for it.

Spent now, he rose and made his way back to the view he'd been savoring before Zoe had arrived. Taking a deep breath of fresh Cypress Pointe air, he suddenly wondered why he'd ever left her at all. Then, just as quickly, memories bombarded him, reminding him exactly why.

He yanked the sunglasses out of his shirt pocket and clumsily placed them over his eyes.

The beach looked the same. The water, still a brilliant blue-green, drawing tourists to the quaint seaside town. So much the same, yet his entire life had been blasted to oblivion. Upended by a decision that had nearly cost him his life.

It seemed like yesterday that he'd started his career here. When Zoe's mother had given him a camera as a way of channeling his boundless energy, he'd taken to it immediately. The natural surroundings of Cypress Pointe had been an inspiring subject. Samantha had taken one look at his shots and proclaimed he'd found his calling. Skeptical at first, he'd experimented by finding different places and techniques to take photos, pleased he'd latched onto something constructive to steer his life. He had been eighteen, rudderless, except for Zoe, and he'd had no idea what his future held.

Eventually, Samantha had begun showing his photos in her art gallery. The popularity of his work had grown and before long, local and then national publications began calling for freelance work. New opportunities opened up. At first, Zoe helped him book assignments, but eventually her causes took over.

When things started to go south in the marriage, he took whatever job he could find just to get away again. It wasn't until he'd left the last time that the job to photograph conditions at the refugee camp had caught his attention. Zoe's kicking him to the curb had probably been a major factor in his choice. But who knew he'd have ended up at the wrong place at the wrong time?

Heavy footsteps pounded over the wooden deck, announcing an arrival. Mitch shook off his thoughts and turned just as Wyatt joined him at the railing.

"You okay?" his friend asked.

"Been better."

"Zoe gave me the evil eye just now."

"You aren't the only one."

"So how did it go?"

"As you'd expect. She's angry but doing a

good job keeping a lid on it." He looked over the water. "Said we need to talk." He eyed his friend. "Never good when a woman says those words."

Wyatt remained quiet.

"Something I should know?"

When Wyatt didn't meet his gaze, a bad feeling curled in his gut.

"Better you have a conversation with Zoe," Wyatt told him.

"Now I have all kinds of what-ifs running around my head."

"Just sit down with Zoe when you get home. It'll be okay."

A motorboat zipped by in the distance. Mitch longed for freedom from his injuries and the past, but knew that jumping in a speeding boat would never solve his problems.

"About that. Seems I need a place to stay."

Wyatt turned his head, his expression incredulous. "She didn't ask you to come home?"

"I'm thinking maybe I don't have a home to go to."

Wyatt blew out a breath. "You can stay with me."

Mitch made a fist and squeezed. "I don't want to put you out."

"It's not a problem."

"Thanks. If you don't mind, I'd rather we left here before the people inside find out I'm back. Talking with Zoe is about all I can handle right now."

"You got it." He yanked a set of keys from his pants pocket. "My truck is in the lot."

Taking one last gaze at the boat, now far enough away to be only a speck on the tranquil waters, questions assailed him again. What would happen now? Old feelings for his wife, mixed with the conflicted emotions he'd stored away when he'd left Cypress Pointe for good, betrayed him.

Mitch leaned heavily on his cane, following his buddy to the parking lot, wondering how long it would be before the hurricane that had managed to wreck his life hit again.

"MOM? WHERE ARE YOU?" Zoe called as she closed the front door behind her.

She tossed her clutch on the couch, then kicked off her shoes and fell back against the cushions, exhaling the pressure that had been working up inside her chest since she'd left the hotel.

Mitch was alive! She still couldn't wrap her mind around it. So many emotions, so many questions. What did this mean? Did she carry through with the divorce? Did they try to fix their marriage, in light of Leo? And why hadn't she told him he was a father?

Guilt and anger walloped her. Yes, she should have told Mitch right away. But after learning he hadn't called her immediately to let her know he was safe and alive, a selfish part of her had held back. She'd tell him later when she went to Wyatt's house to talk to him, but back there at the hotel? She couldn't. Her pride had made her mute about their son, along with the residual hurt that produced reservations about revealing the truth.

"Mom?" she called again. When she didn't receive an answer, she hauled herself up and walked to the back of the house, sure to find her mother holed up in her studio. The southern exposure of light was an artist's dream. Perfect for when Samantha was creating a new piece.

"Hi, Mom."

Samantha never took her gaze from the canvas as she dabbed paint on the project before her.

"Is Leo okay?"

"Of course." Her mother paused to glance briefly at Zoe, then back to her piece. "Why are you home early?"

"We need to talk."

Samantha went still. She didn't like dealing with real-world problems, preferring to let Zoe or an assistant take care of her life. Dealing with critical issues, like Mitch returning from the dead, were not her forte.

"Can it wait?" her mother asked, already looking for a way to avoid the conversation.

"No."

"Let me just get this last shade…"

While she finished her task, Zoe roamed the room, thinking of a way to break the earth-shattering news.

Samantha laid down her palette and brush, then wiped her hands with a paint-spattered towel. "Are you going to explain why you're home? Trouble with Tim?"

Poor Tim. He'd been just as shocked to see Mitch. Barely spoke on the uncomfortable ride to the house she shared with her mother.

"No. Well, yes, but not what you think."

Her mother grimaced. "I knew this dating thing was too soon. You aren't ready. He's not right for you."

Except, he had been. Until less than an hour ago.

"Mom. I don't know any other way to say this without just blurting it out." She took a breath. "Mitch is alive and here in Cypress Pointe."

The color fled from her mother's pretty face. "But… How?"

"I don't have all the details. Apparently, he was in some kind of accident and lost his memory. He was badly hurt and, until recently, unable to travel home."

"Where is he?"

"At Wyatt Hamilton's house."

Her mother tossed the towel on the table. "We have to go get him. Despite your troubles, he should be home."

Zoe reached out to grab her mother's arm as she started to leave the room. "No."

"Why not? He's your husband."

To say she'd been caught off guard when she saw him standing on the hotel deck was an understatement, but it didn't mean an automatic reconciliation. Mitch was the father of her child, yes, and she had to figure out how to handle that, as well as the repercussions of him being back in her life. She could blame her confused emotions right now on the hopes and dreams of the couple she'd just married; it was making her vulnerable and lowering the wall she'd erected when she and Mitch had separated. At least, she desperately hoped that was the case.

Zoe rubbed her temples. "I know." But it was so much more. Did she dare open her son's life to a man who would rather wander the world without a shred of responsibility for the needs of a family? Was Mitch clueless or still only thinking about himself and not how his actions affected others? "First of all, Mitch needs continued medical attention. He looks terrible."

The image of her once-robust husband was overshadowed by her new reality. Mitch had lost weight. The button-down shirt and jeans had hung from what used to be a muscular frame. And his beautiful wavy brown hair? Gone, revealing fresh scalp scars under the buzz cut.

"All the more reason he should be here where we can take care of him."

"I understand you want him here, but I can't. Not yet."

Her mother gasped. "How can you say that?"

"Mitch didn't call us, Mom. He contacted Wyatt, instead. Did what he wanted instead of what was right. Clearly, he hasn't changed."

Uncertainty strained her mother's features. "He must have had a good reason."

"Said he wanted to tell me he was alive in person." Which on the surface made sense, but it was just one example on an ongoing list of ways Mitch always made decisions that suited him, not them.

"Well then, he was looking out for you."

Maybe. "I need time to process all this."

"So, what, you can push him away again?"

Zoe clenched a tight rein over her anger. Once again, her mother was not on her side.

It had always been like this. Samantha and Mitch were like peas in a pod. Artistic. Spoke the same creative language. She'd always felt like the odd one out, never fitting into her mother's world, left out of an important part of Mitch's.

Her mother never understood why she and Mitch had problems, even though Mitch knew early on in their relationship that Zoe didn't want to leave Cypress Pointe. She hadn't kept it a secret from him, and it hadn't become an issue until his career began to take off and she was more involved in town activities. He at least tried to humor her, asking her to tag along, even though in time, a chasm formed between them. But Samantha never seemed to consider Zoe's side of things, just like she'd never shown motherly concern when Zoe had been grazed in the upper arm by a bullet. Hadn't worried about the scars that might form because her daughter had witnessed and been caught in the cross fire of a bank robbery. Samantha had been too preoccupied readying for her first major art show. Zoe could take care of herself, her mother reasoned, just like she'd always done.

"You may not like my decision, but Mitch is my husband. I will deal with the situation as I see fit."

Samantha leaned against the wall. Crossed her arms over her chest. Her expression revealed she knew she wouldn't win this particular argument.

As if just thinking of it, her mother asked, "What did he say when you told him about Leo?"

"I haven't yet."

"You didn't tell him?"

Zoe swallowed the guilt rising in her throat. "I…I was going to, but he looked worn out. I didn't want to shock him with the news until he'd had a chance to rest." To her ears, it sounded like a lame excuse, but it was all she had. Just like Mitch, she'd withheld important information affecting their lives. What did that say about the state of their relationship?

"What if he hears about Leo from some-one else?"

It shouldn't be a problem. She'd passed Wyatt in the hotel just before she'd left, asking him to please keep news of Leo a secret until she could tell Mitch herself. He'd agreed, but by the scowl on his face, she recognized his displeasure. Didn't matter, really. This was her call to make.

"What are you waiting for?" her mother said. "Get changed."

She turned to leave the room, then stopped and faced her mother. "I know you don't agree with my decision, Mom, but please, respect it."

Her mother's eyes grew moist. "I do. We've been given a miracle. Make that two, with Leo."

Zoe would have loved to hug her mother right then, but years of resentment stopped her. When she'd learned Zoe was pregnant, and then of Mitch's subsequent death, her mother had finally broken free of her self-absorption. When Leo was born, Samantha had transformed into the caring and present parent Zoe had always longed to have. It confounded her, but she was unable to deny that she was ecstatic Leo had a grandma, even if she'd never been a mom.

Stopping in the living room to grab her shoes, Zoe made a detour to Leo's room. The cutie lay on his back, breathing lightly, his lion blankie wrapped around his legs. Placing her shoes on the floor by the crib, she gently untangled the blanket and ran her fingers over his downy soft hair, then his warm cheek. An intense rush of love took her breath away. Leo was her child. Hers to protect, even if it was from his own irresponsible father. She'd do anything to keep her son safe. Would never let Mitch hurt Leo like he'd hurt her.

Leo moved in his sleep, settling into another position. Zoe watched him for a few more minutes, then tiptoed from the room.

A few minutes later, she changed into a short-sleeved T-shirt, denim capris and sandals. Before leaving her room, she gathered up a framed picture of Leo to show Mitch. She also had way too many pictures to count saved on her cell phone. He could scroll through her gallery to view dozens of other shots. She tossed the frame in her purse and went to the living room to retrieve her phone from her fancy clutch bag.

Before leaving, she returned to the studio. "Mom, I'm leaving."

Samantha stood by her paint rack, studying a tube of paint. She glanced up, clearly startled.

"Make sure you deliver the news to Mitch gently."

"I will." Zoe bit the inside of her cheek. "You have the baby monitor turned up, right?"

"Yes. Leo will be fine."

Zoe backed out of the room. The less they talked would probably be for the best.

Fifteen minutes later, Zoe sat in Wyatt's driveway. She should have gotten out of the car already, but nerves kept her in place. Could she do this? Really, she had no choice. Mitch deserved to hear about his son from her. But telling him made this new twist in her life real. They were connected forever, no matter the state of their marriage. What would this look like now? Would Mitch want them to live as a family? Would he take off again because, let's face it, he saw each job as an adventure, that might once again cost their family? Cost Leo his father?

Only one way to find out. Heaving in a breath, she opened the door and stepped into the early twilight. Hooking her purse strap over her shoulder, she forced herself to walk around the side of the house to the screened-in porch. Sprawled out in a lounge chair, Mitch was watching boats coming in and out of the marina.

She approached softly, so as not to surprise him, but he'd already half risen from the chair.

"Don't get up," she rushed to say.

He sank down quickly. "Thanks. My leg gave up working for the day. All the traveling has finally caught up with me."

The lines on his face showed his exhaustion. His stiff shoulders suggested he hid a lot of pain. "Sure you're up to this?"

"I've spent a lot of time with only my thoughts for company, so yeah, whatever you have to say, I'm up to it."

She dragged a chair closer to his.

"My mom was overjoyed to hear you're alive."

"Not upset I didn't call?"

She frowned. "Upset with you? When did you ever do anything to make her angry with you?"

Her bitter comment ushered a silence over them. In the distance, the clanging of a buoy rang in the dusk and the chugging of an idling boat engine sputtered nearby. The scent of diesel gas made her nose wrinkle. The temperate evening seemed to close in on her.

"Let's cut to the chase, Zoe. Clearly, you

have something to tell me and I can guess what it is. You're seeing that guy from the wedding and you want me to sign divorce papers."

"What? No."

Trying to come up with the right words escaped her. She dropped her purse on her lap and took out the framed photo. Held it to her chest against the tight band threatening to cut off her breathing.

Mitch pushed up straight against the chair back. "Zoe?"

"I tried to find you, I really did, but it was like you'd fallen off of the face of the earth."

He frowned. "And I already explained that was my doing."

"Yes, but I want you to know I tried."

Leaning forward, Mitch stared her straight in the eye. "Tell me."

She swallowed, pulled the frame from her chest and stared down at her son's precious face. Met Mitch's gaze again.

"We have a son. His name is Leo."

CHAPTER THREE

OF ALL THE things Zoe could have surprised him with, news of a son shocked Mitch to his core. Especially after all the trouble they'd had trying to conceive.

Fingers shaky, he put all his willpower into calming them before hesitantly taking the frame she offered, unsure why he was afraid to look down.

"We tried for years," he said, mostly to himself, attempting to make sense of her news.

She shrugged. "I can't explain it. I only know we have a child."

He angled the frame so he could see the picture. A boy, his eyes bright, mouth curved in a toothless smile. He had a child? His breath lodged in his throat as the reality looked back at him.

"This was taken a few months ago. He's gotten some teeth in since then."

Mitch marveled at the pride in Zoe's voice. Yes, she'd pushed long and hard to have a child. Thought a baby would fix the problems between them when the reality of each miscarriage only made things worse.

"Why didn't you tell me at the hotel?"

An expression that looked suspiciously like guilt flashed over her face. "I wasn't sure how you'd react."

"To the news of my own child?"

"You weren't exactly on board with the whole baby idea."

True, he hadn't been at first but with each disappointment, the distance between them had continued to grow and deepen.

He studied the image again, using his professional eye. Definitely taken in a studio; he could tell by the backdrop. Good lighting. Nice angle. Clear contrast. Professional.

His son.

The reality had him spinning. He handed the frame back to her.

"Why didn't you bring Leo here in person?"

"He was sleeping. The nights have been a bit rough since he's cutting teeth. I didn't want to disturb him."

News of a son had never crossed his mind, but now that he knew, he wanted to meet him in person right away. "Then you should take me to see him now."

He started to rise, clumsily swinging his leg over the lounge chair, groping for his cane and coming up empty. As he stood, teetering to one side, Zoe scrambled to help him by slipping her arm around his waist to hold him upright.

He met her gaze, pity shining in the sapphire blue depths. Her fragrance surrounded him, just as her arms did. This close, he yearned to lean on her. Absorb her strength. Instead, he pushed away, forcing every fiber of his being to remain upright.

"I don't need your help."

She blinked, then quickly looked away. Spying his cane on the floor, she retrieved it.

He snatched it from her, angry because her look made him feel like half a man. He didn't want her sympathy. He'd be better soon. Return to the man he once was.

The pounding in his head called him a liar.

"Mitch?"

Slowing his breathing, it took a few prolonged seconds to answer. "I'm fine."

"My car is out in the driveway."

Gathering up her purse and the picture frame, Zoe moved ahead of him as he hobbled along, holding the screen door open for him. Night had fallen since they'd been discussing his son. He made sure to concentrate where he walked to keep from falling flat on his face in front of her.

Before getting in the car, the overhead streetlight revealed a car seat in the back. A stuffed animal lay beside it. Reality hit him a little harder in the gut.

"Are you okay?" Zoe asked from behind him. "Do you need help getting in?"

Mitch ignored the question and slowly ducked inside. Zoe closed the door for him, making him realize how her news, compounded by his injury, threw him more off balance than usual. He thought the accident was the only event to upend his life. How wrong.

As Zoe drove through Cypress Pointe, Mitch noticed Main Street hadn't changed much. Some of the gift stores were closed for the night, but the local restaurants were hopping with customers. The wind flowing in from the window he'd cracked open carried the scent of burgers, making his stomach nauseous. After settling in at Wyatt's place, he hadn't had much of an appetite. Sometimes the headaches were so skull-crushing he couldn't eat until the pain eased. Tonight was one of those episodes.

The sights grew more familiar the closer she drove to their neighborhood. When she passed by their street, a sense of confusion enveloped him. He closed his eyes, tried to visualize the location of their house. Finally, he connected the dots. "You missed the turn."

She looked at him quickly, then back at the road. "No. I live at my mother's house."

He frowned, an action that brought on another round of pounding in his skull. The doctors had told him stress would aggravate his symptoms. He hadn't believed them until now.

"Since when?"

"After I found out I was pregnant. I had a few…difficult months. I sold the house and moved in with her."

"You sold our house?"

She bit her lower lip, never taking her eyes off the road. "I'm… At the time, it was a good idea. And living with Mom is a great help. She adores Leo."

He started to nod, then stopped. The pain hadn't abated. "I get it," he snapped. With the pain came mood swings he hadn't entirely learned to manage. "I wasn't here to help you."

"No. You weren't."

The tension rose between them and the remainder of the ride couldn't pass quickly enough for Mitch. When they finally pulled into the driveway, he had the door open before she'd completely stopped.

"Mitch. Be careful."

He pivoted out of the seat, ready to send a zinger Zoe's way, just as Samantha came out of the house, joy written all over her face. She drew closer and he was afraid she might try to hug him, so he braced himself in anticipation. When she saw the cane, she slowed. Her eyes went wide at his appearance and she completely stopped.

"Oh, Mitch. Zoe said you were…"

The pity in her voice had him grounding his teeth. He leveled his voice. "Samantha. Good to see you."

He hated looking so helpless, feeling so useless. A shell of the former man.

"Mom, Mitch wants to see Leo."

"He's still asleep," Samantha said.

"We don't plan on waking him." Zoe rounded the front of the car to join them. She glanced at Mitch. "Ready?"

In response to her question, he took a halting step forward, then another. She turned and led him into the house, followed by Samantha. Thankfully, her expression had changed.

They entered the living room of the roomy ranch-style house. He'd spent most of his high school years here, visiting Zoe, but also putting some distance between him and his father.

The memories were a bit fuzzy right now, but he would never forget that this was where Samantha encouraged his gift. Where he'd taken the first steps in realizing a career that had ultimately taken him away from his family and friends.

Your choice.

Yes, it had been. In pursuit of freedom and adventure, his life had taken a dramatic turn. The ultimate price to pay: nearly losing his life.

"This way," Zoe said, leading him down the dim hallway. She pushed open a slightly ajar door and disappeared inside the room. Mitch hesitated. Once he went inside, viewed his son for the first time in person, his life would change forever.

Zoe stuck her head back out into the hallway. "Mitch?"

"Give me a moment."

Annoyance crossed her face, then she was gone again. His world suddenly tilted out of control. He braced a hand against the wall, tried to wrap his mind around the fact that he was a father. Did he have it in him to act like one?

Even when they were trying to get pregnant, the thought of taking care of another life had frequently crossed his mind. He hadn't taken the idea lightly, no matter what Zoe thought. But unlike most fathers, he hadn't had nine months to prepare for his role. In his case, he'd had less than an hour to get ready.

Once the panic subsided, he hesitantly stepped through the doorway. A small lamp set on a dresser sent soft light over the room. The scent of… Was that baby powder? In the corner sat a shelf filled with books. Plastic toys littered the rug in front of it.

Zoe stood beside a crib. From across the room, he could see her leaning over. Attending to the baby? She looked at him, the fierce love etched on her face stopping him from moving. He'd always thought Zoe was pretty, but now, she took his breath away. Becoming a mother had transformed her. She was no longer just his high school sweetheart. Before him stood a full-grown woman, a mother, who had become more beautiful in the time he'd been away.

"Come see your son."

Leaning on the cane, he made his legs move forward. When he came to the side of the crib, he gazed down at the sleeping boy, who had one thumb brushed up against his lips. Mitch's breath caught and completely left him for a moment.

Zoe moved to give him better access. He

stepped closer. Leo's chest rose as he inhaled and exhaled. Mitch stared, then began taking inventory, like he imagined a father would upon the delivery of his child. Ten fingers and toes. Light colored hair, standing on end. Chunky little legs. Rosy skin. Spiky eyelashes caressing his cheek.

A longing, unlike any he'd ever experienced before in his life, pummeled him. This was his son. His flesh and blood. A miracle.

"He's so small."

Zoe fingered the downy soft hair sprouting from his head. "He's actually at the correct weight percentile, according to his pediatrician."

"So he's healthy?"

"Ear infections have plagued him since he first came home, but the pediatrician is on top of the problem. He eats well. Babbles up a storm."

Mitch tilted his head to get a different view. "What color are his eyes?"

"Blue."

He swallowed against the sudden thickness in his throat.

With halting fingers, he reached out. He barely touched his son's arm, so soft and plump, then moved to Leo's face where the tips of his fingers brushed his cheek. When Leo shifted in his sleep, Mitch jerked his hand back to his side.

"He's okay," Zoe said in a low tone. "Just resettling."

Right. People moved in their sleep. Even babies.

She gently pushed Leo's thumb from the proximity of his mouth. "He never took to a pacifier, so I have to keep his thumb away from his mouth."

Mitch didn't know what to say. Taking care of a baby was completely foreign to him.

"I'll give you a few minutes." She pointed to a white radio-looking thing on the dresser. "The monitor is on. Call if you need anything."

As she walked away, Mitch gazed down at his son. His chest swelled. Was this what pride felt like?

"Hey, buddy," he whispered.

Leo puffed out a breath, but instead of panicking at the child's response, Mitch smiled. The longer he stood over the crib, the more a sense of protectiveness seized him. Now that the initial shock had worn off, he desperately wanted to be a part of this child's life. No matter that he and Zoe had made a mess of their marriage, he was thankful they had produced this miracle despite things not working out.

For some reason, thoughts of baseball crossed Mitch's mind. Little League. Rooting for his son as his short legs ran the bases. Wait, was he walking on his own yet? Had he taken his first steps? He'd have to ask Zoe. Before long, he'd tell his son stories about all the cool places he'd traveled to in the course of his career. Eventually, he would take Leo along. Include him in the adventures. Silently, Mitch vowed to be present in his son's life. He would never be like his own father, distant and disapproving.

Yes, he'd continue to travel for his job, but he'd never close himself off like his own father. So rigid in his ways, he'd tried to squelch Mitch's spirit.

As he got older and increasingly curious, Mitch would often sneak off whatever military base they were on and explore the local sights and, more often than not, take off on thrilling adventures. His father never approved. Luckily, when his dad retired, he'd brought the family to Cypress Pointe, although he'd expected his son to carry on the generations-old tradition of joining the army.

Ironically, it had been all those years growing up traveling from base to base that had given Mitch a severe case of wanderlust. So, he would show Leo the world. Give him options. Nurture him in a way his own father never had.

The door opened behind him. Zoe's vanilla and floral fragrance reached him before she did. She took her place beside him again.

"Why Leo? His name, I mean," he asked after a prolonged moment of watching their son together.

Zoe crossed the room to a basket of stuffed animals. Removing a lion from the top, she returned to the crib and held it out for him to see.

"Do you remember him?"

Mitch stared at the small animal with the fluffy mane. "No."

"We were in high school. My mother had missed my debate team competition and I was really upset. A few weeks later, a carnival came to town and you made me go. To cheer me up, you said." A small smile curved her lips as she brushed her fingers over the lion's mane. "You won this at one of the game booths. Told me not to be sad or scared because Leo the lion would look out for me."

Her misty gaze met his. "I found the lion when I was packing up our belongings at the old house to move here. I held on to this little guy and cried, over the memories we'd shared and the reality that I would never see you again." She took a stuttering breath. "When Leo was born, I wanted to give him a strong name. I thought he needed it since he'd never know his father."

Mitch swallowed hard.

He'd missed so much.

And on the tail of that revelation, anger at the events that had kept him from returning home simmered, but he held it in check. He'd deal with it later, when he could sort through his emotions and vent without giving Zoe reason to keep him at arm's length.

"So, what do you think?" she asked.

"I think I can't wait to get to know him."

The frown again.

"What?"

"I just can't picture you staying in Cypress Pointe long enough for any quality time with Leo."

"My priorities will change."

"Really?" Disbelief tinged her voice. "For how long?"

He turned, bit back the impatient retort he wanted to hurl at her. "For as long as it takes. He's my child, too, Zoe."

A mulish expression he recognized as trouble crossed her face. "We'll see."

"Do you plan on giving me a hard time about my place in Leo's life?"

"No. But I won't let you hurt him when you revert back to form and leave for weeks at a time. I won't explain why his daddy isn't here for the milestones in his life."

Did she have that little faith in him that she thought he would abandon their son? The steel in her tone reflected exactly that. She had no faith that he would put his son above his career.

"I'll be here."

She snorted. "Right. Like every other time you made that promise, only to break your word."

"This is different."

Her brow rose.

Yes, he had let Zoe down. She'd never understood his need for adventure to begin with, but she had accepted it as part of the man she loved. However, once she'd wanted a baby, things had changed. With each miscarriage, he'd wanted out of the pressure and the expectations he couldn't deliver on. She'd never stopped to consider how the loss of each baby took a piece of his soul, and because she was suffering, he'd never made his sorrow an issue.

But now that Leo was here, she would never stand in the way of his being a father. He'd make sure of it.

Leo rustled again.

"He senses the tension between us." Zoe adjusted the blanket over him. "Let's leave him be."

Mitch gazed at his son, then at his wife. "This conversation isn't finished."

ZOE CLOSED THE door behind her, waiting for the soft snick. Mitch had hobbled to the living room ahead of her. She took this time alone to center her thoughts and tamp down her frustration.

So Mitch was going to march into their lives and expect nothing had changed? That he had a right to make decisions affecting her son?

Yes. Her son. She'd given birth to him. Raised him. Protected him. Worried over every aspect of his life. Even if Mitch hadn't been injured, she didn't believe he'd have stuck around to help her. His track record spoke volumes.

Squaring her shoulders, she joined Mitch. He paced the room, his agitation evidenced by his clumsy gait. When he passed her, she saw that his face had gone even more pale, if that was possible. He rubbed his temple with his free hand while he leaned heavily on his cane with the other.

"Mitch, there's nothing to discuss."

"Really? I beg to differ."

"You haven't been a part of his life."

"Not on purpose," he said, his words clipped and angry.

She glimpsed the hurt on his face but held firm to her conviction. "I have to look out for his best interests."

"And that includes keeping him from his father?" He made a turn, stumbled and reached out with the arm she noticed he kept tucked close to his body. He leaned over the couch to steady himself on the armrest. A small gasp escaped her, but his sharp look kept her from rushing to his aid.

"You aren't in any condition to take care of a child."

"Not now, but this condition won't last forever."

Maybe she should have felt sorry for his plight, but she wasn't willing to barter the welfare of her child over her sympathy for a man who had left her too many times to count. Did that make her cold? No. It made her a mother.

"So you're going to recover here? In Cypress Pointe?"

"Yes." He tried to walk again, but ended up sinking into a nearby chair. His cheeks were red from exertion now. Zoe knew he was a proud man and pointing out his physical limitations would only make the situation more tense.

"And once the recovery is complete?"

He dropped his head into his hand. Remained silent for too long.

"Mitch? Your recovery?"

His head shot up and he winced. "What?"

"I asked about staying in Cypress Pointe while you recover."

"Yes…that's…ah…the plan."

Unease slithered over her. "Are you okay?"

He rubbed his head. "Don't worry about it."

"Don't worry? Mitch, you want to be part of Leo's life. I have to look out for him."

"And you honestly think I'd hurt him?"

"Not intentionally."

He grimaced.

"Look at it from my point of view, Mitch. You aren't yourself."

"So you'd keep him away from me?"

"No, but I certainly can't leave you alone

with him until you're stronger. He's a bundle of energy right now."

He opened his mouth, presumably to argue the point, then stopped.

She took a seat on the couch near him. Gentled her tone. "Mitch, I don't mean to come across as the bad guy, but Leo is my responsibility. It's not just you and me anymore. Our actions matter now."

"I'm not going to make demands."

"Sure feels like it."

He blew out a breath. "We need to calmly hammer out some sort of…agreement, concerning *our* son."

A shiver ran over her. She knew Mitch enough to know that when he set his mind on something, he didn't give up. Mitch might be okay putting himself in harm's way, but she never would be. And what if Mitch wanted to take Leo out of Cypress Pointe? She couldn't entertain the idea.

"I don't want us to be on opposite sides here, but things are different now," she told him. "This is nothing like our old life."

The defeat in his dark brown eyes nearly undid her, but she remained strong. For her son's sake.

"This is a change of topic," she said, "but do you have a doctor here?"

"I have a referral. I need to make an appointment."

"That's a step." She hesitated. "We aren't together, but I'll try to work something out with you concerning Leo."

The pain in his gaze made her pause. Emotional or physical? She couldn't tell.

His shoulders sagged. Resignation seemed to deflate him. "Please call Wyatt and ask him to come pick me up. I'll wait outside until he gets here."

She rummaged through her purse to find her cell phone. Before she found Wyatt's number and dialed it, Mitch said, "I will be a part of my son's life, Zoe."

His quiet, firm conviction made her fear that Mitch's return from the dead could be the end of the quiet, stable life she'd built for herself and Leo.

CHAPTER FOUR

EARLY THE NEXT MORNING, Zoe paced the living room while Bethany sat on the floor with Leo, feeding him little round cereal oats. She'd turned it into a game, which Leo loved, if his bursts of laugher were any indication.

"Mitch is serious about being present in Leo's life," Zoe said.

"Are you surprised?" Bethany placed another *O* in Leo's hand and clapped when he clumsily tossed it in his mouth. "This is a big shock for him."

"Yes, but he's never wanted to hang around Cypress Pointe before." Which, when translated by Zoe, meant he hadn't wanted to hang around her.

"He's never had a child before."

Zoe ran a hand through her short hair. "I can't believe this whole thing is happening."

"You're going to have to deal with this whether you like it or not."

"I know." Zoe stopped and sank down to the

carpet to join them, smoothing a lick of hair standing straight up on her son's head. "I'm just not entirely sure how I feel about the sudden change."

"Since I'm usually the outspoken one, I'm gonna say it." Bethany placed a hand on Zoe's arm. "No matter what happens with Mitch, you can handle it. When you set your mind on a task, you can accomplish anything. I've been telling you this our entire lives. Why do you think I pushed you to run for mayor?"

"Accomplish anything? I barely leave Cypress Pointe."

"It's not that you can't. More like you won't."

Zoe absently rubbed the scar on her arm. The physical reminder of why she worked hard to make Cypress Pointe a safe place to live. "Why would you say that?"

"Because things in life happen." Bethany nodded at Leo. "You have to be prepared."

"I'm always prepared."

"Okay, that may be true." Bethany ran a finger over Leo's hair. Nodded her head at Zoe's arm. "But you have to stop blaming yourself."

"Who else is there? It was my idea to go shopping. I ran us straight into danger."

"It seemed like a good idea at the time. And in the end, we were safe."

"Tell that to your parents."

Bethany frowned. "It's time they stopped treating you like some kind of evil person. You didn't force me to go along with you the day of the robbery."

Zoe could barely look at her friend. "No, but it still haunts me to this day."

"Bad things happen everywhere, Zoe. We witnessed a bank robbery sixteen years ago. We survived." Bethany sent her a probing look. "You're going to have to deal with the phobia at some point in your life."

Yes, Zoe knew that. She just didn't want to face the truth.

"There's going to come a time when Leo is going to want or need to leave Cypress Pointe. What will you do then?"

Zoe didn't have an answer.

"It's time, Zoe."

She blew out a breath. Her doubts lingered.

"You'll figure this out, my friend, because this little guy is going to force you to." Bethany chucked Leo's chin and cooed in baby speak. "Won't she, buddy?"

Zoe laughed at her friend's ease at doling out serious adult advice, then switching to sweet baby talk.

Bethany glanced up. "Face it, Zoe. Leo will

get you to confront your fears in ways Mitch never could."

In her eyes, Mitch had been in such a hurry to get away from her. Or had he just gotten tired of her refusing to do anything about those fears? It had been easier to blame him than consider she didn't have the backbone to stare her demons straight in the face.

"When did you become so smart?"

"Since you gave me this beautiful godson. I get to spoil him and give him back to you."

"Thanks so much."

"You're welcome."

The evidence of spoiling lay scattered all over the carpet: toys in all shapes and sizes and brightly colored clothing. Bethany had gone out of her way to bring lots of goodies for Leo.

"You might be looking at this from the wrong angle," Bethany said as she handed Leo a block.

"Do tell."

"Embrace that Mitch is back. Help him recover. It's not like that isn't in your wheelhouse. You help everyone."

"In my position as mayor."

"Please, you've been coming up with ways to better people's lives since we were kids. Always planning fund-raisers or donating time and energy to other organizations. Remember our first lemonade stand?"

Zoe chuckled. "If I recall, all the proceeds went to the animal shelter."

"Sounds right. We were in our save-the-mutt phase."

"You always went along with me."

"Because you always had a compelling argument to do good. Who could resist?"

"We did make a good team."

"Until Mitch came on the scene."

Zoe held back a smile. More like Mitch had made a grand entrance into her life.

She'd been at the park, checking off names for a 5K run to support cancer research. The runners had lined up at the start line when all of a sudden a guy with long shaggy hair came careening through the crowd on a skateboard. He barely missed the runners, hopping off the board right in front of her table, stomping his foot on the edge to make the board fly up into his hands. With an unrepentant grin, he asked if it was too late to sign up. She was speechless, but had nodded. After the race, he sought her out and their relationship developed from there.

So long ago. Where had that young love gone?

"He does have a way of making a statement," Bethany continued.

Yes, he did. It served him well when he went hunting for big profile stories to document.

"I suppose I should hear him out. See what he has in mind. You're right. I can't run from this. Now that Mitch knows about Leo, he'll never let me keep him out of his son's life."

"And you shouldn't."

True. But she couldn't stop the worry and the excuses filling her mind since she'd laid eyes on him yesterday.

"Can I risk him taking Leo off on his own? In his current condition?"

"Do you think he's even gotten that far in the process? From what you said, he's dealing with physical limitations. Mitch may have taken off at a moment's notice to cover an event or a story, but he isn't unrealistic. He's got to know that becoming a father to Leo will take time."

Guilt washed over her. She'd been so overly concerned about how Mitch's return would impact her and Leo's life, she hadn't really focused on him. The man who needed a cane to walk. Whose scalp looked like a jigsaw puzzle of scars. Who needed serious medical support. If she'd let herself dwell on his condition, she'd probably have broken down on the spot. Her once healthy, vivacious husband had been reduced to a shadow of the former man. Why hadn't she been more sympathetic?

Because you don't want him to hurt you again.

Maybe. But what person didn't at least try for a little more compassion in a situation like this? Certainly not a selfish person. Is that who she'd become?

"I should ask him more questions when I see him again. He mentioned he had a referral to a local doctor."

"Zoe, you guys have a long history together. I witnessed the crushing hurt you went through while trying to make things right with Mitch and it wasn't working. The agony of deciding to divorce. I get that you're afraid to remotely consider laying your heart on the line with him, either by co-parenting or helping him get through the recovery process." She paused and met Zoe's eyes. "But you have a big heart, my friend. No matter the personal stuff between you two, you can't keep yourself from pitching in to aid those in a bind."

At that moment, Leo rolled onto his knees and pushed up. Zoe held his hand when he staggered and plopped down on his diaper-clad behind.

"He's going to be running before you know it," Bethany said.

"Like his father," Zoe whispered and just like that, the reality of their current situation hit like a ton of bricks.

Her husband was home. Alive. Injured. Wanting to know his son. It was all too much.

Bethany asked, "Hey, you okay?"

Zoe blinked and took a breath. "I'll be fine."

"Good. I don't want to have to worry about you while I'm gone." Bethany glanced at her watch. "And on that note, I have to run. I've got calls to make, then brunch with the family before I head to the airport."

After she rose, Bethany scooped Leo into her arms.

"I'm going to miss you," Zoe said as she stood. "Who else can I talk to about all this?"

"Mitch?"

Zoe shot her an annoyed look.

"Just a suggestion."

"Which I will take under advisement. Now—"

The doorbell cut off her next words.

"Who could be here this early on a Sunday morning?" she wondered out loud, walking to the door while Bethany cooed her final baby goo-goos.

When the door opened, her eyes went wide to find Mitch on the porch, a white bag in one hand, a white-knuckle grip on the cane in the other.

"Good morning, Zoe. Hope you don't mind that I stopped by."

"Without a call first? Why would I mind?"

He winced at her sarcasm.

"If you'd asked you would have known."

He opened his mouth, then closed it. When Leo squealed from the living room, his shoulders slumped. Along with her displeasure. What a shrew she'd turned into.

"C'mon in," she said, opening the screen door to let him in.

"Sorry. Next time, I'll make sure to check with you first."

As she closed the door, Mitch hobbled into the room. Leo hid his face in the crook of Bethany's neck, but Bethany's lips curved into a big smile.

"Mitch. I wanted to see you before flying out again."

"Same here."

Zoe came around Mitch and took Leo from Bethany's arms. Once her godson was taken care of, Bethany wrapped Mitch in a gentle hug.

"I'd say you're looking good, but…"

Mitch responded with a startled bark of laughter. "Truck wrecks will do that to a person."

Bethany stepped back. "Really, it is good to see you in one piece."

Leo squirmed and kicked. Zoe set him down among his toys.

"Good timing. Bethany was just about to leave."

"Yep. Places to go. People to see." Bethany hugged Zoe, then grabbed her purse from the couch. Pointing a finger at them, she said, "Play nice, you two."

Silence mingled with crackling tension after Bethany closed the door behind her.

"I brought breakfast." Mitch held out the bag. "Bagels and cream cheese."

As if understanding the bag held food, Leo grabbed Zoe's leg and tried to stand, one hand turned up as if reaching for the tasty treats. Zoe lifted him into her arms again.

"Would you like some coffee? I made a fresh pot."

"Thank you."

With Mitch following, she entered the kitchen, grabbing two empty mugs from the cabinet with her free hand. Leo bounced on her hip, a sign he wasn't happy with his current location, so she settled him in the high chair and sprinkled cereal on the tray.

"Your mother remodeled," Mitch commented as he set the bag down and leaned a hip against the counter.

"The kitchen was hopelessly outdated when I moved in. Mom finally decided to get the work done."

The golden seventies look had been replaced with crisp white Shaker cabinets, a bold granite countertop and a dark floor.

He gazed around the room. "Samantha always had a flair for colors."

"Actually, I picked out the color scheme. She wanted to go with red and black." Zoe shook her head. "Too dark. We battled over that decision."

A fleeting smile curved Mitch's lips. "Your battles were pretty epic."

Mitch shifted his weight from the one leg that Zoe noticed he favored. He sagged a bit, then straightened before moving to the high chair to shove some of the cereal closer to his son's chubby hands. Leo grabbed Mitch's finger and tugged, his nonsensical babble catching Mitch off guard. He froze, as if not sure what to do. Her breath caught in her chest as she watched. When Leo dropped his finger to capture the cereal, Mitch backed up to his original position, looking pleased.

"I did some thinking last night," he said.

Zoe resumed pouring steaming coffee into the mugs and brought Mitch's to him. He didn't reach out to take it, still distracted by the interaction with Leo, so she set it on the counter, ignoring the subtle spicy cologne that she associated with him. How many times had she sniffed his pillowcase after he went missing, hoping for the sensory connection that triggered her memories? Making her feel he was still with her. Right up until the day it faded completely, leaving her bereft and filled with renewed sorrow. After that, she didn't like to go into his closet for fear the scent on his clothing would bring her to her knees.

She hadn't been sure how to process her life back then. She still wasn't sure today.

"And what did you come up with?" She grabbed her mug and carefully sipped the too-strong brew.

"I agree that physically I can't take care of Leo." He glanced at his son and smiled before turning his attention back to her. The smile disappeared. "I'll call and make an appointment with a local doctor first thing tomorrow."

Okay, this was progress. She was all about

taking action to get things done. "Can I help in any way? Drive you there? Sit in and listen to the treatment plan? Two sets of ears are always better than one, especially at a doctor's visit."

"That would probably be a good idea. I'm…" He cleared his throat. "Retaining information is still a little iffy."

Her heart squeezed. He'd lowered his head when revealing that truth. Mitch had always been so sure of himself. To see the doubts reflected on his face broke her heart, but she knew he wouldn't appreciate her sympathy.

"But I meant what I said yesterday. I want to be a part of Leo's life."

Upon hearing his name, the baby looked across the room to Mitch and sent him a goofy grin. Before she realized he was moving, Mitch inched closer to wipe the drool from Leo's chin with his bib. These were all firsts for him.

"I get it, Mitch. But, I'll be honest. I have to be cautious about whatever we decide, so let's take it slowly."

She took another sip of coffee to hide her reaction. Seeing father and son together was more complicated and heartrending than she'd anticipated.

Mitch settled against the counter again. "Thank you. I didn't mean to come across so strong yesterday, but I need to know where I stand. You get that, right?"

She did.

"What about us?"

She nearly choked. "Us? There is no us, Mitch."

"So that's it? You've closed the door on any possibility that we can work things out?"

Did she want to rehash the past? No. Too much had changed since he'd left. "We made our decision."

He stared down at his untouched coffee mug.

"Let me ask you a question, Mitch. Are you planning on going back to work after you heal?"

She nearly held her breath as she waited for his answer.

"I have to."

Hurt swamped her, but she shoved it away. It wasn't like she'd expected any other answer. "Then my response is still the same. There is no us."

Leo began to fuss, an I-need-my-diaper-changed expression making his face red.

Zoe strode to the high chair and removed her son. "I need to take care of Leo. You know the way out."

As she passed, Leo reached out for Mitch.

She tugged her son closer and escaped the bleak expression in her husband's eyes.

MITCH STOOD IN the empty kitchen.

He rubbed the ache throbbing in his temple. He hadn't slept last night, instead sitting on Wyatt's porch, trying to come up with solutions but only managing to muddle through the fog in his brain. His thoughts were fuzzy, as if he were looking at the world through distorted glass, never able to completely focus. He could see things moving on the other side, but they never came into clear definition. It was annoying, to say the least, while frightening at the same time.

He'd dwelled a lot on Leo, experiencing joy and fear in equal measure. Zoe was right. How was he going to take care of his son? Not just physically, but emotionally? He could barely figure things out for himself. His own emotions varied day to day, depending on how he felt or how much he could corral his dizzy thinking. Some days, he flew off the handle. Others, he was calm to the point of not being able to get off the couch. And financially? Would he work again as a photographer? That was the biggest nightmare of all, but not for the reasons Zoe would naturally accuse him of.

Yes, he'd seen the betrayal in her eyes that

always appeared when he said he would go back to work. But things were different now. He had a son to support. The decision to continue in his career had nothing to do with ego or getting out of Cypress Pointe.

When he'd first started traveling, he enjoyed the freedom. Once he began buying into the fame, the excitement, jetting around the world, it crept under his skin. When he tried to explain the reasoning to Zoe, she didn't understand. But he was hooked.

Now, his decisions had to be based on everything to do with the little boy he'd fallen in love with at first sight. Travel or stay put, it didn't matter. He needed to provide for his child. If Zoe didn't get that, then maybe things were finally over between them.

With a sigh, he pushed away from the counter, leaning heavily on the cane. On his way through the living room to the front door, he heard music floating from Samantha's studio.

He changed direction and slowly hobbled to the back of the house. The scene he came upon was familiar, yet vastly different from the last time he was here.

Bright light filled the room. Samantha stood before a canvas, feverishly dabbing paint on a half-finished work. Colors bombarded him, from the bright yellow walls to the rainbow of different colored paint tubes on a rack to the canvases in various stages of completion scattered around the room. A jar of brushes in differing sizes and shapes lay on its side on the table. A clear glass held murky blue water. Cleaning fluid tinged the air. He leaned against the door frame, closing his eyes as memories assailed him.

Showing Samantha his first photographs and waiting for her evaluation. Picking Zoe up and twirling her in a circle after accepting his first real paying job, her laughter ringing in his ears. Arguing about the future and what would happen to their marriage. If he could remember all that, why not the events of an accident that had put him in this current situation? And why couldn't he shake the sense of urgency to unravel the truth?

"Mitch. I didn't know you were here."

He opened his eyes, catching Samantha lowering her brush to wipe her fingers.

"I came by to check on Leo."

"He's something, isn't he?" Pride infused her tone, surprising him. She hadn't been very motherly with Zoe.

"He is. I'm excited to get to know him."

"You will. Don't let Zoe railroad you." She pointed a paint-speckled finger at him. "You're Leo's father and have every right to enjoy that child."

"Railroad?"

Samantha cleaned the brush she'd been holding. "Yes, railroad. Since she's become mayor, she's gotten bossy."

Any more bossy than she'd always been?

"It's not that the power has gone to her head, exactly. More like she has the power to get things done and won't take no for an answer."

"Zoe has always been passionate." That was one of her many qualities that he'd been attracted to. Still admired her zeal to get the job done despite their differences over the years.

"Well, now she has a title to go along with it."

"Why do I get the feeling you aren't thrilled about that?"

Samantha shrugged and got that elusive look that she used with art critics and dealers when she didn't want to answer a question.

"It's different."

Meaning Zoe didn't have time to take care of her. He recognized her pout.

"You always knew she was destined to run the town."

"It was inevitable, I suppose."

This would explain the tension he felt when the two of them were in the same room yesterday. At least one thing hadn't changed.

She waved her hand. "But enough about me. Are you going to work while you're home?"

He raised a brow. Hadn't she noticed he wasn't exactly in any shape to go out and scout locations to take pictures?

"I don't have a camera right now."

His words earned him a stunned expression.

"Zoe mentioned you were having problems remembering what happened the day of the accident?"

"Yes."

He still could only piece together a few details of that day. Leaving the camp and driving the old pickup truck to the prearranged spot for…for what? It couldn't have been work related since he'd left his credentials behind. Did it have to do with the refugees he'd been helping? Even his passport went missing, which held him up at the consulate when he'd wanted to return home. He really needed to talk to someone who was there. But who? He couldn't remember even one name.

A fuzzy image flashed through his mind,

only to disappear. Shadows obscuring a face? He blew out a breath in frustration.

"Mitch. Did you hear me? You can get another camera."

Sure, he could. And then what? He certainly was in no condition to pick up where he'd left off. And even when he was ready, had his ability to pick out a subject been affected by the head injury? The blurriness he'd lived with for weeks after the accident had finally receded, but what if his vision was permanently damaged? He couldn't consider that possibility. He'd built his life around a keen eye and sharp instincts. If they had been destroyed in the accident, what would he do?

"Mitch? Are you listening?"

He shook off his innermost fears and tried to pull a convincing smile.

"Sorry. I zoned out there for a minute."

Sympathy crossed his mother-in-law's face. He'd come to really resent that particular look. On anybody.

"I'm sure once you remember, you'll get the camera back."

To be honest, he was almost glad it had gone missing. Soon, though, he would have to find out if he could still take photographs.

"You're probably right."

Pleased by his answer, Samantha went on to fill him in on town happenings. He'd missed a lot while he was gone; only this time, it mattered. After nearly two years, he wanted to catch up on events in Cypress Pointe.

"Your parents will be stunned to see you. What do you think your father will say?"

He shook his head. His dad would probably berate him on how his foolish "hobby" had nearly gotten him killed.

He pushed away from the wall. "I need to run. It was good catching up with you."

"Don't let Zoe discourage you, Mitch. You belong here."

"Yes. I know."

On wobbly legs, he made it to the front door. At the last moment, he paused. A strange sensation niggled at him. He turned to find Zoe watching him from the kitchen entryway. Her closed expression made him curious. Once, he could read every emotion on her face. Not any longer.

"You'll call me about the doctor's appointment?"

"I said I would."

She nodded. "We'll make plans for you and Leo after the visit."

He nodded and walked out into the bright

sunshine. He didn't want to argue. The visit had taxed his strength and he wasn't up to exchanging words with her. It was enough that she would accompany him to see the doctor. Her presence alone would give him the moral support he was, if a little begrudgingly, acknowledging that he desperately needed.

He'd already had enough negative diagnoses to last him a lifetime. *You may never walk without a cane. Your memory may never resurface. Your brain may never function properly.*

Maybe this was all true, but it was not going to keep him from his son.

CHAPTER FIVE

PUTTING THE CAR in Reverse, Zoe mulled over the last few hours. The doctor's visit turned out to be more complex than she'd expected.

Not that she'd had any clue as to what would happen. But after listening to Dr. Warren evaluate Mitch, Zoe didn't know what to feel. To avoid a sense of helplessness, she'd taken notes while Mitch sat beside her, taciturn, with few comments to share. The doctor had tried to get Mitch to engage, but that stubborn frown never left his face. He'd always been a horrible patient.

When Mitch had called her with the appointment date for Thursday, the reality of his health became tangibly real. She'd jumped on the internet to find out all she could about brain injuries, only to be overwhelmed by the information. She had no idea where Mitch was in the recovery process, nor what treatments he'd already undergone. He was tight-lipped about his time overseas, so she could only imagine what he'd endured prior to returning to the States.

"How do you feel about this doctor?" she asked as she pulled out of the medical complex once they'd finished setting up future appointments.

Mitch stared out the window. "Fine."

"Considering he didn't have any records from when you were previously in the hospital, he seemed to sum up the situation well."

Mitch shrugged.

As they had talked, Mitch revealed that he'd had to relearn how to walk once he'd woken from the coma. Her chest had hurt as she listened to his monotone voice relay the early days after the accident. He'd spent hours, first with a walker, shuffling up and down the hospital hallways, until he'd graduated to a cane. He couldn't be sure of the timeline since his memory was still spotty.

His vision, Mitch admitted, had been affected but was getting better. She'd been shocked because he never mentioned the problem. The doctor concurred after an examination. With one good checkmark next to his name, Zoe could breathe more easily.

The doctor ordered a CAT scan to evaluate the progress of the brain injury, along with physical therapy for Mitch's leg and arm, as a beginning treatment plan. Once he read the scan, he hoped to have an additional diagnosis but was clear about them not getting their hopes up yet. When he mentioned seeing a neuropsychologist, Mitch's shoulders had gone rigid.

"Dr. Warren said the CAT scan will probably give him a better idea of your prognosis."

Out of the corner of her eye, she saw Mitch idly rubbing his scalp, his face still a blank mask.

"Next week, we'll have a better idea of your recovery."

Silence filtered through the car, heavy and uncomfortable, before Mitch finally spoke.

"Just drop me off at Wyatt's and we'll call it even."

Zoe pressed her lips together. Held her tongue. All this was new to her. Mitch had been dealing with doctors and hospitals and who knew what else on his own for months now. She didn't want to add to his stress by asking endless questions.

"Sure. Do you want me to drive you to the imaging center next week?"

"Don't you have to work?"

"I can juggle my schedule."

His voice grew tight. "I'll let you know."

She pulled into the driveway of Wyatt's cottage and put the car in Park. "Do you need any—"

"I can take care of myself," he snapped.

She tried not to show any outward sign that his mood upset her. From what she'd read, patients with these types of injuries were sometimes irritable, likely to lash out at those caring for them.

Which she was barely doing.

Guilt consumed her. They'd agreed to get Mitch set up with the doctor before trying to deal with their personal problems. She'd thought that was a good idea at the time; but now?

Pasting on a sunny smile, she said, "Well, call me if you need anything."

"I'd like to see Leo."

Another area where she had to tread lightly.

"The sitter is with him this afternoon. If you want, I can swing by after work and bring you to the house."

"You don't trust me with him?"

"He doesn't know you yet."

"And he won't if you keep me away." His good leg bounced in place. She'd noticed this week that when he was tense, he grew fidgety.

The dark circles under his eyes, the restlessness and the way he favored the cane had her worried, but she also knew Leo was the one bright spot in Mitch's day. But until they had a better idea of his recovery, she couldn't chance leaving Leo alone with him.

"Are you sleeping?"

He looked away.

"Eating?"

No answer.

Shaking her head, she put the car in Reverse.

He sat forward in his seat. "Hey, what're you doing?"

"Taking you to get some food."

"I'm not hungry."

"Really? When was the last time you had a decent meal?"

"Zoe," he nearly growled. "Leave it alone."

"Can't. Not if you want to be in better shape to spend time with Leo."

He clamped his mouth shut and sank back against the seat. Yeah, it was low using their son to get him to go along with her, but it was the only leverage she had.

An hour later, he'd devoured a big late-morning breakfast and she'd driven them to the beach-access parking lot. She turned off the ignition and shifted in her seat to face him.

"Not hungry, huh?"

"Don't start."

"Then, from now on, be honest with me, Mitch."

After a couple of long static seconds, he nodded.

"Want to go sit on the bench by the sand?"

Instead of answering, he opened the door. She quickly scrambled from behind the wheel. He was already heading to the bench when she joined him, but she made sure to let him make his unsteady way on his own steam.

They sat for a few minutes, watching the scene play out around them.

Little children scampered about, mostly followed by mothers with a frazzled look Zoe recognized. Leo was already too curious for his own good; she couldn't imagine what it would be like when he could really toddle around.

The green-blue water lapped against the sugary white sand, calm in the sea-scented breeze. Seagulls squawked, hovering in the sky until finally diving to snag food just below the water's surface. One little boy held up what Zoe thought might be a sandwich, but his mother quickly snatched it away. If the gulls knew there was human food offered nearby, they wouldn't leave the youngster alone, which created a mess for everyone in the vicinity.

"Do you bring Leo here?" Mitch asked.

"Sometimes. He's still too busy putting everything in his mouth so I err on the side of caution."

"Sand isn't the most appetizing."

"The one time he did get some in his mouth he tried spitting it out. I was trying hard not to laugh at his hysterical facial expression while at the same time telling him, no."

"He listens well?"

"He does, but he is very inquisitive. I'm constantly watching him so he doesn't get himself into trouble."

"Isn't that part of growing up? Making new discoveries?"

"He's only a year old," she replied, tone dry. "He still needs guidance."

Mitch sent her a black look. "Are you laughing at me?"

She grinned. "Not really. I just know if you had your way, you'd encourage him to try new things, even though he's still too young."

"Believe it or not, I'm not totally clueless. I can wait until he turns two."

Zoe glanced at Mitch's handsome face. Despite the paleness and general look of exhaustion, she saw real humor light his eyes for the first time since he'd been home.

"I always imagined I'd have to keep an eye on you two. I have a feeling there are going to be a lot of don't-tell-Mom moments in my future."

"Does that mean you won't fight me about being active in Leo's life?"

"Not unless something happens to warrant it."

Zoe reached out to touch his arm, then pulled back. Touching probably wouldn't be a good idea. Not yet.

"Mitch, I get the feeling you'd rather not talk about it, but at the doctor's visit today, you didn't seem very…interested with your treatment."

He gazed out over the water. "I've had my fill of being poked and prodded."

"But you do want to improve, right?"

"More than you know." His words, though impassioned, where spoken so quietly she had to strain to hear his voice.

"So you do what the doctor says."

"I think I have a much more detailed concept of what my prognosis will entail. Therapy. Tests. Appointments. And all the while questioning if I'll remain in this condition permanently."

"Which you'd hate."

"Exactly."

A shout drew Zoe's attention to the water. A boy splashed his mother while she tried, unsuccessfully, to scold him.

"At the risk of sounding overly optimistic, think positive."

"I'll try," came his droll reply.

"Seriously, Mitch, do you feel any better since the accident?"

Mitch tapped his cane against his good leg. "The biggest positive change is my vision. Otherwise, I'm not healing as quickly as I'd like."

"See, that's a step in the right direction."

He stopped tapping and gazed in her direction. "You always were a cheerleader."

"You make it sound like a bad thing. I've always been a glass half-full."

"And what happens if my recovery is half-empty?"

"Then we keep working."

His gaze captured hers. "We?"

Her stomach fluttered—was it because she didn't want to discuss the state of their marriage, or admit she still found his dark brown eyes compelling? For all they'd disagreed about the direction of their lives near the end, there was no denying they shared wonderful memories as well. "We, as in for Leo. So his dad can be a healthy part of his life."

Mitch turned away, his easygoing features now gloomy. "Right. Part of Leo's life."

Zoe thought about how bad stress was for Mitch and decided to change the subject. Since they hadn't made any decisions, now was not the best time to start. He'd had a tough morning, and with the future appointments lined up, it wouldn't get easier anytime soon.

"So, there's a bonfire Saturday night," she said instead.

"Wyatt mentioned it."

"Maybe you'll go?"

"I…" He tap-tap-tapped his cane. "Probably not."

"You should go."

"And you shouldn't push."

She held her hands up in retreat. "Fine. I just thought being around people might be good for you."

"To give them fodder to cringe and try to make small talk when they don't know what to say? Like Lucy at the restaurant today?"

Their waitress, a friend to both since high

school, had been nosy and took too many fur-
tive glances at Mitch. Since his hair hadn't had
time to grow out yet, the scars were still visible. He'd lost weight, his skin tone sallow. If
Lucy had been tongue-tied, maybe Mitch was
right, and other friends would have the same
reaction.

"You're underestimating people."

"And you've always lived in a bubble."

Okay, that was true, but hurtful, because he
probably didn't mean it in a good way.

"On that note, it's time to leave," she said
in a crisp tone. "There are people in Cypress
Pointe who actually value my opinion."

He winced as he pushed himself up from
the bench to lean on the cane. "Sorry, Zoe."

"No, I don't think you are. You always
thought my projects were cute while you were
off gallivanting with the rich and famous. I
make a difference here, Mitch. A difference
you'll notice if you bother to stick around."

Face hot, she turned and stomped back to
the car. *Remember, he's lashing out because
of his injury.* That may be true, but it didn't
hurt any less.

He probably shouldn't have come to the
bonfire tonight, but Mitch needed to make

amends. Zoe had been faithful about coming to his doctor appointments, and what had he done? Given her a hard time. She didn't get the pain he lived with daily, but that didn't mean he should push her away. They were practically divorced. At least, he thought they were. Zoe hadn't been clear on the status of the paperwork, a detail he needed to get to the bottom of. And she had a job. She didn't have to be chauffeuring him around from one consultation to the next.

But he was relieved she'd volunteered.

Why? When spending time with her would only make the final split, when it came, more painful? Because it would come. She'd been clear about that. They may be parents, but they wouldn't be filling the roles as one happy family. Besides, he couldn't be the partner she needed, not when his future health challenges were looking dismal. He hadn't been the best husband when he was healthy. What did he have to offer her now?

In light of the constant pain and uncertainty of his recovery, he wanted some part of his life to be familiar. To have Zoe around, like it had once been. Even if it was only to drive him to the medical center. The fact that she was willing to put up with him gave him hope that he might be okay as a father even if he'd flunked at being a husband.

And right now, he needed hope above all else.

Standing on the edge of the rowdy group surrounding the just-lit fire, Mitch debated the wisdom of showing up this evening. Young guys traded jokes and talked sports while the moms and dads talked about their kids and their jobs. So different from the world he'd been living in six months ago. There, people worried about where they would live or if they had enough food to survive. Could he make the transition back to this life as he'd once known it?

He had to try, for the sake of his son. So, he'd pulled on a pair of worn jeans and a black polo shirt, then slipped on a pair of comfortable shoes. Sitting alone on Wyatt's porch wasn't an option tonight. Part of getting back to normal was at least trying to act normal, at least he assumed. Between the accident, finding out he was a father and returning home to a wife who had lost all faith in him, normal was a relative term.

He'd grown tired of his own company, especially as he racked his brain for a tiny piece of the puzzle that was the accident. The sense of uneasiness he'd experienced ever since leaving Jordan hadn't abated. And what made it worse was that he had no idea what to be uneasy about. He remembered driving away from the camp, but to where? He recalled laughing with someone, but whom? The inability to call his memories into play frustrated him more than his physical limitations. His gut churned with an urgency he could not ignore.

And if he brought this up? People might surmise it was because of his head injury. That he didn't want to face the reality of the accident. But he knew better. Something was up.

Last night, he'd just started to doze off when a strange thought had filtered through his brain: *This was going to be your last assignment. You were returning home to fix things with Zoe.*

He'd awoken with a start. Repeated the thought over and over in a nonstop loop. Was it true or wishful thinking? He needed to get his memory back for more than solving the mystery of what had happened that day. He needed to find out if the thoughts about Zoe were what had driven his last actions. And if the words were indeed accurate, he needed to figure out what fixing things for them meant. Coexisting? Co-parenting? He didn't have a clue.

Through the throng of townspeople, a figure approached Mitch.

"Heard you showed up at my wedding reception. The polite thing to do would have been to come inside and congratulate me."

Max Sanders stopped before Mitch, a grin belying his serious gaze. Yeah, this reaction was exactly what he'd hoped to avoid.

"Couldn't have a dead man crashing your party."

"It would have been memorable."

"Somehow I doubt Lilli would have agreed."

When Max held out his hand, Mitch shook it, surprised at how much he appreciated the token. He and Max hadn't been close confidants, but they'd had a friendship Mitch missed.

"Heard you're staying at Wyatt's place."

"Yes."

"Sorry, man."

Mitch nodded. The depth of his and Zoe's marital woes were not common knowledge in Cypress Pointe.

"If you need anything, let me know."

"Thanks. I've got everything under control."

A dark brow lifted over Max's eyes, but he let the comment go.

"You probably heard that I can't recall the accident."

"Small-town rumors always make it to my ears."

"If at some point I need an investigator, can I call on you?"

Max owned a private investigative firm located right in Cypress Pointe. Mitch knew his reputation and trusted him. By the curiosity on his face, Max was intrigued.

"Do you have reason to believe your accident was anything but?"

Mitch ran a hand over the back of his neck. "As of right now, no. But my gut says otherwise."

"Call whenever you want. Even if it's just to hash things out."

"I will."

More people were arriving and through a break in the crowd, Mitch noticed Zoe. She laughed, her eyes and her smile bright, as she chatted with friends. Dressed in a loose-fitting gauzy blue top, black leggings and flat shoes, he couldn't drag his gaze away. Something in his chest shifted until a tall guy, the one he'd seen with Zoe at the wedding, came to stand by her, resting his hand on the small of her back.

Every instinct he thought long gone screamed for the guy to get his hand off his wife.

Max must have noticed his distraction. He turned to take in the scene around them.

"Tim Bellows. Firefighter."

A hero. How was Mitch, broken down as he was, supposed to compete with the guy?

"From what I understand, they recently started dating."

Great. Another sure sign Zoe was moving on.

Why had he been so stubborn about taking jobs Zoe hadn't approved of? What had he been trying to prove back then?

"Just to be clear," Max continued. "I'm on Team Mitch."

His lips curved, even though he wanted to send Tim packing. "I didn't realize there were sides, but thanks for the vote of confidence."

"We need to stick together."

Indeed. Spying Zoe and her male friend, he came to the conclusion he would appreciate having friends to lean on in the future. Still, his pride revolted at the idea. Emotional support on top of everyone's pity. Now would be a good time to turn tail and head home.

"Don't let him run you off."

Mitch shot Max an interested glance. "You think I'm worried?"

Max chuckled. "I've seen that look before, so, yeah."

So much for thinking he'd kept his misgivings hidden. He was about to speak when Zoe turned in his direction and caught his eye. Their gazes met and held. Heat washed over him and even from a distance, pleasure crossed her features before she closed off her expression. She said a word to the group and headed in his direction.

"That's my cue to leave," Max said. "Good luck."

"I'll need it," he muttered.

As she sauntered over, she greeted Max. "Your wife is looking for you."

A self-satisfied grin Mitch remembered carrying himself a long time ago spread over his friend's lips. "She can't stand it when I'm gone for five minutes."

Zoe laughed and waved him on.

"I'm surprised to see you here," she said.

"You were right. I needed to get out."

Her eyes crinkled in the corners. "Did I hear that correctly? You actually admitted I was right?"

"I'm not always trying to fight you." He held

up his hand when she started to argue. "That was the old me. This Mitch is willing to take your advice."

"Did someone beam Cypress Pointe into an alternate dimension and forget to tell me?"

"Is it hard to accept I might have a new outlook on life?"

Her gaze sobered as it swept over him, then back to his face. "You've only been back a week. I think I need a little more time to make my decision."

He breathed out a sigh. "Fair enough. We have to start somewhere."

"And somewhere is the bonfire?"

"Good enough place as any."

"Even though—" she angled her thumb over her shoulder "—I came with someone else?"

"Yes. You've made your position about us clear."

She cocked her head. "Okay."

"I've only ever wanted the best for you, Zoe."

Her eyes grew dark. "I should, um, return to the…group."

He reined in his impatience. "You do that."

Confusion evident, she backed up before turning to walk away.

It was all Mitch could do not to run after her.

How crazy was this? She couldn't get away from him fast enough.

During the time he'd spent talking, the purple twilight had faded into dusky shadows. Red sparks from the spitting logs shot into the air before turning to ash and slowly fluttering back down to the ground, clogging his throat in the process. Voices suddenly grew louder and distorted, as if he were in a tunnel. He closed his eyes, transported back to the refugee camp.

Fear and uncertainty had been a mainstay. Families had lost their homes, children their parents. He'd taken pictures, memorializing the suffering of a community, yet this time it had been personal. He shared their pain, even if it had been to a lesser extent. Hadn't he lost his family when Zoe had pushed him away?

A loud shout shook him from the vision. Confusion overwhelmed him. He blinked, trying to orient his surroundings. The temperate night turned too warm. Sweat broke out on his brow. He tugged at the collar of his polo shirt, trying to catch gasps of breath. The air turned thick and the scent of burning trash filled his senses. Crying children running for cover and safety flashed before his eyes.

He reached for the camera, like a phantom

limb, letting the cane fall. But there was no camera dangling from the strap circling his neck. His good hand only grasped air as his other arm shook. Dizzy now, he staggered, his stomach swirled and his vision went cloudy at the edges. Where was he?

He heard his name repeated over and over, the urgency pulling him from the trancelike state. But instead of coming out of it, he felt the sudden impact of a crash, followed by pain, then blackness.

"Mitch. Please. Talk to me."

He blinked. Once. Twice. The haze began to clear in his mind until Zoe came into view, frantically trying to get his attention. He swayed. Would have fallen if Zoe hadn't been quick on her feet and caught him, her slight frame taking the brunt of his heavier build. He took soothing breaths before easing some of the pressure off her.

"My cane," he sputtered.

She glanced around, finally locating the wooden lifeline. Crouching down, still laboring under his weight, she snatched the cane's end and pulled it close. Once she had a grip, she passed it to Mitch. He tightened his grip on the handle and moved his weight to his good leg. His blood pounded as if he'd just finished a 5K run. What had just happened?

"Mitch. Are you okay?"

He focused on Zoe, taking in her worried features. "I'm not sure."

"You seemed to blank out there for a few moments."

"I thought I was back at the camp."

She frowned. "You're in Cypress Pointe. Surrounded by friends. You're safe, Mitch."

He shook off the fear, his heart rate finally slowing. Whatever had triggered that…flashback, he had to get away.

"I'm okay, Zoe. I'm going to leave now."

"You don't look anywhere near fine. Your hands are shaking and your face is as white as a ghost's."

"I just need to sit." He tried to move but his legs nearly buckled.

Zoe slid her arm around his waist. "I'll take you."

"No." He gently pushed her away, straightening his shoulders. "You came here for a good time. Not to help an invalid."

Her lips pressed together and he noticed a bright sheen in her eyes. Great, on top of flipping out, he'd upset Zoe.

"Just go back to your friends."

She opened her mouth. He took a step back, ready to turn, but stopped. The voices and laughter around them had faded to silence, the pop of burning logs the only sound he heard. Mitch looked around, appalled to find all eyes on him. Eyes filled with pity, revulsion and curiosity.

This was his life now? The town oddity?

Anger and embarrassment surged through him. With controlled precision, he turned on his heel and limped away from this nightmare come true. Swallowed the bile rising in his throat. He now had concrete proof that he was half a man, certainly one unable to care for his wife and son. He'd lost Zoe long before tonight. Had his meltdown now cost him his son?

CHAPTER SIX

Zoe hurried alongside Mitch, nearly losing her own footing in the sand as she tried to stay out of his path. "Where are you going?"

"Far away from this crowd."

"Mitch, slow down. You'll fall."

Her words only made him move faster, increasing her frustration level. Why wouldn't this man ever listen?

"Please."

Her tone must have finally registered as he slowed his clumsy gait to a snail crawl. When he finally stopped, she halted beside him, trying to slow her racing heart. "What happened back there?"

Running a hand over the back of his neck, Mitch stared at the ground. "I…ah…think I had a flashback."

"You're not sure?"

He glanced around. "Can we discuss this away from curious eyes?"

She glanced over her shoulder to find they

were the center of attention. "Sure. Where did you have in mind?"

"For now, let's just walk."

She sent a doubtful look over his leg.

"I can manage," he bit out through clenched teeth.

The first couple of minutes were spent in silence. Mitch pushed himself and she tried not to hover—well, hover as much as one could while walking. Mitch stopped every once in a while to adjust his grip on the cane or rub his forehead. When he did, Zoe looked over her shoulder. The crowd had receded in the distance, but the bonfire remained a bold beacon in the spring night.

"You can start explaining anytime," she told him as they began moving again.

A flashback. He shook his head as if trying to remove the cobwebs weaved over his memory. "The scent of the fire triggered a response. I guess it reminded me of the refugee camps I'd worked in."

"Any chance it's connected to the accident?"

"Might be. At the end, I felt an explosion. Obviously not real, but it sure seemed like the real thing in my mind."

"Was there was an explosion at the crash?"

"The medical team never said anything. I

must have been mixed up when I got to the hospital. Kept saying, 'He's behind me.'"

"Someone was after you?"

"Again, I don't know. Or why, if that's the case. I was doing humanitarian work, taking photos of a refugee camp, not covering a story."

Zoe's eyes went wide. "Humanitarian work?"

He shot her a sideways glance. "You aren't the only altruistic one in the family."

Surprised by his disclosure, she was at a loss for words.

By now, they'd reached the north end of the beach. This area was more secluded. Besides the stars sparkling in the sky, the only light to be found came from the illuminated windows of the homes they passed. Before long, they came upon a small cove curved into the very end of the beach. From here, they would have to scale rocks and jetties before reaching another smooth stretch of sand.

"Mind if we sit?" Mitch said, his breath heavy from exertion.

"Of course not."

Making sure Mitch didn't topple over as he lowered himself onto the sand, Zoe sank down beside him. The water, reflecting the light of the three-quarter moon, was calm tonight. The cool sand sifted beneath her fingertips. Nearby, sea oats swayed in the breeze, the air scented with a mixture of briny moisture and damp earth.

"Do you remember this place?" Mitch asked.

How could she not? "We used to hang out here in high school. Usually after one of us had a fight with our parents."

"I'm surprised it hasn't been developed."

"The original owner still keeps this property as natural as when he first moved here."

Mitch stretched out his injured leg, massaging the thigh muscles. "This is the most I've walked in days."

Zoe picked up a small shell and rubbed the rough texture with her fingers. She hadn't wanted to ask, hadn't thought he had answers due to his memory loss, but now, finally, seemed like the right time to question him. "What happened over there, Mitch?"

He stared over the water.

"You saw me. I lost it."

"No. I mean overseas."

His shoulders sagged as if diverting her questions took too much energy. "I was covering the conditions of a refugee camp at the Syrian border. The conditions are... Let's just say, you wouldn't want Leo living there. But it's home for many people. The kids—" His voice broke for a second. "It would have broken your heart, Zoe. Yet the kids were resilient as only children can be."

When he paused, she wanted to reach out, put an arm around him, but she didn't want him to stop telling the story.

"One of the boys, Hassan, heard his father had been forced to another camp by local rebels after a bomb attack near their home. Supposedly, this small camp was just over the border, about twenty miles from our location. A few of us gathered together supplies to deliver, just in case the reports were true. Hassan wanted to know if his father was there and if he was, begged us to bring him back when we returned."

When Mitch didn't elaborate, Zoe finished the story for him. "Only you didn't return."

"No." He dropped his head in his hands for long seconds, then lifted it again, not meeting her gaze. "It's like every time I start to think about the trip, I get so far and, bam, a door slams shut. I remember driving, then nothing."

"Were you alone?"

"There were…two others, maybe?"

"They weren't at the hospital when you woke up?"

"No. If there had been others there, maybe

talking to them would have jogged my memory."

Zoe shook off the sand between her fingers. "Dr. Warren seemed positive about you getting your memory back. Once the injury heals."

"And while I appreciate his take on my recovery, he isn't the one racking his brain to come up with one little detail that hopefully opens the floodgate."

How on earth was he coping with all of this? She didn't know if she could be so matter-of-fact if she were in his shoes. As much as she wanted answers, Mitch wanted them more and pushing him wasn't going to bring results, only frustration on his end.

"I'm sorry I suggested you come to the bonfire tonight."

"You had no idea I'd have a meltdown."

"I should have considered how being around old friends might affect you."

"Zoe, I'm not upset with you."

She lowered her head. "You should be."

He exhaled loudly. "So what, every time I have a setback you're going to take the blame?"

Her head popped up. "No. I mean, I guess if I caused it."

"You were trying to help."

"I'm not sure how to help you, Mitch."

"Look, helping is your thing, but we both need time to figure out what life looks like from here." He took the end of the cane and started poking the sand with a vengeance.

"How about we table the discussion on where we go from here. Just for a while."

"Sounds good." He looked up at the stars for a long while, so did she. "Tell me more about Leo."

Her heart lifted and a smile curved her lips. "He was a surprise, Mitch. When you left the last time, I just knew my chances of having a child were over. Boy, was I wrong."

He shifted, bending his good knee to balance his weight. Zoe noticed the slight grimace he tried to hide.

"You said you moved in with your mother because of health issues?"

"I had a tough time in the last trimester. Bed rest was ordered. Instead of Mom always coming to my place, she set me up at her house to take care of me. After Leo was born, I didn't want to go back to the empty house, especially when it didn't seem like you'd be returning, so we packed up and sold it."

"Sorry about that."

"It's actually been a good thing. For the most part, Mom and I have learned to coexist. My parenting style is a complete one-eighty from hers, but she's encouraging. A surprise, I'll admit, but we're working at making things better."

"What does she think of you being mayor?"

Zoe let loose a laugh. "I'm the establishment now. Completely blows her away."

"If she'd paid attention to you growing up, she would have seen how you and this job were made for each other."

His words of praise lifted her spirits. They'd always been on the same page until the last couple of years. It still saddened her the way they'd drifted apart.

"It's a good thing she never figured out we used to hang out here," Mitch continued. "You needed a place to unwind when she went for days on a painting spree."

Those times had been hard. Her mother had been right on the cusp of making a legitimate name for herself as an artist after many years of shows and reviews and getting her work in front of the right people. She'd throw herself totally into a project, forgoing all else, at the expense of Zoe's childhood. With the money her paintings were earning, Zoe had had to pay the bills her mother forgot about to ensure the studio had light for her to work by. Zoe had bought groceries, cooked, cleaned, you name it. While she should have been at high school football games and school dances, instead, she was making sure her mother didn't fall into a depression over a negative review. Until they'd hired Maria, her mom's assistant, Zoe had made sure her mother met her deadlines at the same time as she was studying for tests.

"It all worked out."

"I heard the gallery has done well. National artists show their work there?"

"Maria is responsible for that. You remember when she took over. I'd had about as much of the art world as I could handle. Maria and my mom clicked and both had a similar vision. So yes, the gallery is quite successful."

A band of loosely formed clouds passed before the moon, obscuring the light. The temperature dipped, but it was still warm enough to enjoy the seasonable night.

"Have you talked to your folks?" she asked, dreading the answer.

"My mom. I'm not ready for a reunion with my father. I'm sure he'll love telling me how weak I am."

Zoe's back went stiff. Mr. Simmons was a bully. She'd never liked the man.

"You can't help you were in an accident."

"Some way, Dad will turn it around and make it my fault."

"I make sure your mother sees Leo pretty regularly. Not so much your dad."

"He's probably not interested, anyway."

He wasn't, but Zoe didn't want to dump salt in the wound by confirming it.

The breeze picked up and the clouds broke free from the moon. In the milky light, Zoe could make out Mitch's brow furrowed in thought.

"Your mom is good with Leo."

Mitch smiled. "I don't doubt it. She was a great mother to me."

"The past is the past, Mitch. We can focus on Leo now. Make sure he has the best life any kid can have."

He started poking at the sand with his cane again. "What if I can't?"

"Mitch, it's still early. The doctor even said so."

"Zoe, I want to be there for him, able to help him ride his first bike or to shoot hoops in the driveway."

"And you will. You'll get better physically." She paused, hated to voice her next nagging thought. "But when you are better, you'll have to decide if you want to leave again. If you do, you'll miss those milestones."

Mitch stared into the darkness, then said, "I don't want to let him down."

Like he had her?

"Mitch, just love him."

"Is that what you've learned?"

"Yes, in my vast experience of one year." She glanced at him. "Parenting takes time. We learn as we go."

"I want that."

She had no doubt. He might want to gallivant around the world, but she'd seen the love in his eyes when he'd looked at their son. A deep kind of love they'd both let slip away from each other.

"He's starting to take more than a few steps before falling. This morning, he made it from the couch across the living room to the arm-chair."

"He'll be on a skateboard before you know it."

"Please. Don't rush things."

Skateboards and fast cars were a part of Mitch. She silently prayed Leo didn't inherit the reckless gene.

"Feeling better?"

Mitch rolled his shoulders. "Yeah. Headache's eased."

"Do you get them often?"

"Every day."

And reality returned with a slap in the face. "Ready to head back?"

"I suppose."

As they stood, a memory jolted Zoe. "I won't let you fall."

Mitch's head jerked in her direction. "That's what I used to tell you."

When they were younger, Zoe refused to get on a skateboard. She'd fallen off once, scraped her knee pretty badly and wouldn't try again. But Mitch had hounded her, insisting she'd be fine. Finally giving in, she'd gingerly pushed the board with Mitch by her side. When she got enough nerve to pick up speed, he was running with her, ready to catch her if she wavered and fell. He'd been like that back then, pushing her beyond her boundaries, sure she could balance on the board like a pro. But when their marriage wavered and fell apart, neither had been able to pick up the pieces.

They'd taken a few steps when Mitch stopped. "Something wrong?"

"This is the place we shared our first kiss." Her stomach fluttered. He was right.

With the life-altering events of the past week and watching Mitch's near meltdown just a short while ago, Zoe had forgotten. How could she have failed to recall such a momentous event?

"It was junior year." Mitch grinned at her. "We'd been flirting and I was determined to make us a couple. When I suggested it here, you got all teary, said yes and then I kissed you."

Okay, if she were truthful, maybe she didn't want to remember that night. The sweet memory brought a pinch of pain in the vicinity of her heart.

"That was a long time ago."

"Doesn't make it any less memorable."

She didn't want to talk about the good times, because that would ultimately lead to a discussion of the bad times. Of wondering how they could have let such a young, fragile love grow and bloom, then not tend it and watch it wither and fade. Yeah, she couldn't go there.

"I think the best thing for us is to focus on Leo."

"Yeah." His voice went hard. "The best thing."

They continued walking, uneasiness building a wall between them.

"Who is watching Leo tonight?"

"My mom. She's not a fan of bonfires."

"After that year she decided her work was derivative and tossed all her newest paintings in the fire, I can see why."

"One of her more epic mood swings."

"She said she had the evening all planned. Then she started getting all giggly. She loves Leo, but this was odd. Like something else was going on."

"Something she didn't tell you?"

"We might get along better than we did when I was a kid, but she still doesn't tell me everything."

"That's your mom."

And it still drove her crazy.

"By the way, I checked my work calendar," she told Mitch as they approached the dying bonfire. Wispy white streaks of smoke curled from the few logs left aglow on the pile. The crowd had thinned, with it the prying eyes of speculation. "I can take you to your appointments."

"If you're sure."

She placed a hand on his arm. "I mean it. Your recovery is important to Leo."

A shadow dimmed his eyes. "Right."

Before she could say anything more, Tim walked up to them, his eyes on Zoe.

"You guys okay?"

"Oh, Tim. Sorry. Mitch and I… We needed to talk."

"Thanks for your concern," Mitch said, voice tight.

"No problem." Tim sent him a quick glance, then shifted back to Zoe. "Ready to go home?"

"I…um…came with Nealy." Awkward. She felt Mitch's eyes on her but refused to meet his gaze.

"She left. Asked me to make sure you got home safely."

"How neighborly of you," Mitch said.

She recognized that tone. Deceptive in calmness, concealing mounting displeasure. Time to make a getaway. Fast. "I'll call you, Mitch."

"Great."

She turned and walked away, with Tim beside her. It was all she could do not to look over her shoulder. She didn't like being in this situation, but Mitch had put her here, right? When he'd left, then supposedly died. She'd just been getting her life in order when he'd returned.

So why did she suddenly feel like she was in limbo all over again?

MITCH WATCHED HIS wife walk away with another man, his gut burning. How had he let himself get to this low point?

"Young Mitch would have had words with Tim," Wyatt said as he joined Mitch. "And the guy wouldn't have liked what you had to say."

"Yeah, well, this Mitch walks with a cane and can barely keep himself together, so…"

"Just sayin', buddy."

"I appreciate the support, but Zoe has a say in the matter, too."

"So you're just gonna let it go?"

"You know, we're headed for a divorce."

"You guys keep saying that, but no one's filed." His friend regarded him for a moment, then said, "You do want the divorce, right?"

"Sure. I mean, Zoe's the one who really pushed for it, but I agreed."

"How come I don't believe you?"

Mitch rubbed his temple. The headache that had abated when he was with Zoe had returned with a vengeance. "I don't know what to tell you, Wyatt."

"Now you're really faking it."

He sighed. Leaned more heavily on the cane and wished he was anywhere but at a bonfire that transported him back to the refugee camp.

"I have this fleeting memory from before the accident."

"About what led to the crash?"

"No. Those events are still fuzzy and pulling

at me, but this was different. Like something was prompting me to come back and make things right with Zoe."

"Your subconscious?"

He shrugged. "At this point, I can't be sure. With everything still mostly a blur, I don't want to act on what might be pure imagination."

"And if what you remember is accurate?"

"Then I need to consider Zoe's feelings. She's moved on."

"Tim might not be the right guy for her."

"And I am? She asked me repeatedly to stay in Cypress Pointe. Or at least limit my travels to within the States. The last thing she said to me was 'I never want to see you again.'"

Wyatt cringed. "C'mon. She didn't mean it."

Mitch rose a shaky hand to rub his temple. Exhausted now, he asked, "Why are you pushing the issue, Wyatt?"

"Because I'm living with the shell of a great guy. I get you have injuries but, man, this thing with Zoe had taken the life out of you. Where's the guy who was up for anything? The one who'd drag us off on a grand adventure and never look back?"

"Lost in the desert somewhere."

"Well, you need to find him. Before you lose what you had with Zoe for good."

"I'm starting to get tired of rehashing this conversation. Zoe doesn't want to be married to me."

"She never filed the papers."

"She thought I was dead. There was no need."

"You've been back a week and she hasn't brought them to the lawyer."

Mitch turned to his friend. "And you know that how?"

"Jenna."

Jenna Monroe. Wyatt's girlfriend. A former celebrity chef, she'd settled in Cypress Pointe with her adopted twin daughters and captured Wyatt's heart.

"She and Zoe are friends. After you left, they bonded and if Zoe had indeed filed the papers, Jenna would know."

"Right now, I'm more concerned with Leo. I want to get to know my son."

"I get it. The girls certainly changed my life."

Wyatt's own son had been killed in a freak boating accident years ago. Mitch hadn't thought his best friend would ever recover emotionally, or want children again, but Abby and

Bridget, along with their mother, had shown Wyatt that old wounds could be healed by the power of love.

"Look, I get you're a changed man. I'm happy for you. While your path to happiness worked out, I don't see Zoe and I reconciling."

"You never were a quitter."

"And that was the main source of our problems."

A log snapped in the pit, a final brief flame flaring before the embers died. Much like Mitch's roller-coaster emotions since returning to town.

"Okay. I'll lay off."

"I'd appreciate it."

"I'm going to take Jenna home. Need a lift?"

The prospect of going back to Wyatt's cottage just to camp out on the porch and obsess over his life didn't appeal. "Thanks, but I'm going to hang out here a little longer."

Wyatt gently slapped him on the back. "Call if you need a ride."

Mitch ground his teeth together and nodded. He hated this helplessness, the need for others to taxi him about.

Maybe his father's prediction had finally come true.

His stomach in a knot now, he made his way

to a bench just out of view from the stragglers still partying by the fire. He lowered himself and heaved out a sigh.

The road to recovery loomed before him, but his patience was beginning to wear thin. Right now, he wanted to race full-speed down the beach, the humid wind against his face, his feet stomping the sand. A way to release the pent-up energy coursing through him. And even if he could? He'd get twenty feet and run out of gas. If he couldn't run down the beach, what made Wyatt think Mitch could convince Zoe to give them another try?

She had a full life. A job she loved. A child to dote upon. The only hindrance in her life right now was him. She'd been great about helping him out but pretty adamant they had no future. Is that what he wanted for their relationship now?

I never want to see you again.

Words spoken in the heat of an argument. Why had he been so stubborn? And why hadn't he put her first? Maybe he needed to see a therapist for more than his nonexistent memory. But he remembered the pain in her eyes when she'd thrown those words at him. He'd put it there. He'd been sure he could take off for parts unknown and she'd be okay with it. But she hadn't been. The truth lay in the scattered ashes of their marriage.

Did he dare wonder if that flash of memory was really accurate? That he had been thinking of a way to make things up to Zoe? First, he questioned himself, what would have caused the turnaround? And second, why had he waited and taken a job that had landed him in danger? Zoe had always been afraid he would get hurt while he'd thought he could laugh off death. Boy, had he been wrong.

He'd pushed his wife and lost.

But now he had a son. Could this be a second chance? And if it was, how would Zoe weigh in?

The image of her walking away with the firefighter twisted his belly. If he were a bigger man, wouldn't he be happy to see her move on with her life?

The headache moved from his temple to cover his entire head. The more he thought, the worse the pounding became, which brought him back to square one. What did he have to offer her now?

Nothing.

Except vowing to be the best father for Leo.

As he sat under the dark star-filled sky, drinking in the natural beauty surrounding him, he thought, *Staying here might not be the worst idea ever.* Yes, his years abroad had given him access, opened many doors for him, but he could use all of that here—everything he'd seen and learned—to do good, and still be close to his son. Much like the way Zoe backed her causes. Maybe if they had something in common, their wounds would heal. And after the healing, they could decide what their future looked like.

There was only one way to find out.

Besides being forever connected by Leo, had fate allowed them a second chance?

CHAPTER SEVEN

"GO AHEAD. OPEN IT."

Mitch looked down at the gaily-decorated box sitting on the coffee table. He'd called first, then stopped by to spend time with Leo, while Zoe attended meetings and took care of her mayoral duties. He found Samantha holding Leo on her hip, practically dragging Mitch inside to show off her surprise.

He knew Samantha enough to recognize what was in the box. You'd think by the way he took a step back it was a box of snakes, but it most likely contained a camera. Just as scary.

Leo squirmed to be let loose. His grandmother lowered him to the carpet where he plopped down. Mitch thought he might cry, but then Leo smiled that toothy grin. Mitch's heart expanded and he forgot all about the box. He gingerly lowered himself to the floor and met Leo's gaze on an equal level.

"Hey, buddy."

Leo tilted his head, glanced up at Samantha, then back to Mitch and inched closer.

Mitch went still as his son placed a chubby hand on his cheek. His chest tightened like a belt twisting tight; he wasn't sure he was capable of another breath. Love, strong and pure, washed over him and for the first time in months, Mitch thought his future might just be okay.

Deciding Mitch was not a scary stranger, Leo started babbling and before Mitch realized what was happening, dropped into his lap.

Now what did he do?

Samantha laughed. "Just give him a hug, Mitch."

Taking advice from the expert, Mitch wrapped his arms around Leo and hugged. Leo giggled, resting his head against Mitch's upper body. His son felt warm and sturdy in his arms. The magical scent of baby powder surrounded him. He inhaled, closed his eyes to savor the miracle of his baby son so close to his heart.

"Feels good," Samantha whispered.

Mitch had to clear his throat before answering a croaked, "Yes."

Leo, quickly bored, scampered out of Mitch's embrace to toddle over to a basket of toys. When he wavered, Mitch reached out his arms as if to steady the little guy. To his relief, Leo stayed upright and then dug in to find a toy to play with.

"Zoe told me he's started walking."

"He's getting better every day." Samantha paused. "I'm glad you'll see him grow up, Mitch."

He blinked watery eyes. "Me, too."

Leo picked out a red block and carried it over to Mitch. When Mitch took it, Leo giggled and ran back for another. This went on for six trips until Leo wandered toward the kitchen.

"Now we need to set up a baby gate," Samantha said as she swung Leo up and set him back by the toy basket.

"Can I help?"

"Sure. Zoe is supposed to pick one up at the store. I'm sure she'll appreciate you helping assemble it."

Would she? Mitch hoped so, because after holding his son, he wasn't going anywhere.

As Leo brought over another toy for Mitch, he noticed the child's gaze catch sight of the brightly colored box on the table. Leo bellied up to the coffee table and reached out, his fingers merely grazing the box. His brows angled and his cheeks went red before announcing his displeasure with a loud cry.

"You'd better open the box so Leo can play with the wrappings."

"Is it okay? For him to play with the paper, that is?"

"For a whole minute before he goes off to something else."

Mitch leaned over and slid the box closer to Leo. He broke the tape on one flap, loosening the gift wrap. Leo caught on quickly, grabbing the paper and pulling. It ripped and revealed part of the box. Leo giggled and grasped for more.

Before long, the paper was in a pile on the carpet while Mitch studied the box, which indeed contained a new camera.

"Surprise," Samantha sang. "I couldn't let you go on without one."

Actually, Mitch had been just fine cameraless. Now he'd be forced to find out if the accident had affected his abilities.

"This is way too generous," he said.

"It's my way of letting you know I'm thrilled you, and your talent, are still here with us."

Mitch set the box on his lap as he read the details on the side. He was looking at a digital SLR camera, with an additional portrait lens and another smaller lens, along with a carrying case. By the description, he learned it was more high-tech than the one he'd lost, weatherproof and durable, definitely a tool he could use indoors and out.

All in all, a really nice camera.

Leo came over and began slapping the top of the box. Mitch moved it out of range. "Sorry, little guy. This isn't a toy."

Leo's face went red again and Mitch waited for an outburst, but instead, Leo sank down by Mitch's feet and messed around with the wrapping.

"He'll like playing with the empty box."

"Really, Samantha, this is too much."

"I disagree, so don't argue with me. You'll only lose, anyway."

That much he remembered.

"Thank you."

"Before you know it, you'll be out capturing photos the world will want to see. Since you're still healing, start out slowly and see what happens."

"I can't make any promises."

"A talent like yours is intrinsic, Mitch. I believe in you. So much so, I'll sponsor a show at my gallery."

"Now you're really putting the cart before

the horse. I have no clue what the future holds for me."

He still had trouble with his equilibrium. The headaches still disabled him in their intensity. He knew there would be more therapy and doctor's visits to come. When would he have time to take photos?

Suddenly, everything about his situation overwhelmed him and he was afraid he might experience another meltdown. His palms grew sweaty. Inhaling, he calmed his frazzled nerves while waiting for his racing heart to slow down.

"Stick around Cypress Pointe while you decide," Samantha continued, unaware of his rocky condition. "There are plenty of locales to capture right here in your own backyard."

Hoping to cover his physical reaction, Mitch set the box on the couch, out of Leo's view, and played with his son. He soon discovered Leo was a definite balm to his soul. Like a healing gift. Samantha went back and forth between the living room and the kitchen, seemingly unconcerned about leaving Leo in Mitch's care. He didn't know whether to be thankful or, if anxiety hit again, terrified.

A little past noon, the front door opened and Zoe blew inside, wrestling a large box.

When she saw Mitch on the floor with Leo, she blinked a few times before closing the door with her foot.

Her cheeks were rosy, from carrying the load, he guessed, and her hair was attractively mussed. Her pretty blue eyes met his, then dropped away. But not before he caught... Was that embarrassment? Had she been thinking about their conversation at the beach? Or how she'd left him for another guy?

Yeah, that little tidbit had kept him awake for two nights in a row.

"Mitch. Hi." She looked around. "Where's my mom?"

"In the kitchen," Samantha called out before stepping into the living room.

"I...ah...didn't expect to still see you here."

"Don't worry," he told her in a measured voice. "Leo is just fine."

She dropped the box. "I can see that." She met his gaze, this time more composed. "I didn't mean to imply he wasn't."

He shrugged. She might say otherwise, but he still read the uncertainty in her eyes.

Samantha picked up the box. "Oh, good. The gate. I was just telling Mitch we needed one."

Zoe captured Leo and scooped him into her

arms, rubbing her pert nose against his. "Because speedy racer here needs boundaries."

Leo let out a squawk and wiggled until Zoe set him down. He toddled to Mitch and sat down beside him.

"We're getting to know each other," Mitch offered.

"That's good."

"How long are you here?" Samantha asked.

"About forty-five minutes. I have a town council meeting later."

"Then let's get lunch going. Mitch? Any requests?"

"Anything is fine." He rolled to his side to lean on the coffee table before pulling his bum leg up. In the past few days, his arm had gained strength, so he wasn't as leery about using it to help brace himself. When he looked down, he found Leo mimicking him. A startled chuckle escaped him.

Samantha took Leo's hand. "Come on, half-pint. Cut-up hot dogs and bananas are calling your name."

As the two disappeared into the kitchen, Mitch couldn't miss Zoe's discomfort.

"You're getting along with Leo?"

"Like best buds."

A frown wrinkled her forehead.

"Why do I get the impression you're not happy?"

Her gaze jerked to meet his. "It's not that I'm unhappy. I just haven't had to…"

"Share him?"

She let out an uneasy laugh. "Bingo." She waved a hand. "Don't mind me. This will all seem normal soon."

"Zoe, I can't swoop in here and take your place. I wouldn't want to."

"I know. I'm just being silly."

"You've had sole responsibility for a year. I get that. But now we can share. You don't have to shoulder the load."

"Leo isn't a burden."

"I didn't say that. I meant now you have someone to help you."

She looked unconvinced but remained silent.

Mitch shifted, moving his cane from one hand to another. When he moved from the couch, Zoe asked, "What's in the box?"

"Your mom got me a new camera."

"Your old one?"

"Lost after the accident."

"That explains things. I mean, it was weird seeing you without it. I just assumed you weren't working, so you didn't need to tote it around."

"I'm still not working. Don't know if I will again."

His comment caught her attention. "What do you mean?"

"I don't know if I can take pictures."

"I don't understand. Can't you just pick up the camera and shoot?"

He sent her a brittle smile. "There's a little more to it."

"Sorry. I knew that."

A burst of laughter came from the kitchen. Leo to their rescue.

Mitch hobbled to the next room, Zoe close behind. Samantha set plates on the table with a loaf of bread and two different types of cold cuts and cheeses.

"Help yourself," she urged.

They made sandwiches and ate in strained silence until it was time for Zoe to get back to the office. As she was preparing to leave, Mitch noticed Zoe pull her mother into the living room and heard muted voices. He braced his legs, lifted Leo from the high chair, surprised and pleased when Leo didn't want Mitch to set him on the floor. Balancing Leo's weight on one side, the cane on the other, he successfully carried him toward the other room.

"Mom, what were you thinking?"

"That Mitch needed a new camera. A reason to get better."

"Those are the key words—*getting better*. Until then, we can't push him. We have to remember he can't function like he used to."

He nearly stumbled at her words. Leo croaked and the two women looked his way, surprise on Samantha's face, guilt crossing Zoe's.

Is that who he was now? The injured guy who couldn't function?

"Don't worry, ladies. The invalid isn't planning a major photo shoot anytime soon."

MORTIFICATION GRIPPED ZOE. She hadn't meant for Mitch to overhear. Not that she'd said much, but enough for Mitch to suspect Zoe had her reservations about his future intentions. Whenever mention of a camera entered a conversation, all she could think about was Mitch choosing his career over her. Some things hadn't changed.

Leo, sensing the rising emotion in the room, squirmed. Mitch set him down, teetering, then stabilizing himself with his cane. Would he always need extra assistance? She hated thinking of Mitch this way, but the truth stood before her, a thundercloud shadowing his features.

"I'll get out of your way."

"Mitch—"

Leo toddled over and tugged on her leg. She lifted him, settling him on her hip. Leo buried his face in her neck and she rubbed his back, taking comfort in her bundle of joy.

Mitch walked past her, his expression now under control, even though she could feel the waves of tension as he passed her.

"What about your playdate with Leo?" Samantha asked.

"I'll come back another time."

He sent Zoe a glance, one she couldn't decipher, and left the house.

"Mom," Zoe railed. "Mitch doesn't need this kind of pressure."

"What he needs is to feel productive. To work again," Samantha countered.

"Right. You know this because you're such an expert on the career of Mitch Simmons."

"Obviously, I comprehend that part of him better than you do."

Zoe tightened her grip on Leo as she carried him to his room to ready him for his nap. She laid him on the changing table and unsnapped his little pants to change his diaper.

"Like I don't know my own husband," she groused, handing Leo a small stuffed animal to hold his attention while she went to work.

Being a pragmatist, Zoe had struggled to grasp the passion of an artist's soul. She'd had her own projects to throw herself into, fighting for ideals and ways to make people's lives better. Mitch had never gotten that.

Think again.

Startled by the thought, remnants of the conversation with Mitch at the beach taunted her. *You aren't the only altruistic one in the family.* What had Mitch meant by that remark? Before she could dwell on it longer, she finished changing Leo. Settling him in his crib, she played with him for a few minutes. She was already pushing the constraints of her lunch hour, but she didn't care.

"This is all so confusing."

Leo stared up at her, his eyelids drooping.

"You have a daddy," she whispered. "And I have my husband back."

But did she? Would the chasm between her and Mitch ever be bridged? Did she want it to?

It was a decision she would have to make soon, for all concerned.

Once Leo dozed off, Zoe forced herself from her place by the crib. For once, meetings and agendas and doing good didn't excite her. If she wasn't so booked, she'd call the office and inform them that she wouldn't be back. But she had an obligation to the town.

Hoping her mother had escaped to her studio, Zoe bit back a groan to find Samantha waiting for her, seated on the living room couch.

"Mitch left his camera behind."

"You know where he lives."

"And it doesn't bother you that he's living somewhere else?"

Zoe silently counted to ten. "I don't want to have this conversation with you."

"You never do." Samantha rose. "You're afraid he'll leave again."

Her accusation wasn't much of a revelation. Anyone who knew Zoe well knew how she felt about her husband traipsing across the globe. "It's only a matter of time."

Samantha skirted the coffee table. "I don't think so. Something is different with Mitch."

"Yes. He's injured."

"No. It's more than that. Of course, Leo has already grabbed his heartstrings, but I sense something more profound."

She had to agree with her mother on that point. There was a change in Mitch. Their conversation at the beach had been eye-opening. Mitch had cared for a young refugee boy. Someone who wouldn't advance his career. Acted more like…Zoe when she was bent on helping a cause.

The idea baffled her. Yet made her proud.

Zoe grabbed her purse. "I have to get back to the office."

"You can't run from this, Zoe. Mitch will get better. And he will remain in your life, one way or another."

Why, after all these years, did her mother have to be so perceptive?

And why did the chills coursing down her spine make her question everything she thought she knew?

Right now, though, she needed to fill her mind with something other than her messy personal life.

By 4:00 P.M., ZOE had successfully completed her entire schedule, except for the final meeting, which she was actually looking forward to. Nealy Grainger and Jenna Monroe were coming in to discuss Zoe's latest charity event, a fund-raiser for the food bank.

She straightened up her desk, tucking notes in files and placing a pen in the cup holder, when the phone buzzed and the door opened simultaneously.

"It's just us," Nealy said as she swept into the room.

"Being completely rude by barging in," Jenna added as she followed.

"It's fine. You're my last appointment of the day."

Nealy pulled a notebook from her leather briefcase. "Saving the best for last?"

"Always."

"We just need to finalize some details," Jenna confirmed.

"I have my final list." Zoe handed a copy to each of the women.

"Number of invites, check. Decoration theme, check. Time and location, check." Nealy looked up. "Why did you even hire me?"

"Because I may be the idea person, but you're the best party planner in town."

Nealy grinned. "This will be a very tasteful, very successful fund-raiser."

Her words soothed Zoe.

Jenna perused her section of the list. "Appetizers and drinks are good. Everything we already talked about. Comfort food to remind donors where they came from and how much others need their help."

"I spoke to the folks setting up the food bank and they're thrilled to have all the exposure. We're two weeks out, but Mr. Michaels, the director, told me to call if we need anything."

Nealy flipped through the pages of her notebook. "I have his contact number. I'll call him tomorrow and make arrangements to take one last walk through of the space we're using." She tapped a finger on her chin. "Have you thought about using some sort of visual aid to show the guests how the food bank works?"

"I have." Zoe popped up from her chair and hurried to a bookshelf. She grabbed a thick catalogue, opened it and placed it on the desk where Nealy and Jenna rose to look as well.

"This catalogue is full of different shelving units and containers and just about anything needed to store the goods we've been collecting for the bank." She flipped through until she found the page she'd flagged. "This three-shelf unit would be perfect to place just inside the door of the gymnasium as the guests enter. I was thinking about having a couple of the high schoolers already working the program stand beside the unit and answer any questions."

"Good idea," Nealy said. "Can I borrow this?"

"Sure. I'll order the unit ASAP and we'll get

it delivered next week. Afterward, we'll add it to the collection room."

"Awesome. One more thing to cross off my list." Nealy slashed her pen to paper in a flourish.

"I really want this to be a success and draw new donors," Zoe told them.

When she had been running for mayor, she'd had conversations with single parents, but one woman in particular had resonated with her. The woman had three children, and while her children qualified for the state-funded lunch program during the school year, it wasn't enough to cover weekends when her paycheck didn't stretch far enough to buy extra food.

Zoe remembered those days. Samantha, so immersed in her painting that Zoe had to be creative when it came to planning meals, especially since most of the food was from a can. The woman's plight had struck a chord and she'd been determined to help somehow. Once elected, she'd approached the town council who was one hundred percent on board with the plan. The food bank was going to be housed at the high school, used as a community project for students and made available for anyone in Cypress Pointe who needed it.

"This is one of your best ideas, Zoe. How

can anyone turn down supporting a community project like this?" Jenna reasoned.

"And when I called every person on the list to confirm," Nealy said, "plus others I added, not one person declined attending the event."

"I've been talking it up as much as I can," Jenna went on to say. "I'm also proud to be a sponsor since I make my living with food and stress how important it is to have healthy choices for low-income families."

"And a little star power never hurts." Nealy nudged Jenna with her shoulder.

"I'll be honest, I really promoted it the last time I filmed a cooking segment. Told anyone who wants to donate to the cause to get in touch with me." Jenna reached into a magenta-colored tote with *Charming Delights Catering* stitched in black and lime green, her company colors, and removed an envelope, which she then handed to Zoe.

"Some of my regular catering clients have already donated. They can't attend the fundraiser so they sent the checks to pass along to you."

Zoe's spirits lifted. "I'll be sure to contact them personally to say thank you."

Jenna, with her short blond pixie-cut hair

and bright green eyes, beamed at her. "They'll be thrilled."

"Dane has gotten corporate sponsors, too. Owning the Grand Cypress Hotel has its advantages." Nealy ginned at Zoe. 'See, this is all working out."

Swallowing the huge lump in her throat, Zoe reached out to hug her friends. They'd been with her during the tough time after Mitch had left, through the dark moments when they'd thought he was dead, to her difficult pregnancy and then the joy of giving birth to a healthy son. "I don't know what I'd do without you two."

"Same here," Nealy sniffled.

Jenna blinked away tears.

Zoe took the tissue box from her desk and passed it around. "Okay, enough tears. This is supposed to be a planning session."

After wiping her nose, Nealy said, "I almost forgot. Lilli called last night. She and Max went out of town, but will be back in time for the fund-raiser."

"Good. Her mother is a brilliant fund-raiser, but she scares me." Zoe shivered.

The matching looks of fear she observed in Jenna and Nealy confirmed she wasn't alone. How Celeste calmly talked others into doing her bidding, and not taking no for an answer, was a lesson in itself; one, Zoe had to admit, she'd emulated at different times as mayor.

"So, the principal said we could set up Friday prior to the event," Zoe confirmed.

Nealy tossed her wavy mahogany-colored hair over her shoulder. "Dane and I will be there early."

"As will Wyatt and the girls," Jenna chimed in, then blurted, "I can't stand it any longer." After a taut second, she squealed, "Wyatt and I finally set a date." She danced up and down on tiptoe. "We're getting married next month."

Both Zoe and Nealy screeched. Zoe hugged her friend, but Nealy held back.

"Wait. A month? How am I supposed to plan your wedding?"

"You don't have to. It's going to be very small. Family and just a few close friends, like you guys, will be invited."

Nealy parked her hands on her hips. "I still need to work my magic."

Jenna nodded. "Absolutely.".

"And how about you and Dane?" Zoe asked. "The last holdouts."

"We've decided Las Vegas is looking better and better all the time," Nealy said.

Zoe's mouth fell open. "No way!"

"Way. Ironically enough, we don't care about the wedding, just being married. We eloped once. Twice is the charm, they say."

After high school, Dane and Nealy had eloped but quickly had the marriage annulled. Thankfully, they'd found their way back to each other.

Jenna's eyes went dreamy. "I know what you mean. About being married, not eloping. We wanted to wait until Lilli and Max had their big day before setting our own date, but we are so ready to be married."

Zoe's heart cracked just a bit at their words. Once, she'd been starry-eyed and in love. Now? She wasn't so sure.

They finished tying up the loose ends of the meeting. Nealy closed her notebook and met Zoe's gaze head on. "So, what's going on with you and Mitch?"

Nealy was never one to shy away from showing concern for her friends' personal lives, so Zoe wasn't surprised at the change in topic.

"Same."

"And I suppose he's thrilled about you dating Tim?"

"We haven't exactly had a sit-down about our dating lives."

"He can't like it."

"He doesn't have a say."

Nealy scoffed. "Really? You're going to deny your husband the chance to redeem himself?"

"What makes you think he's redeemed?"

"I hear things."

Like the fact that Mitch had helped refugees by documenting their lives? The more Zoe thought about it, the more intrigued she became. What had happened to make him see beyond the lens? Why that boy and why at that time?

"Actually, Jenna told me."

Jenna's eyes went wide. "Thanks for throwing me under the bus."

"Hey, Mitch told your boyfriend."

Zoe glanced at Jenna, her brow raised in question.

"The other night, Wyatt asked Mitch what was up. He didn't go into detail, but he did tell Wyatt a story about a little boy he'd been trying to help. Wyatt was impressed by his compassion, which ultimately led to his accident, and Wyatt mentioned it to me."

This wasn't a fluke? Mitch was really that invested in helping others? She'd never have imagined he'd be drawn to a cause—other than Zoe's own initiatives, anyway, and that was always secondhand. He'd gone along with her passion to make the world, or at least Cypress Pointe, a safer place. Supported her, even if his heart hadn't been that into whatever organization she was involved with at the time. No, he'd been all about his career, right? And if he'd really changed, if things were less about Mitch and more about the world around him, how was she going to resist finding out what, exactly, had caused this turnabout in her husband?

CHAPTER EIGHT

MITCH BRACED HIMSELF against the wooden frame of the town gazebo, scanning the view stretching out before him. From this vantage point, he could see the sparkling gulf waters and a swath of the beach to his left. To his right, the park ran parallel to Main Street where townspeople hurried along the sidewalks, busy with their daily errands or sightseeing. Deciding to go with the beach for inspiration, he lifted his new camera.

Samantha had personally delivered the gift he'd left behind a week ago, after he'd stormed out of Zoe's house. Since then, he'd made sure Zoe was out when he stopped by the house, not wanting his time with Leo tainted by the tension created when he and Zoe were in close proximity. He still wasn't sure how to handle the new normal of his life.

Refocusing on the task at hand, he opted to see if he still had an eye for choosing a subject. He hefted the camera.

A jogger passed by, calling a greeting his way. He waved, recognizing an old neighbor. Thankfully, she didn't stop to chat. Being in public more and more now that he was feeling settled, he still cringed when he received curious looks from old friends. The looks that all said the same thing: damaged goods.

He'd vowed to change those first impressions. Damaged? Not if he had anything to say about it.

He still experienced killer headaches, but his hair was starting to grow out, covering the scars. His leg wasn't cooperating, but his arm was regaining strength daily. He was still frustrated, fidgety and restless, and his memory hadn't returned except in very blurry flashes, but he was determined to overcome it all.

So in order to make progress, the prior week he'd allowed himself to be examined, x-rayed and pushed in physical therapy beyond his endurance.

And this was just the beginning.

Doctor visits were his job right now but wouldn't be forever. He would prove that to Zoe and anyone else who questioned his ability to be whole again.

Which also meant taking photos.

Blowing out a breath, he picked out a few

areas of the local landscape he thought would capture well and lifted the camera. With shaky hands, he aimed and clicked. After taking a few photos, he checked the screen to see how they'd turned out. A little out of focus, but not horrible.

Encouraged, he continued. It wasn't long before he turned his attention from the beach to the sidewalk. Hours flew by and for the first time in a very long time, he was in his element. Forgetting the reality waiting for him once he was out of the zone.

A shout caught his attention. He glanced over his shoulder in time to catch sunlight reflecting off a car window. He blinked, suddenly thrust back to the day of the accident. He fought to make sense of the images.

Driving along a rutted dirt road. Sand drifting in through the open window, grazing his face. Someone yelling at him to go faster. The scent of gasoline and sour food. Looking in the rearview mirror to see a dust cloud trailing the beat-up truck. Light reflecting off the windshield of the vehicle gaining behind him. A sense of urgency and fear.

Mostly fear.

The images started to fade and Mitch willed

the vision to continue. He squeezed his eyes shut, waiting for more.

Suddenly, he remembered he was alone in the cab; the others with him sitting in the truck bed, the hot midmorning sun beating down on them. The temperature had risen in the cab, an uncomfortably sticky heat. Mitch had wiped his eyes, then turned his head to check on the passengers, his stomach dropping at their frightened expressions. Who was after them? And why? As he grasped for more information, a fuzzy face slowly came into view from the other side of the window. His features clear as he yelled words Mitch couldn't hear.

But just as quickly as it formed, the image and the sound of the voice disappeared, locked in his mind where Mitch didn't have access.

C'mon, Mitch, he inwardly screamed at himself. *You can do this. Remember!*

"Mitch. Mitch?"

Someone called his name, but it wasn't a male voice. Confused, Mitch opened his eyes, transported back from the hot, dusty road to a beautiful, lush park in Cypress Pointe, Florida. He shook his head, wanted to cry out in frustration that he hadn't connected a name to the face before it had all gone blank.

"Mitch, are you okay? Are you having another flashback?"

Disappointment tasted bitter on his tongue. He'd been so close to remembering.

"Mitch, answer me."

Taking a breath, he turned to find Zoe, face pale and eyes wide.

"I'm okay," he managed to say without letting frustration bleed into his voice.

"I kept calling your name but you didn't respond."

"Sorry." He ran a shaky hand over the top of his head.

"It was a flashback, wasn't it?"

"Yes."

"Do remember anything more?"

He glanced at his wife, at the intent expression on her face. What he'd just experienced in that flashback had him reeling. He had to go over it when he was alone, pick apart each nuance he'd remembered to try to make sense of what he was seeing. Zoe had enough responsibilities at the moment. No way could he tell her that the danger he'd initially only imagined was turning out to be very real, indeed.

"A few bits and pieces," he finally answered, giving her a sliver of information to satisfy her.

"Did it help?"

"Not really." He shook his head, sensing a headache creeping up on him. He noticed that stress and confusion triggered the pain. He breathed like the doctor had suggested when Mitch mentioned the symptoms.

"I'm sorry, Mitch. I know you want to figure out what happened that day."

Exhaustion washed over him. He lowered himself onto one of the steps leading into the gazebo. "It'll come to me, Zoe. With time."

She took a step toward him, then hesitated. He patted the step beside him. "Join me?"

At his invitation, she sat, angling herself to face him. Vanilla and flowers surrounded him, her signature scent. Mitch never forgot it, no matter where he traveled.

"I didn't mean to bother you, but I was running an errand and stopped when I saw you." She nodded at the camera he'd set down on the other side of him. "My mother told me she'd delivered her gift."

"I was doing a test run."

"And?"

"I won't be booking any jobs based on the work I did today, but it felt good to do something familiar. To keep busy."

A pained expression crossed her face. "I'm sorry about that day we saw each other at the house. I didn't mean to imply you'd never work again."

"It's okay."

"It's really not."

He grinned. "I'm glad you said that. To be honest, I was pretty ticked at you."

"I was mad at myself." She clasped her hands in her lap. "I had no right to interfere with your decision to go back to work or walk away."

"Very true, but I get the feeling your reservations had more to do with Leo than my brand new camera."

"Yes. I… When I came home and saw you two sitting side by side on the floor, it was like a mirror image. The way you both hold yourselves, the lift of an eyebrow or a tip of your lips. It's uncanny."

Warmth crept through his chest.

"It's an amazing thing, to see yourself in your children. Leo's going to look just like you when he gets older."

"He has your eyes. I noticed that right away."

She lit up. "Really? I look at him and swear I don't see any resemblance at all."

"He has your laugh, too."

Her smile widened.

"This week has been a revelation. Every

time I stop by, I try to keep up with him but he's one tiny ball of energy. Did your mom tell you we went out back to kick a ball around? Even though he's just started walking, he has some serious balance."

"She didn't give me details, just that the two of you are settling in. Leo is comfortable around you. He feels safe."

Which was very important to Zoe. More than creature comforts or a large income. She wanted to keep her son protected from the ills of the world. After experiencing a bank robbery, her outlook had changed from carefree to super vigilant in watching out for those in her life. And he'd caused her way too much heartache by purposely heading into reckless, sometimes dangerous situations as part of his job. It went with the territory. He'd never considered that his actions weren't fair to her, until his accident.

He got it now. Too little, too late.

Mitch didn't have the heart to tell her that sometimes, no matter how careful or diligent you were, bad things happened. He wouldn't burst her bubble today.

Instead, he said, "I know I'm a little biased, but he's awesome."

Zoe laughed, a tinkling sound that lilted straight to his heart. "I agree."

It was all he could do not to take her hand in his. She'd made it clear he didn't have that privilege any longer. It was about time he respected her wishes.

The topic of Leo having played out, Zoe morphed into serious mode. "So, I really stopped here to run something by you."

"Shoot."

"There's a fund-raiser Saturday night at the high school. We're raising funds and awareness for a community food bank. I was wondering if you'd be available to take pictures of the event."

His brow rose. "Really?"

"Like you said, you want to get back to work. It's not high-profile like you're used to, but it's important to us. What do you say?"

"My first reaction is no."

Surprise flashed in her gaze. "Why?"

How to explain when he hadn't quite figured it out himself? "I'm still readjusting. I'm not sure jumping into the deep end is the best scenario."

"Look at it like your sticking your toes in the water. It's an opportunity to ease back into your career."

A career she hated. Did she want him to get better and leave again? So she could continue with the new life she'd built for herself without him in the way? It would sure make it easier on everyone, but the stubborn streak in him rose and heartily opposed the thought. She was giving him an opportunity to try out his old life. Prove he wasn't damaged goods. He'd be a fool to pass it up.

"I have to say, based on conversations we've had in the past, I'm surprised you're asking me."

She held up a hand. "For the sake of your recovery, I'm willing to suggest a truce."

"Interesting."

She sent him a self-deprecating grin. "While I'm not a fan of the past disagreements between us, you are talented and I would like the event documented professionally. It's important for Cypress Pointe. So, will you come?"

"If you promise this isn't a pity job."

Her brow wrinkled, producing a frown. "Look, I agree I messed up the other day. And I apologized. But I do want you to take the photos. Okay?"

He wasn't sure he believed she didn't feel sorry for him, but he had to take her at her word. As he mulled it over, he decided he needed to try to do everyday things. Attending this event would do just that. And maybe show people he could handle this simple job.

"You aren't going to boss me around, are you?"

Her eyes went wide in mock dismay and she placed a hand over her chest. "Me? Whatever are you talking about?"

He chuckled. "I know you."

"Then you know that was a silly question."

A balmy breeze lifted the ends of her hair and he got lost in the depths of her blue eyes. What would she do if he closed the short space between them and brushed his lips over hers?

For a moment, the world around them went blank. He drank in the sight of her, realizing how much he'd missed her. Missed what they'd once had together.

Zoe sensed the shift in the atmosphere around them. Softened. Her eyes became heavy lidded like they did just before a kiss and she swayed in his direction. But then, catching herself as she leaned toward him, dismay colored her face. She cleared her throat and stood.

"So you'll do it?" she asked, her voice raspy.

He held back a sigh. "Yes. I'll be there."

"Great." She rattled off the time. "I'll see you there."

He nodded.

She took a few steps backward, spun and hurried back toward Main Street.

She'd been as affected as he had been by their near kiss; he could read it in her eyes. Yet, she'd still pulled away. As much as he'd hoped for a different outcome, he wasn't surprised. Zoe wasn't entirely ready to let go of the past.

And if she had any inkling of the danger Mitch sensed during his recent flashback, she'd never trust him again. Until he had put together more pieces, he'd keep silent. No use making trouble when he couldn't decipher what the images meant.

He only hoped that once he learned the truth, it wouldn't destroy the fragile bond he was beginning to experience with his wife.

SATURDAY NIGHT, PEOPLE filed into the high school gymnasium. Excitement vibrated in the air, voices and laughter rose and carried in the vast space. Tables were set up around the room, filled with program literature, secret auction items or bakery goodies. Near the back of the room, Jenna was busy setting out her delectable hors d'oeuvres. Those who were familiar with her culinary skills were already lining up for a sample or two as soon as the aroma wafted around the room.

"Looking good," Nealy said as she sidled up beside Zoe.

"The space looks awesome. For a gym."

"That's why you hired me. I get results."

Indeed, she did.

The room was tastefully decorated with floral arrangements, candles and subdued linens covering the tables. Folks could roam around to look at displays the kids had created explaining the food program, or sit at a round table and chat with friends. The two top volunteers for the food bank program stood beside the three-shelf unit Zoe had ordered, which had been stocked with typical donations like canned goods and boxed items. Balloons were tied to the top shelf and hovered cheerily over the unit.

"Your ambassadors are talking up the program."

"Thanks for that, Nealy. I appreciate you mobilizing the gang."

Lilli and Max worked one side of the room while Dane and Wyatt, until their significant others were free, worked the other. Her friend Kady, owner of The Lavish Lily floral shop, had delivered beautiful flowers in gorgeous vases that would be auctioned off later. The point of the evening was to not only bring awareness but also solicit donations.

"I gave them a rousing pep talk before we opened the doors."

"It's working."

Zoe blinked back hot moisture. Her friends had always been supportive of her causes. What would she do without them? Or without the wonderful folks of Cypress Pointe?

She wiped a stray tear with the back of a finger, looking around for something to dry her eyes with. Even a napkin would do at this point.

"Here." Nealy handed her a tissue she'd pulled from the pocket of her stylish dress. "I'm always prepared."

Zoe took the proffered tissue and dabbed. She didn't want to ruin the makeup job she'd spent an inordinate amount of time on or leave stains on her new aqua-colored sheath dress. The chunky bracelet at her wrist slid down her arm, the matching necklace swinging as she moved. When she'd looked at herself in the mirror before leaving the house, she'd refused to answer the question of why she'd been so particular about her appearance tonight. This was a fund-raiser, just like the other dozen or more she'd headed up since becoming mayor.

Except tonight, Mitch will be here.

The thought kept rattling around in her brain. This was the first time he'd see her not only in her role as mayor but as a woman. Would he be impressed? Surprised? And, why did it matter?

"Now," Nealy went on to say. "Pull yourself together. Jamison Prichett, CEO of Prichett International, just entered the room. He's expressed interest in making a substantial donation to the food bank. You don't want to be all weepy around him."

Zoe straightened her shoulders. "Sorry."

"No problem. Now, go get 'em."

Smoothing the fitted skirt of her dress, Zoe took a breath and headed in the direction of the Prichett entourage. She'd met Celina Prichett six months ago at a city-planning meeting and the two had become fast friends. Celina had been enthusiastic about the food program and had promised to get her husband on board.

She weaved through the crowd to her destination when Mitch stepped into her path, his camera clicking. "Zoe."

"Mitch."

She'd only had a glimpse of him when he'd

arrived earlier, setting his bag behind one of the tables and moving around to get shots before the crowd showed up. Then she'd gotten busy and lost track of him. Which was good, because she couldn't get the scene in the park a few days ago out of her head. She was positive he'd wanted to kiss her and much to her dismay, she'd almost let him. Not a good move when she was still trying to determine what their relationship was going to be.

"Quite a turnout."

She tried not to beam, then thought, *What the heck*. This was a good turnout. "I'm pleased. Everyone who agreed to attend is here, plus others who were on the fence."

"It's a worthwhile cause."

"It is."

She met his intent gaze and chills ran over her bare arms. He'd dressed in a dark button-down shirt and slacks. His hair was combed back and his brown eyes seemed clear of pain. As he stood beside her, the cane rested against his leg, a reminder of what he had suffered and the healing he continued to work toward.

Why, recently, was a brand new attraction overshadowing her confusion about the man?

"Thanks for doing this, Mitch."

"My pleasure."

Was it her imagination or had his voice gone rough when he said those words? His intent stare never left her and suddenly she felt more self-conscious than she had in a long time. When she looked closer and saw a flicker of appreciation in his eyes, the goose bumps returned and she felt…beautiful. The past few years had taken their toll and here she stood with a handsome man's full attention. Okay, it was her estranged husband, but she liked it just the same.

Someone brushed up against her, causing her to bump into Mitch. His tangy cologne enveloped her and stirred her senses. As she caught his arm to steady herself, she couldn't ignore the lean muscle flexing under her fingers.

Oh, boy. This was not good.

She made space between them. "Well, I need to speak to some of the donors."

Mitch angled his head toward the crowd. "Go do your thing."

Before she had a chance to step away, Celina Prichett came into her line of vision.

"Zoe. What a wonderful event," her friend said, taking one of Zoe's hands in hers. "When you told me you were holding the fund-raiser at the high school, I never imagined it would be in such a lovely setting."

Zoe silently thanked Nealy.

"I'm happy you could come," she told Celina.

Celina dropped her hand and reached over to pull her husband into the group. "This is Jamison."

Zoe held out her hand. "Pleased to meet you. Celina has so many wonderful things to say about you."

Jamison sent Celina a sidelong glance. "Then you must have caught her on a day when I wasn't scheduled to hit the golf course."

Celina tucked her hand into the crook of her husband's arm. "You know I don't complain." She glanced at Zoe. "He works hard. I don't begrudge him a golf game here and there."

The couple, so worldly and attractive, couldn't have been more down to earth. The nerves she'd expected upon meeting the CEO quickly subsided.

"I'm sure Celina has told you all about our program?"

"Yes. And the teens who met us by the door were very knowledgeable. I'm quite impressed."

Zoe tried to keep from doing the happy

dance. Now all she had to do was get Jamison to sign on as a donor.

"So, we have many—"

"Hold on," Jamison cut in. "Isn't that Mitch Simmons?"

"I…um…" Zoe lost her train of thought. "Yes, it is."

"I'd heard he was killed while on assignment."

"Thankfully, it was a false report."

"I'm a big fan of his work. How on earth did you get him to cover this event?"

Zoe brushed back her exasperation. "He's a Cypress Pointe resident."

"Really?" Jamison glanced at his wife. "I'd love to meet him."

Pasting on a steady smile, Zoe nodded. "It just so happens I can make that happen."

Pushing down the rush of emotions— annoyance, jealousy and something old and festering she didn't dare uncover—Zoe went to fetch Mr. Hotshot Photographer. Tonight was supposed to be about helping families who needed food, not fodder for Mitch's career.

Zoe walked the few measured steps to Mitch.

"Got a minute?" she asked, proud that her voice came out steady.

"What's up?"

"I have a CEO who'd like to meet you. He's a potential sponsor."

"Sure, I'll talk to him."

She led the way, stopping beside the chatting couple. With a flourish, she said, "Mitch Simmons, meet Jamison Prichett."

Jamison stuck out his hand. "Good to meet you, Mitch. I'm a fan of your work."

"Really?" Mitch said, sounding surprised. His gaze darted to Zoe and then back again. She hoped her irritation wasn't visible.

"I have a signed series of prints you did of the anniversary of Cook's travels to Antarctica a few years ago. The shots were magnificent."

"Thanks for your interest."

"More than just interest," Celina drawled. "He made a trip there to check out the place for himself."

Mitch looked truly astonished. "That's terrific. I'm flattered."

"Tell me, what are you working on now?"

"Actually, the food bank is my newest project."

Now it was Jamison's turn to look surprised. "You're staying here in the States?"

Mitch glanced at Zoe. "That's the plan."

As much as she hated the limelight being

taken off the food bank, she had to admit Mitch's uncertainty bothered her. He'd always been proud of his work, but never puffed up and impressed with himself. Somehow he'd found a balance, which even she admired. His work was incredible, no matter her personal opinion of his extensive traveling to get the outstanding photos.

"I'd love to talk to you about your travels," Jamison went on to say.

"Right now, I promised to give Zoe's event my undivided attention. This program is important to the community, so I'm here to work. Perhaps another time?"

"You bet."

Zoe's heart squeezed at his words. He'd worked the conversation back to the cause at hand.

Mitch started to turn, then stopped. "You know, Mr. Prichett, you just might be getting in on the ground floor of a sweeping movement here. I can envision these types of food banks at schools all around the area. You should talk to Zoe about it in more detail."

Disbelief flooded her. She'd had that very thought in the back of her mind, but hadn't fleshed out the logistics of such a project yet. How had Mitch known?

"I believe I will."

Mitch nodded and moved away as quickly as he could while toting a camera and using the support of a cane.

"Amazing to see him," Jamison said as Mitch disappeared into the crowd. "I was leaning on supporting the food bank before we got here, but knowing Mitch is involved has sealed the deal. We'll sit down and go over the numbers next week."

Zoe's excitement wilted momentarily, but she kept her smile strong. "That sounds wonderful."

"Oh, Jamison," Celina said, tugging her husband's arm. "There's an item I want you to bid on. C'mon."

Celina winked at Zoe and dragged her husband away.

Zoe rubbed a hand over her brow. As upset as she was about Mitch taking the spotlight, he'd managed to steer the conversation back to the reason they were all here to begin with. She would get corporate sponsorship. Should it matter how it had come about?

No. Mitch was helping, just as all her other friends were doing tonight. Instead of letting old wounds keep her from being overjoyed at the outcome, she should applaud Mitch's effort and count it as a victory.

As soon as she had a minute with him, she'd thank him properly.

She took a few steps and Mitch came into view. He'd been speaking to someone and had started walking in her direction before spotting her. He stopped. Even from a distance, she could see the attraction in his eyes. For her. Just like the first time they'd met, only now they'd had years of memories together. And even though she wanted a divorce... She still wanted the divorce, right? There was no mistaking that Mitch still wanted to be her husband. That near kiss in the park had spoken volumes.

Unsure what to do, she jumped when a voice sounded beside her.

"Hey, Zoe. Sorry I'm late. Just finished my shift."

She turned to find Tim, the man she'd thought she wanted to date, with a big grin on his boyish face. His eyes lit with expectation and he held a single-stemmed red rose out in her direction.

Oh, boy.

"For me?"

He shrugged. "Just wanted you to know I was thinking about you."

Her head darted back to look for Mitch, her heart sinking as she watched him turn and hobble in the opposite direction.

CHAPTER NINE

MITCH WRAPPED UP his assignment before the event started to wind down. While it felt good to be doing something constructive—adjusting the brightness and contrast on his camera, performing light checks and focusing on the subjects—a headache hovered. Add in a new suitor for his wife's attention and, yeah, he was done for the night.

Folks said hello, but thankfully left him to sit at a corner table, alone. Small talk had become uncomfortable. He could see his friends wanted to ask questions about the accident and why he'd stayed away for so long, but by his terse responses, they usually let it go. There wasn't much to tell them beyond what everyone already knew. It wasn't like he'd had any more insight into that day, no matter how often he concentrated on the few new memories he'd gleaned from the latest flashback.

Curious gazes hovered longer than necessary on the cane at his side. His leg injury bothered him less and less, but because his balance was still sketchy, he relied on the cane. If anyone asked, he claimed his leg was weak, hoping to keep conversations about his brain injury to a minimum. Especially with Zoe. He didn't want her babying him or worrying about the residual results any more than she already did.

Leaning back in the metal chair, breathing deeply to keep the headache at bay, he watched as his friends laughed with ease. Max and Lilli exchanged a secret joke. Nealy ordered Dane around while he smiled. Wyatt helped Jenna lay out her culinary creations. How long had it been since he'd chuckled over something? Shared a secret? Touched the woman he loved on the arm just because he could? Long before the accident, for sure, when he and Zoe hadn't been at odds and constantly fighting. No wonder she was interested in a new man.

The subject of his thoughts hurried by, heart-stoppingly beautiful in a fitted dress that looked like it had been designed specifically for her. She stopped an older man in an expensive suit, chatting him up about making a donation, he assumed. He watched her animated face, not for the first time tonight realizing that his wife had changed as much as she'd stayed the same. Motherhood had given her a different glow and brought out a confidence that hadn't been there before. Her short hair had won him over. It actually suited her much better than the long locks he'd encouraged her to grow because *he'd* liked them.

When had she become such a poised, self-assured woman? While he was away, chasing his dreams? And while his interests were different, her passion for a cause remained.

A slight smile curved his lips as he watched her work her fund-raising magic. No wonder more than one guy wanted to carry on a conversation with his wife. She might see it as furthering the cause, but he didn't miss the interest on more than one man's face. The most astounding fact was that Zoe was oblivious to her appeal. Which made her more desirable. And Mitch more depressed.

He continued to observe his wife before instinctively lifting his camera. In all the years they'd been married, Zoe had never been a subject of his work. Tonight, she deserved recognition.

He adjusted the shutter speed and looked through the viewfinder. After a half dozen shots, he reviewed them on the digital screen. Nice candids. When he glanced up again, Zoe had moved and it took a few seconds to find her. She stood apart from the crowd, viewing the happenings on the sideline. Mitch lifted the camera. Clicked the moment of vulnerability when all the hard work of the night caught up with her. Her face softened, and she let herself be. The moment was over quickly when she shook herself and went back to work.

Mitch checked the screen again. Priceless. A picture no one but him would ever see. His personal reward for tonight's job well done.

"Glad to see you here. Zoe was right to ask you to cover the event."

Mitch lowered the camera and looked up to find Wyatt standing beside him.

"Just like she corralled all of you?"

Wyatt chuckled. "It's what she does."

"Seems I've missed quite a bit in my wife's life."

Wyatt pulled out a chair, turned and straddled it, his arms resting against the top of the back. "It took everything in her to keep going after we thought you were dead."

Mitch glanced at his friend's solemn face. If anyone could relate, it was Wyatt; having lived through much the same experience after his young son had died. "Once she found out she was pregnant, that's what gave her the power to carry on. Leo saved her."

"Unlike me, who caused all her problems?"

"I'm not saying that." Wyatt ran a hand through his hair. "You guys had hit a dead end. And to be fair, it wasn't only you. Both of you had your fair share in the failing marriage."

There had been more than one night of Mitch sleeping on his good buddy's couch.

Mitch caught sight of Zoe again. "She's something else."

"You have no idea."

"Guess I should find out."

"I wasn't gonna come right out and say it, but yeah. You need to figure out what you want and make it happen."

Mitch sent him a sideways glance. "Is that what you did with Jenna?"

Wyatt's brow rose.

"Heard you set a wedding date."

His friend's chest puffed. "Yep. And since you mentioned it, I can officially ask you to be the photographer."

Surprise struck Mitch. In all his career, he'd never covered a wedding. Or baby and family photos. Not that he had anything against the domestic angle, but his path had taken him in a different direction. But this was Wyatt, a good friend to him through the years.

"I'd be honored."

"Thanks, man. I'll give you the details when I find out more."

"You mean Jenna hasn't already started the grand plans?"

"No. We both agreed on small and intimate."

"Congrats."

Wyatt grinned as he stood and replaced the chair in its original position. "Can't wait."

As his friend walked away Mitch thought back to his and Zoe's wedding. They'd been out of high school a few months. Their mothers had been on board, his father a holdout, as usual, insisting they were too young to make such a huge commitment. He tried one last-ditch effort to convince Mitch to enlist in the military before, as he put it, Mitch ruined his life. Which had been a great big bust because, yeah, in time, his career had wrecked the marriage.

His father had boycotted the ceremony. Mitch always told himself it didn't matter, but deep down it had hurt when his father hadn't shown. Another moment in a long history of episodes where a son disappointed his father and vice versa. The more his father disapproved of Mitch's decisions, the more Mitch went after his career with a vengeance.

Look where that got you. You never speak to the man and your marriage suffered because you were trying to prove...what? That you knew better than your old man?

Running off to the far ends of the earth hadn't fixed anything, and now he had a broken marriage as a result. Did he want that kind of childhood for Leo? A father in and out of his life? Could his own father have been right about so many things? Mitch didn't even want to ponder the possibilities.

"You look like you have the weight of the world on your shoulders."

Zoe plopped down in a chair beside him and kicked off her high-heeled shoes. She reached down to massage one foot. "Ah. Much better. My toes went numb."

"You probably walked five miles tonight."

She sat up and waved a hand. "My calves will hate me tomorrow, but it was worth it."

The crowd began to dwindle. The big donors Zoe had been courting left, mostly those remaining had worked on the event. Jenna had cleaned up after her food disappeared in record time. A few of the teens were starting to collect the decorations for Nealy as the event planner instructed Dane to pull out the plastic bins she'd hidden so they could pack up for the night. Other helpers blew out candles, whirls of smoke lifting toward the fluorescent lights above, carrying with it a waxy residue smell.

"Are all your events this successful?"

She grinned, unrepentant. "You bet."

He chuckled. "Well, I for one am impressed. I can't believe the way you worked the room."

"It goes with the territory."

"Really, Zoe. You did great."

She lowered her eyes. His chest grew tight when a cute red flush covered her cheeks. Confidence mixed with the humility. Very attractive.

She met his gaze. "I hope you got some good pictures tonight."

"I'll go over them tomorrow. Get back to you to see which ones you want for your promotional needs."

She nodded, all business again. "I have a list. The local newspaper, the chamber of commerce and the city website. Some other sites that cater to those who want to lend a hand in feeding those in need. We can meet in my office next week."

"You really have turned into the mayor."

"Like you had any doubt?"

He shouldn't have. Cypress Pointe was her safe haven. She would do anything to make the town the best it could be.

"Not really. It was just amazing to watch."

She met his gaze and all he could think about was kissing her. Until a shout pulled her attention elsewhere.

"I'll be right back," she said as she jumped up and hurried over to talk to Nealy. After an in-depth group discussion, most everyone cleared out. The gym suddenly seemed cavernous. The voices of the few teens removing the canned goods from the display echoed and the wheels from a large trash can rumbled as the janitor rolled it into the room for the final cleanup.

Zoe gathered her belongings, placing them on the table before collecting her shoes. "Well, we can officially call it a night."

Mitch didn't miss the single rose lying beside her small clutch purse. He nodded toward it. "So, where's Tim?"

She looked away as she pulled on her heels. "Got a call."

"Huh. Happen often?"

She sat up. "I wouldn't know."

"I thought you were dating?"

"More like…talking."

"Talking?"

"That's what the kids say when they start to get to know someone before actually dating."

He chuckled. "The kids, huh?"

"You hang around teens, you pick up a thing or two."

"So, you and Tim?"

She exhaled. "I don't know what you want to hear, Mitch."

"How about the truth?"

Her brows angled. "You want the truth? Okay. Here it is. I don't know where we stand. I like Tim. He's a nice guy. We have fun together." Her expression turned dark. "But you and I aren't divorced, so to be honest, I have a hard time agreeing to go out with him. He says it doesn't matter, but... Well, it does."

Mitch digested her words, silent for a long moment. "Why didn't you file the papers?"

She sighed. "You were dead. What was the point?"

"And now that I'm very much alive?"

She met his gaze again. Spoke softly. "I don't know."

Tension stretched between them.

"He picked the wrong color," Mitch finally said.

She looked at him, confused. "What?"

"The rose. Yellow is your favorite, not red."

Surprise replaced her look of puzzlement. "You remember?"

"I didn't lose my entire memory. And just because I haven't given you flowers in a long time doesn't mean I forgot what you like."

She gaped at him, pulling herself together when one of the teenaged girls approached them.

"Sorry to bother you, Mrs. Simmons. I just wanted to let you know my mom won the bid for me on your Spend a Day With the Mayor silent auction. I've always been interested in politics."

Zoe smiled. "I can't wait, Ashlee. Give my office a call and we'll set up a day."

"Thanks." The teen looked from Zoe to Mitch and back. "I should go."

"Be safe," Zoe called out as the girl joined her friends before leaving the gym.

"You're a mentor, too?" Mitch teased. "How do you have time for it all?"

"I manage," she said, trying and failing to hide her pleasure. "Besides, I like working with young people. I love their energy and ideas."

"Then it's a good thing you offered your services."

"I learned a while back that silent auctions pull in a lot of extra revenue. And people love to outdo each other in the bidding."

"Tell me about it."

She raised a questioning brow.

Mitch reached into the camera bag and pulled out an envelope. Handed it to Zoe. "Watching you bustle around all night wore me out. I won this for you."

She took the envelope, fingered the flap to pull out a certificate. Her face lit up. "You bid on a spa day?"

He shrugged. "Maybe you can take a couple of your friends with you."

She glanced at him. "Why would you do this?"

"Like I said, you work hard. You're a mom and the mayor. A couple of hours being pampered is the least you deserve."

"Okay, where is my husband and what did you do with him?"

"WHAT? I CAN'T give my wife a gift?"

She'd hurt his feelings. She could see it by the disgruntled scowl and the stiff set of his shoulders. But why wouldn't she be surprised? She wasn't used to this selfless side of Mitch.

To say his gift caught her off guard was an understatement.

"I'm sorry."

"Are you, Zoe?"

Was she? Her mind had been in a constant state of flux ever since she'd found Mitch on the deck at the Grand Cypress Hotel. She'd finally accepted his death, and there he was, in the flesh and very much alive. So, sue her for being confused. She'd been angry with him when he'd left, and if she were completely honest, she was angry at his sudden return. She'd gotten into a routine, a new way of life with Leo, but now felt like she was on an emotional teeter-totter. Her husband was back and she was sixes-and-sevens about what to do with all the changes.

"I seem to say all the wrong things around you."

He blew out an exaggerated sigh. "It's not like I haven't made things difficult for you."

"Not so much difficult as perplexing. I'm afraid I'm not handling all this very well."

The janitor returned and moved the mobile trash can on rattling wheels, reminding Zoe that they should leave and let him get to work.

"Do you need a ride home?" she asked as they both rose.

"No. I've got a ride lined up." He glanced at his watch. "Should be here in fifteen."

"I can stay with you until then," she said as Mitch pulled the strap of his gear bag over his shoulder and they exited the gym and walked down a dark corridor.

"You don't have to. I can take care of myself and besides, you probably want to go home and kiss Leo."

Her heart expanded. Any mention of Leo brought her immediate joy. "I do miss him when I'm away from him for long periods."

"I get that now." He moved with less of a limp, she noticed, even though he still leaned on the cane. "He's captured my heart."

What about mine? she wondered. Despite all they'd been through, did he still hold her heart in the palm of his hand? Better yet, did she want to give him that privilege?

"Do you remember where our lockers were?" Mitch asked, thankfully changing the subject.

"I haven't thought about high school in years." She looked around to get her bearings. "Down this hallway?"

"Looks right."

Instead of continuing outside, they turned left. The old familiar scent of cleaning supplies masking the odor of leftover remnants of sweat and dirty gym clothes took Zoe back to those long ago days. The light grew even dimmer, obscuring the scuffed floors and leaving the trophy case at the end of the corridor in shadows. She ran her fingers over the cold metal of the lockers, could still make out the numbers on the doors despite the limited light. "Twenty-three, twenty-four... Here we go. Twenty-five. My old number."

"Wonder if the combination is the same."

"Who even recalls those numbers?"

"I do. Yours was ten-fourteen-one."

She stared at him, incredulous. "How, after all this time, can you rattle off my combination?"

"Certain things are imprinted on my memory."

His words and intent features sent chills over her skin. Looking away, she tried the number sequence. "No luck."

"It was fun to try."

It was. In fact, she hadn't had a whole lot of fun in a long time.

"What else do you remember about high school?"

"Let's see." He glanced up at the ceiling, then back to her. "Skipping English."

"Which you would have failed had it not been for me."

"True." He thought more. "Playing basketball."

"I never missed a game."

"Taking pictures for the yearbook."

She forced away a frown. When she thought back, his intensity on the yearbook committee should have been a clue to how serious he would take his career. They'd been young, not thinking about the future. She'd ignored, or at least hadn't recognized, the warning signals when he'd started traveling early on. Learned the signs only too well in the subsequent years.

"We should probably leave," she said. "Someone will be locking up the building soon."

"Before we leave, let me tell you the most important thing I remember."

She swallowed.

"Meeting you here every morning before the first class bell rang. Kissing you was the only way to start my day."

This was the second time he'd mentioned kissing. It shouldn't have mattered, yet her stomach flopped and her heart raced in anticipation.

"And your point is?"

"I'd like to kiss you again. See if there's still a spark."

No. Oh, no, no, no. "I don't think—"

"Chicken?"

"Of course not," she sputtered even as her belly swirled harder.

He moved closer. Captured her gaze with his. Held it while her breathing grew labored.

"Sure about that?"

His words brushed over her lips. Before she could stop her reaction, she leaned closer, easily ignoring the reasons she shouldn't kiss him. Seeing her agreement, Mitch touched his lips to hers.

Slowly, at first. Almost like savoring a distant memory.

She moved in, responding to the tug of tenderness, angling her head to deepen the kiss. This, she could never forget. The heat. The man. The years they'd shared together as a couple, dating. Their wedding and the hope of a long future together. All shattered because Mitch had wanted a career that took him from Cypress Pointe, leaving her behind, aching for a child she thought she'd never be able to have.

"Wait. I… This is too much."

He took a step back, giving her room. The

distant jangle of keys reminded her where they were and why. "We really need to leave."

Increasing their pace now, they exited the building into the flower-scented night. A full moon lit the sky. There were only three cars in the parking lot. A dog barked in the distance. An ordinary night, except she was more emotionally topsy-turvy than ever.

She needed to get home.

"It must be getting late. Will your ride be here soon?"

"Should be. Go on."

"If you're sure…"

He nodded.

Yes, she had a tendency to control her surroundings, especially when off kilter, like right now. "Right." She opened her clutch to remove her keys. Realized something was missing. She looked around her feet.

"Lose something?"

"Yes. Um, the rose."

"You left it on the table," he said, his tone low.

"And you didn't tell me?"

"Figured if it was that important you wouldn't have left it behind."

She narrowed her eyes but couldn't tell if he was playing games with her or not. He'd made his point, though, because she hadn't given the rose from Tim a second thought.

"I'll see you next week when you come by the house to visit Leo?"

"There's nowhere else I would rather be."

"Speaking of places to be, have you come up with a plan yet? You know, for work?"

"I'm not leaving Leo. That means I'll find something local." He held his arms out. "I can't go anywhere like this. Who knows when I'll be medically cleared to travel."

"The doctors seem positive."

"They do. But I still have to put in the time and effort."

She opened her mouth, but he held up his hand to stop her. "You can't do this for me, Zoe. Just let me go to my appointments and work with the professionals."

"You're right."

"Leo and I will find plenty to do."

Her son had enough energy to keep most people busy, but how long would that hold Mitch's attention? He may not admit it, but he needed more. He'd always been that way, craving nonstop activity, for as long as she could remember. Once he started feeling better physically, he'd need a challenge. Otherwise, he might leave her again. And not only her, but their son as well. He might say otherwise, but she would only believe him when she saw his words in action.

Glowing headlights angled into the parking lot. The vehicle headed their way.

"That's my ride."

She squinted, trying to recognize the car and driver.

"Uber," Mitch told her.

"Okay," she said. "Thanks again, Mitch, for helping out tonight."

"I'll call you when I've edited the images. Hopefully I captured what you wanted."

"I'm sure you did."

"Good night." Mitch opened the car door and nodded over the roof. "I'll wait until you take off."

"Good night."

Keys in hand, Zoe swiftly walked to her car and slid inside. Surprised her fingers were trembling, she started the ignition and put the car in gear. She crossed the parking lot, the headlights behind her until she turned left to head home, the car with Mitch heading in the opposite direction. She blew out a breath, wondering at her shaky condition. Was it the walk down memory lane? The kiss? Mitch reminding her to ease off trying to help him get better?

All three, but mostly the kiss.

What had she been thinking to let him kiss her? Okay, she'd been curious. Mitch was right—there was still a spark there. Boy, was there a spark.

Still, until she knew for sure what Mitch's intentions were, she had to keep their relationship on hold. Once he was healthy and sure about what road he wanted to travel down, she'd decide to pursue this…kissing or file the already drawn-up divorce papers. She didn't want to put pressure on Mitch, but their future was in his court.

Ugh. Basketball term. Now she had visions of a younger Mitch running back and forth across the gymnasium floor, racking up the points. Truth be told, she found this mature version of Mitch much more arresting. Why? Was it the way he conducted himself now, as if his actions mattered? Or the scars that were now a part of him? Could she call it…character? Only time would tell.

She turned down Main Street on her journey home. The few restaurants that stayed open late were dark, along with most of the other businesses. Even the lights at Charming Delights Catering were off, indicating Jenna had headed home. Just how long had she let Mitch sidetrack her?

At least she'd discovered one thing tonight. She had to stop putting her foot in her mouth when it came to conversations with him. Her purpose was never to hurt him, yet she seemed to do so on a regular basis. She'd be dealing with him professionally now and needed her wits about her.

Before turning off Main, her eyes lit on an office space at the end of a block. She blinked, then the wheels in her head started turning. A plan formulated. Her lips curved in satisfaction.

After some research, she'd approach Mitch. He might not be on board, nor willing to make more changes in his uncertain future, but she had to try. That's what she did, right? Help people? Whatever his answer, she'd get a better idea if he was really planning on sticking around Cypress Pointe. Because the longer he remained in town, the more she needed answers. For both her sake and Leo's.

Besides, he'd done something nice tonight by bidding on the spa day for her. Wasn't it right to return the favor?

CHAPTER TEN

"Surprise," Zoe sang out after she'd unlocked the front door of a downtown building just a few days later. Leo, nestled on her hip, chattered in a language only he understood. She juggled their son and diaper bag with practiced ease while she flicked on light switches after leading her husband inside.

Mitch moved slowly. Curiously glanced around.

Today, he'd met her at the old photography studio on Main Street dressed in a navy polo shirt and a pair of jeans, most notably without the cane. Was he finally on the mend? It was all Zoe could do not to ask. With reason. He'd been much too quiet the last time he'd stopped by the house to visit Leo. She wasn't sure if he was preoccupied or having trouble with his therapy. She ought to be thrilled by the lack of a cane, but the stronger he became, the less sure she was about their future. Either way, she couldn't miss the back-off vibes radiating from him whenever he sensed she was going to question him.

"It's a portrait studio." Zoe stated the obvious after trying to control her nervousness.

"I can see that." He tucked his sunglasses into the neck of his shirt and walked to an area set up with a backdrop screen and a stool placed on a large square of carpet. Lighting equipment lined a wall. A large reflective umbrella took up another corner. "Why are we here?"

"Mr. Haynes is retiring."

The only in-town photographer, the older man was eighty if he was a day. While his mind was still sharp, his body had slowed. His retirement had given Zoe a perfect opportunity to help get Mitch back on his feet.

"That's nice for him but doesn't explain the field trip."

Zoe bit her lower lip. Oh, boy. This was going to be tricky. She really should have planned this better, but when she'd come up with the idea while driving home from the fund-raiser, it had seemed solid.

"You worked here a couple of summers when we were growing up."

"Sure. It was a great experience." His voice

carried over his shoulder as he checked out the equipment.

She took a breath. Hugged Leo closer. He let out a squeak and she loosened her hold. "I talked to him about the possibility of you taking over."

"Taking over what?"

"His business."

Mitch turned on his heel to face her, shock etched on his face. "You did what?"

"You seemed to be making progress by taking pictures at the beach, then at the fundraiser. Why not take it a step further and run this place?"

"Because I'm not a portrait photographer."

She frowned. "I don't understand. You take pictures of people everywhere you go."

The shock slowly turned to irritation. His tone, when he finally spoke, was exasperated. "Yes, to tell a story. That's what a photojournalist does."

"You don't have to talk to me like I'm in the first grade."

"And you know the difference between working in a studio and out in the field."

Leo squirmed, picking up on the tension. Zoe lowered him to the floor, using the break in the conversation to come up with another tactic. Her son plopped on his bottom, then grabbed her pant leg to lug himself up, eager to explore the brand new world around him.

"You're right. I do know the difference." Zoe set the diaper bag on the floor beside her. Smoothed the flowing shirt she'd thought was pretty and feminine, and wondered why she'd bothered. By the glare aimed at her, he wasn't going to notice her carefully selected outfit. "To be honest, I always felt candid shots were your strong point. No matter the backdrop."

He moved around the room, his steps purposeful, yet stilted. Had he been too hasty in giving up the cane?

"You could set your own hours," she went on. "And you don't always have to be closed up inside. Mr. Haynes also did weddings, outdoor graduation shots, birthday parties. With a little creativity, you could carve out a niche for yourself."

"If I wanted to stay in Cypress Pointe, you mean?"

She'd come prepared for this argument. "You said yourself you can't predict the outcome concerning your health. How it will impact your career. If you take over the studio, it gives you time to get well. No need to rush into your next step. And as an added bonus, you'll be able to spend time with Leo."

At the mention of his name, Leo looked up from a small basket of animals Zoe assumed Mr. Haynes used to distract his younger subjects. Leo garbled a few words, then went back to work, tossing anything of little interest onto the linoleum floor around him.

Mitch circled the room before stopping to stare out the large front window with *Haynes Photo Studio* emblazoned across the glass in gold leaf. Though he stood perfectly still, he lifted a hand to rub his temple. Swayed momentarily.

"Mitch?"

Squaring his shoulders, he turned. "You should have talked to me about this, Zoe."

"I am. Now."

"And I suppose Mr. Haynes is waiting for an answer?"

"Well, um, I kind of implied you'd be interested."

His eyes went wide. "Why would you do that?"

"To help you."

He ran a hand through his hair. "I'm not one of your charity projects, Zoe. I can make my own decisions."

"I know. But when I talked to Mr. Haynes he was getting ready to put the business up for sale. I wanted you to get first dibs."

"Again, you should have asked if I'm even interested."

"It's not like you have other plans."

"That you're aware of," he said, voice tight.

Her confidence slipped. "You have other plans?"

"What does it matter if I do? You never asked." He shook his head. "The only thing we seem to have in common right now is our son."

"Who needs his father in his life." She hesitated to take a step toward him. "I know things were difficult when you left. But, Mitch, we thought you were dead." Her voice caught. She looked down at her son, carrying on a conversation with a stuffed dog. "I thought Leo would grow up without knowing you. That the only way he'd learn about his dad was through family stories and seeing your work when he grew up. But you're here. That changes everything."

Okay, this wasn't going well. She hadn't been one hundred percent certain that Mitch would be on board, but she'd hoped for a little less friction at the idea. Time to bring in the big guns.

She lifted Leo and set him on the stool, steadying him with her hands braced at his waist. He glanced around the room from his new vantage point, sending his father a gummy grin as he bounced in place.

"Don't you think kids make the perfect subject? Think about the families who come in here, wanting a lasting memory. You can give it to them."

"I memorialize people whose pictures I take for a story."

"But you don't know them. You don't have a personal connection."

"Really? You know this because you've always been so tuned in to what I do?"

She frowned. "What do you mean? You've always wanted to take pictures."

"Maybe you aren't the only one who thought their work could make a difference."

"When did… I never…"

"That's right. You never asked. You always just assumed you were the only one in this relationship to do any good deeds."

Her chin rose. "Don't put this on me. You couldn't wait to get out of town and take pictures of the world."

"Yes. But somewhere along the way, it became about more."

She blinked. When had this happened? Had she been wrapped up in her causes, in her perceived hurt, that she'd missed this? Or had she ignored it so she could use the disappointment of not being able to have a baby to keep him at arm's length? Is that what he'd meant when he'd said she wasn't the only altruistic one in the family?

Leo started to babble, holding his arms out to Mitch. Taking a few steps to close the gap, Mitch gripped his son's small hand in his. Leo filled in the silence between them, his very presence the last conduit linking them.

"You're not playing fair, Zoe, using Leo to make your pitch."

"Why shouldn't I? Your decisions affect Leo as much as they do me."

"Does this big idea mean you want us to get back together? If I stay in town, we'll work on our marriage?"

After that kiss the other night, that's all she'd been able to think about. Them, together. It felt comfortable. But was it right if the core problems between them still existed?

"This is a good way to find out where we stand," she hedged.

"I get it. If I take over the studio and stay in Cypress Pointe, then our marriage might be saved. But what if I decide to travel? Pick up where I left off? Just because you don't want to leave town doesn't mean I have to stay."

She bit her lip again. "I simply want to give our family a fighting chance."

"No. You want to make sure I remain in Cypress Pointe. I understand that you like to get things done. Be in control. But I have to say, I really don't like this side of you, Zoe."

He bent over Leo, kissed him on the top of his head and met her gaze over their son.

Shame. That's what she felt. Were his words true? Was she really such a bad person to want her family in one place? All the years of taking care of her mother when she was younger, the day-to-day uncertainty of life, had left its mark on her. The fears after the bank robbery had stymied her. She wanted—no, needed—to take care of every situation, because she'd always been the only one she could count on. She'd discovered if she took a problem by the horns, she could figure out a way to solve it. But had she stepped over the line with Mitch today? Forever? She didn't know anymore.

"You need to decide what you really want," he said, giving Leo another kiss before leaving the building.

MITCH MADE IT as far as a wooden bench a block away from the studio before the dizziness leveled him. Clutching the back, he eased his way around the bench and sank down. His head pounded. Closing his eyes usually gave him solace, except today when it made the swirling worse. His stomach rebelled and the steadying breaths his therapist suggested he use during times of extreme stress didn't help. He silently prayed he didn't throw up on the spot.

"You doin' okay there, son?"

Mitch gently moved his head upward. Bob Gardener, the town police chief, stood before him, blocking out the stabbing rays of the late morning sun.

"Forgot my sunglasses," he said in way of explanation.

"They're right there in your shirt," the chief pointed out.

Right. He yanked them from the collar and slipped them over his nose.

"That sunshine can be a real pain," the chief said.

Literally, in his case.

"Need me to get you anything? Water? A ride home? An ear?"

Mitch frowned. "I have a therapist, thank you."

The chief chuckled. "Yeah, but that therapist hasn't known you as long as I have."

Right now, all Mitch wanted was to sit on Wyatt's back porch—away from the stress and obligations of life that tended to make him irritable when things got out of hand, or made him physically sick.

Bob lowered himself onto the bench beside Mitch. "Listenin' comes with the job."

"Is that what you call it?"

The chief chuckled again.

"Sorry."

"Been around guys sufferin' from head injuries. No offense taken."

Mitch chanced a look. When his stomach didn't revolt, he began to calm down. "Where have you been around men with brain injuries?"

"At the VFW. Lots of stories about guys coming back home after combat, tryin' to get on with life. You aren't alone."

"Those guys were injured in the military."

Bob shrugged. "Don't matter where it happened. Same struggles."

"What are you saying?"

"One day at a time."

"Which would be easy if I knew what to expect on any given day."

Down the street, a car revved its motor, pulled onto Main and promptly slowed when the driver got a glimpse of the chief.

Bob nodded his head in Mitch's direction. "No cane?"

"I'm trying to depend on it less."

"Leg stronger?"

"Yes, but the cane's for balance. Still having trouble in that area."

"Along with your wife?"

Mitch narrowed his eyes. "What are you up to?"

"Lookin' out for you at a friend's request."

Anger surged through him. "You can tell Zoe to stop managing me."

"Not Zoe."

"Then who?"

"Samantha."

Zoe's mom? He frowned. "I didn't realize she was concerned enough to get local law enforcement involved."

"She knows you're prickly about talkin' things through. Thought another man might be easier to confide in."

"Is everybody in town privy to my private business?"

"Just family, far as I know."

Great. It was bad enough Zoe was trying to guilt him into sticking around. Before he knew it, his father would drop by one day and want to "talk about their feelings." He shuddered at the thought.

"No pressure. You know where I am."

"At Samantha's?" Mitch asked with a sudden glimmer of insight.

Bob cleared his throat.

"I thought she was acting weird. I noticed her talking on the phone when I visited Leo, giggling like a teen."

"Giggling?" the chief asked with interest.

Now it was Mitch's turn to chuckle. "How long?"

"About six months."

His brow rose. "I take it Zoe doesn't know?"

"Her mother would like to keep us a secret right now."

"Why?"

"Not real sure. I'd announce it to the entire town if I had my way."

The only thing Mitch knew about the chief's personal life was that he'd been a widower for a very long time. And Samantha had never been serious about a man, at least in the time

Mitch had known her. In an odd way, he could see them as a couple.

"Good luck breaking the news to Zoe," Mitch said.

"You'd think the girl would be happy for her mother."

"They have…issues."

"And Zoe's technically my boss."

A reluctant grin tugged at the corner of Mitch's lips. "Funny how life turns out."

A scratchy squawk came from the lapel mic on the chief's collar. "Duty calls." He stood. "It don't really matter who asked. I'm here for you if you need anything, Mitch."

"I appreciate it."

The chief nodded, pressed a button to speak into the mic as he strode away.

The conversation with the chief had at least taken his mind off his physical limitations. His head only mildly ached and the dizziness had subsided. Now would be a good time to head back to Wyatt's.

With his destination in mind, Mitch rose. A car blew by, swerving to miss a pedestrian crossing the road. The movement caught Mitch's eye and suddenly he was thrust back to the day of the accident.

He closed his eyes, feeling the sense of fear

and urgency. Wishing he'd called Zoe before leaving the camp to let her know he wanted to compromise— that he would cut back on his schedule to be home more, that this would be his last overseas trip for a while until they worked things out.

Whoa. Mitch opened his eyes and staggered. That trip had been his last?

Closing his eyes again, he pushed the limits of his memory.

The truck behind him drew closer, no matter that Mitch was standing on the gas pedal. He had a death grip on the steering wheel as they lurched over a rocky road. Voices cried out from the bed of the truck, urging him to go faster.

"I'm going as fast as I can."

"They're gaining," came a shout.

A gunshot rang out, shattering the rearview mirror on the driver's side. Mitch ducked instinctively. Glanced back in the mirror. "Everyone okay?"

"Keep driving!"

Another shot sounded. Then another. The third striking the tire. Mitch lost control of the truck, first fishtailing, then picking up momentum on a downward incline.

"Hold on," he yelled.

The steering wheel jerked, throwing Mitch

off balance. Another shot. The truck hit something hard, went airborne for a long, terrible moment before crashing to the ground. Mitch tried to correct the wheel, but suddenly the truck leaned and flipped before landing on the roof, sliding to a stop.

Mitch shook his head. The sound of steam escaping the engine sputtered, then went silent. The radiator must have blown, evidenced by the pungent smell invading the cab. In the distance, a car door slammed. Low voices carried.

Mitch tried to move, pinned in place. A sickly metallic taste coated his tongue. His head pounded and when he looked down, he saw blood spattered about him. Groaning, he tried to make sense of what had just happened.

"Mitch," a shaky voice called from behind him.

"I can't move."

"I'll be—"

The sentence abruptly stopped.

"Jack! Answer me."

A shadow loomed beside Mitch and a blurry face filled his vision. "Jack can't talk right now."

Then a massive blow to the head and everything went dark.

Mitch's eyes flew open and he gasped for air.

Someone had deliberately caused the accident. Shot at him. But who? Why?

Rattled, he lowered himself back down to the bench. He'd wanted to remember, but now the memories caused more questions. Who else had been with him? What had been their fate?

He froze.

Jack.

He remembered. Jack Parsons. Had he worked with another refugee aid group? Mitch had met up with him when he'd offered to help find Hassan's father—the reason they'd ventured away from the larger camp to begin with.

A car horn honked, startling Mitch from his revelation. He had a name to go with the face now. Tangible information as he pieced together that day. As soon as he got back to Wyatt's place, he would start his search.

With his mind only on his mission, he nearly careened into a man standing a few feet from the bench.

"Sorry. I'm in…"

The words died on his lips. His father, deep lines in his pale face, eyes sunken, stared back at him.

"Mitch."

"How… What are you doing here?"

"I was running an errand for your mother. I noticed you on the bench."

His wits returned to him. "And decided to walk by?"

"No. I was trying to think of a way to approach you."

"You're my father. Do you need a reason?"

"You haven't returned my calls."

Uncomfortable now, Mitch wanted to run, but his father's expression stopped him. And then he recognized the brightness shimmering in his gruff father's eyes.

"Dad?"

"My son is alive," Todd Simmons whispered. "I never thought I'd get a chance to talk to you again."

Great. Another lecture on the horizon? Mitch wasn't inclined to defend his life or his decisions to his father right now. Not when the puzzle pieces were falling into place.

"Your mother has encouraged me to come visit you."

"Yet, I haven't seen you."

The older man swiped at his eyes. Color returned to his cheeks. The man who had always seemed so much bigger than life looked beat-up and weary.

"We have a lot to catch up on."

"Really? Because I only recall you wanting to run my life. And when that didn't work, putting me down."

His father looked away. Swallowed before returning his gaze. "I was wrong. It took losing you to make me see how wrong I'd been."

Doubt coursed through him. His dying had gotten his father to see that all his hard-nosed ways hadn't worked? *Convenient*, mocked Mitch's inner cynic.

"Dad, I have to get moving."

"Oh, right." Uncertainty, an emotion he'd never associated with his father, dimmed the older man's eyes. "We'll catch up later."

Indecision clawed at him. Why? Was it that hard to believe his father might have been affected by Mitch's accident? After all, he thought he'd lost a son. Could it be that complicated, yet at the same time, so simple?

He saw the hope written on his father's face. It was like looking in a mirror. Didn't he want to prove much the same to Zoe? That he had changed?

"Ah, yeah, we will."

His father smiled. "Thank you, son."

Confused and feeling awkward, Mitch quickened his stride as he hurried down the sidewalk. Since the accident, he'd felt like he was residing in an alternate universe: He'd never thought he would come back home to his life; never thought he would have a son; could try to make things right with his wife; never, ever, thought he would have a decent conversation with his father. Yet in the span of a month, all these things had taken place.

Had the accident been fate compelling him to take a hard long look at his life?

The headache that had eased returned, but Mitch powered through it. He had too much to do. Wouldn't let the pain keep him from his task. Not if it meant getting to the bottom of the mystery that had hounded him since the day he'd woken up in a hospital bed weak, broken and lacking memories of how he had gotten there.

By the time he reached Wyatt's house, he'd come to two conclusions.

One, he'd walked to town and back without any incidents. No falling. No stumbling. Yeah, he was dizzy, but he could function.

And two, maybe the studio job was just what he needed. Work had always cleared his mind and he had a lot of decisions to consider. He didn't want to get Zoe's hopes up that he would totally walk away from photojournalism to be a portrait photographer. He wasn't sure that's what he wanted to do long term. For now, it would keep him busy. Give him purpose each day and help him sort out the memories, which he was visualizing in more clarity each time he remembered.

He needed to figure out who had shot at him and why. There was more at stake than he'd initially considered. The chance to win his wife back and prove he was a man worthy of Zoe's trust. Watch his son grow up. Protect them both from danger.

He wouldn't let anyone take that away from him.

CHAPTER ELEVEN

"You're awfully quiet. It's not like you."

Zoe glanced over at Nealy, lounging on her right, not able to read her friend's expression under the thick moisturizer slathered on her face and the cucumber slices hiding her eyes. They'd met up to take advantage of the spa day Mitch had won in the silent action at the fundraiser.

On the other side, Jenna rose to lean on her elbow, lifting one cucumber slice to view Zoe while the other slipped to her lap. Lilli, on the far side, cocked her head, waiting for Zoe's answer.

"This is supposed to be a fun girl's day," Jenna said. "What's up?"

Zoe sighed. Did she want to rehash her last conversation with Mitch? He was right. Her actions didn't exactly place her in an altruistic light. For the past couple days, she'd been searching her soul, wondering if indeed she was trying to boss Mitch. So far, she hadn't come up with a sure answer. She liked to think she was more evolved than that, but the guilt niggling her made her question her motives. Maybe some girl talk would help straighten her out.

"I think I made a mistake with Mitch."

Nealy, reclining comfortably on her back, snorted. Lilli emitted a loud sigh.

Jenna angled on the soft leather lounger to face Zoe, confusion crossing her features. "I thought things were good between you guys."

"Good is a relative term."

"Didn't we talk about you cutting the guy some slack?" Nealy asked.

The sad thing was, she thought she had been.

After a bone-melting massage, including a hot-stone treatment, Zoe's muscles were so relaxed she could hardly move. The girls had then been cleansed, exfoliated and soothed with an aromatic body scrub. Now, wrapped in fluffy robes and reclining in very comfortable lounge chairs, lulled by scented candles and rhythmic New Age music, they were waiting for the deep moisturizing facial mask to do its magic before finishing up the visit with a manicure.

Zoe snuggled into the robe, secretly glad

her friends had called her out. Mitch had paid a pretty penny for this spa day, plus, he was watching Leo while she enjoyed being pampered, making her feel even more guilty over her actions.

"Mr. Haynes is retiring. I talked him into letting Mitch take over his studio."

At this revelation, Nealy removed the green slice and peered at her with one judging eye. "Without asking him first, I assume?"

She cringed. "Yes."

With a scoff, Nealy replaced the cucumber. "I'm thinking he didn't take it well?"

"No. I guess I don't blame him, but when I got the brain wave, it just made sense."

"To you."

Zoe sank into her chair a little farther.

While Lilli sat up, Jenna swung her bare feet over the foot of the lounger. "What was your thinking process?"

Grateful to be able to voice her motivation, she took a quick sip from the tall glass of herbal tea on the table beside her.

"There's no way Mitch can travel right now, but he needs something to pour his energy into. I get that being stuck inside a building all day might not be his thing, but I felt he needed purpose. A steady job gives him that."

"And keeps him in Cypress Pointe," Lilli added.

"Well, yes." Zoe paused. Might as well spill the rest. "So I made the arrangements and had Mitch meet me at the studio where I told him the good news."

"Without Mr. Haynes there so Mitch couldn't tell him no?" Nealy asked, questioning the brilliance in Zoe's plan.

Zoe frowned. "When you put it that way…"

"There is no other way," Nealy harrumphed, crossing her arms over her chest.

Jenna shot Nealy a stern look, the move lost by the vegetables covering Nealy's eyes, then softened her features when she looked back at Zoe. "I understand your desire to help him, but the delivery…"

"Granted. Not my best moment."

Nealy brushed off the cucumber slices and propped herself up. "Let's cut to the chase. Now what?"

Good question. Mitch was obviously still miffed with her, if his chilly greeting this morning when he came to babysit Leo was any indication. She'd wanted to explain, but his body language made her take pause. Plus, she was running late. Leo had been up half the night, fussy over the eruption of a new tooth, tugging at his ear and causing her to fall seriously behind.

"I'm sort of between a rock and a hard place. I told Mr. Haynes that Mitch would take over right away and he's made plans to go on a cruise. In the meantime, I have no idea if Mitch will honor my word. If he doesn't show up at the studio, who will I find to fill in?"

"Then you should have—"

Zoe held up a hand to cut Nealy off midsentence. "The worst part is Mitch told me I need to decide what I want, and he's right. Do I want my family intact even if Mitch is unhappy about my interference? Or does he travel again and I go ahead with the divorce? There's no easy choice here."

A spa attendant poked her head into the room to check on the women. After assuring the attendant they were fine, they all sat in silence for a few moments.

"Why do you need to rush things?" Lilli asked in her quiet, subdued tone. "Just be thankful Mitch is back, alive. It gives you both a chance to fix your marriage. If that's what you want." She paused. "That is what you want?"

Zoe's eyes teared. "Mitch has really changed. He's said things, done things that show me he realizes how bad our relationship had become. Acknowledges the issues between us. Why can't I seem to find the grace to accept these changes and work with him?"

Nealy took her hand. "You don't want to be disappointed again."

Jenna took her other. "You don't want to lose him again."

Her gaze went back and forth between her friends. "Wow. I'm pretty pathetic, aren't I?"

"No. Rightfully conflicted." Nealy straightened the neckline of her robe. "Mitch's return was as much of a shock as was the word of his dying. You've been on an emotional merry-go-round for a long time now." Her lips curved into a rueful frown. "I can't imagine the confusion muddling that busy head of yours."

"I have to agree with Nealy," Jenna added. "You're borrowing trouble by forcing events and some kind of normalcy in your lives. Yes, it goes against the nature of Zoe, but you can't control this, my friend. Let time work out the answers."

Could it be that way? Did she have the patience to wait out what would become of their marriage? Their family? Did she have a choice?

The attendant returned to inform them that it was time to remove the masks and move on to the next pampering phase. Before they left the room, Zoe stopped her friends.

"I appreciate your honesty. All of you. And I will let time take its course. I promise to work on that area of my life."

Her friends beamed at her.

"Starting tomorrow."

Nealy's smiled faded. "What did you do?"

"I might have asked your significant others to stop by and check on Mitch and Leo while we were out. My mom has an art show and I didn't think the boys should be home alone."

Nealy let out a low whistle.

"Why didn't we know?" Jenna asked.

"Because I swore them to secrecy. Asked them to make it look like a spur of the moment idea to stop by the house."

Lilli closed her eyes and shook her head. "Mitch is not going to like this."

"And I'm betting he'll figure out it was my doing."

"Good grief," Jenna puffed. "You don't know when you have a good thing."

"What do you say after the manicure we go have lunch?" Zoe suggested in a bright tone.

"And let you off the hook?" Nealy's eyes narrowed. "No way."

"Nealy's right on the money today," Lilli

said. "However unpleasant, you need to go home and face the music."

"I was afraid one of you would say that."

"And so do our guys." Lilli shook her head. "What were they thinking?"

"They all kinda owe me."

All three women stared blankly at her.

"Dane needed a building permit expedited and I spoke to the right people. Max needed information for a certain case he's working on and I steered him in the right direction."

"And Wyatt?" Jenna piped up.

"He owes me for keeping Mitch's return a secret. I'm still not over the fact that the two of them didn't include me in the news."

Lilli tilted her head and considered Zoe. "You're downright scary."

"Maybe, but I get the job done."

The attendant entered the room again, her voice urgent. "Ladies, we need to get the masks off your skin now."

Lilli and Jenna followed the woman dressed in white. Before Zoe could join them, Nealy took hold of her arm and pulled her aside.

"You do understand the message you sent Mitch, right?"

"I do."

"You won't be able to talk or steamroll your way out of this one."

"I know that, too."

"What were you thinking?"

"That I'm a mother who has to watch out for her son."

"From his own father?"

"From a father who is not one hundred percent healthy."

Nealy dropped her hand. "You crossed the line this time."

Zoe knew it. Knew she'd have to face up to her actions. Hoped Mitch was a bigger person than she apparently was turning out to be.

THE FOUR MEN were poised in various locations around the living room. All eyes were on the little guy sitting in the middle of the floor, staring back at them, his cheeks flaming red and wet, a thumb stuck defiantly in his mouth. Leo had been fussy and fretful since Mitch had arrived earlier that morning. Having the other guys show up had done nothing to ease Leo's mood.

He'd already had one tantrum and cried until he couldn't breathe, freaking Mitch out in the process. The guys had tried to distract him with toys and games, but nothing had worked.

Leo had now decided to sit silently, daring them all to continue the staring contest.

"Now what do we do?" Dane asked in a low tone.

Max shrugged. "You got me."

"He's only one little kid," Dane continued. "How is he getting the best of us?"

Wyatt pushed off from the couch to lift Leo. "You guys are clueless."

"Clearly. You're the only one with experience," Dane volleyed back.

At the head of the clueless pack sat Mitch. He rubbed his aching temple. Took into his arms the drooling baby held out before him by his buddy. "It's okay," Mitch cooed into his son's ear once he got Leo settled on his lap. "Daddy's got you."

"Looks to me like you're getting the hang of this thing," Max commented.

Mitch raised an eyebrow, his voice filled with amusement. "Right, because you guys just happened to stop by to see my parenting skills in action."

The guys exchanged guilty glances.

"Fess up. Zoe sent you."

Dane caved first. "It wasn't like we had much choice," he groused. Then realized what he'd said. "Not that we minded coming by," he amended.

Wyatt chuckled. "Just stop."

"Really," Max interposed. "For a guy coming back from the dead to the shock of finding out he's a father, you've taken it in stride."

Mitch glanced down at Leo and was rewarded with a drooly grin. "The more time I spend with this little guy, I can't tell if I'm gaining ground or totally inept."

"You aren't the first parent to question their abilities," Wyatt said, the only man in the group with any kind of daily interaction with children.

"I'll admit, Zoe sending in backup rankles, like she still doesn't trust me." Leo sagged against him, close to sleep, Mitch guessed. Hoped.

The guys moved the conversation to sports, which suited Mitch just fine. He'd suspected Zoe of dispatching his friends to the house from the off. At first, he'd been annoyed. She really had to get a grip on this whole control thing. But when Leo started fussing, it was a help to have three other men trying to soothe the baby. Humorous, almost. But a good feeling. One of belonging. Something he'd given up when he'd gone on the road. Zoe had always understood this village mentality, which brought him back to being annoyed again.

Did she still not trust that he had Leo's best interests at heart? Every time he started to get comfortable, she pulled something like the guys showing up today. Was she thinking he'd mess up? Prove he didn't have what it takes for the long haul?

Before he could answer his own questions, a knock pounded on the door and the police chief let himself in. Leo jumped at the commotion, then held out his arms when the burly man stepped into the living room. The chief said a general hello to the room then stopped to ruffle Leo's hair.

"Samantha forgot one of her paint boxes. I'll be in and out in a jiff."

The baby kicked against Mitch, reaching out to the chief. Mitch rose and followed the older man to the art studio.

"Sure Samantha didn't send you to check up on me?" Mitch asked as Leo bounced in his arms.

"Nah. She did forget something." Bob searched the room littered with all types of art paraphernalia, finding the sought-after box in the corner. "Usually Samantha needs a second pair of eyes before she leaves for a show, but I met her there." He retrieved the box and held it up. "See?"

"Sorry. Zoe asked the guys over to make sure everything was okay here, so I'm a little peeved. It's like she still doesn't trust me with our son."

"It's gonna take time. She's been the lone parent for a good long time now."

"I get that, I just…" Mitch shook his head.

Leo nearly bounced out of his arms. Mitch handed him over to the chief.

"Actually, I'm glad you stopped by." Mitch rubbed his temple. "I was going to call you this week."

"What's up?" Bob asked as he chucked Leo's chin.

"After we spoke the other day, I had a flashback that gave me more concrete details about the accident. I remember the name of one of the guys with me that day. I'm trying to find his whereabouts, but I wondered if you had any advice."

Bob's serious gaze met his. "How about be careful?"

"I think that's a given."

"Really, Mitch. There's no tellin' what might happen if you contact this man. You might be stirrin' up trouble"

"Or getting answers. If I don't find him, I keep on second-guessing."

"That is true." Bob pulled his finger away from Leo, who had grabbed on and was trying to stuff it in his tiny mouth.

"I think what I really want to ask is, can I call you if I feel like I'm getting in too deep?"

Bob's gaze pierced his, straight on. "You know you can. We're practically family."

Mitch grinned. "Things are progressing with Samantha?"

"Now that you're back, she worries less about Zoe. Which means she pays more attention to me, so yeah, things are moving to the next level."

"You'd better tell Zoe soon."

"When Samantha is ready. Speaking of which—" he handed Leo back to Mitch and the baby let out a disappointed whimper "—I'd better get going before she wonders where I ran off to."

"Thanks, Chief."

"You bet." He stopped. Placed a beefy hand on Mitch's shoulder. "You got a room full of friends out there that'll help same as me. And Max has contacts. You might want to include him in this search of yours."

Mitch had thought about it, but once you

told two or more people, you lost control of how and where the information went. He didn't know enough yet to get Max involved. He especially didn't know enough to risk Zoe finding out.

"I'll keep that in mind."

"Good." Bob lightly slapped his arm. "Now I'm off."

Mitch went back to the living room. One by one, the guys took off, busy with Saturday morning errands. Soon a quiet calm settled over the house and Mitch sank onto the sofa, a drowsy Leo snuggled up against him. Before he knew it, the two of them had dozed off. The next thing he knew, Zoe stood over them, a soft smile lighting her face.

"Hey," he said.

"Hey back." She lightly touched Leo's head. "Things okay here?"

"You mean since your accomplices are gone?"

Her face colored. "About that…"

Leo shifted, sensing his mother nearby. He opened droopy eyes and mumbled.

"Let me get him to bed," Zoe said as she lifted him from Mitch's lap. "Then we'll talk."

While Zoe put him down, Mitch went to the kitchen to start a pot of coffee. He glanced at the clock on the wall. Midafternoon. Where had the day gone?

Shaking off the cobwebs, he watched the dark brew fill the pot. The bracing aroma started to perk him up as he gathered his thoughts. He and Zoe needed to get on the same parenting page. Today.

"Leo went right back to sleep," Zoe said as she came into the kitchen. "With that tooth he's cutting, none of us got much sleep last night."

Mitch took two mugs from the cabinet and poured. Handed her a steaming cup then leaned back against the counter while Zoe took a seat at the table.

"I owe you an apology," she started.

"How about an explanation?"

She blew on the hot drink, obviously biding her time.

"You've got to let your guard down, Zoe. I won't hurt Leo."

"You're just now getting back to normal."

He was a long way from normal. His leg was stable enough that he used the cane less, his arm strong after therapy, but the headaches and dizzy spells continued to hit him without warning. He was well aware of how far from normal he still was. But he would never intentionally compromise his son. If he felt a headache coming on, he'd made arrangements to keep his mom on speed dial.

"Take the health factor out of the equation. Do you really think I would put Leo in danger?"

He watched her swallow. Ran a hand through his hair. He had been holding out on her, hadn't he? Not admitting that as he uncovered more about the accident, the gravity of the situation was as debilitating as the headaches that plagued him late at night?

"Zoe, life happens. We won't always be able to control every little aspect of Leo's life. Especially when he gets older."

She rubbed the scar on her arm. Always the reminder of what happened when things spun terribly out of control.

He closed the space between them and took a seat beside her. Took a chance and reached to grasp her hand and held back his relief when she didn't pull away. "Right now you, we, are Leo's whole world. But that won't last. Are you going to limit him by playing it safe his entire life?"

"And what do you suggest? That I let you take him to parts unknown?"

"I'm not saying that. I merely want a chance. Between not wanting to leave Leo alone with me or finding me a job you deem as suitable, something's bound to go wrong."

"That's your opinion."

He let out a long sigh. "Which leads me to believe this is another fruitless conversation."

She met his gaze. He read the turmoil there but also the gentleness. "I was wrong to send reinforcements today. You are doing great with Leo."

"But…?"

"No buts. I mean it."

"Every time you orchestrate our surroundings, you undermine my confidence."

Her eyes went wide.

"You've had time to get used to having a child. Had time to figure out the ins and outs of parenting. You're ahead of the curve while I'm desperately striving to catch up."

Unshed tears glistened in her eyes. "I'll work harder at letting go of some control."

"It has to stop, Zoe. We're in this together, whether we stay married or not. Agreed?"

She puffed out her cheeks. "Agreed."

"And I'll keep making strides in the parenting role. Together we should be able to make positive progress."

A lone tear slipped down her cheek. Without thought, he reached over to thumb it away.

When he touched her satiny soft skin, they both froze. At that moment, nothing could have forced Mitch to move away. He leaned forward, his intent to kiss her clear as he cupped her face. She moved in, until their lips brushed. Tenderness tugged at his chest. This is what he'd been hoping for, a chance to renew their relationship, not second-guess each other.

Zoe angled her head and the kiss became deeper. She held on to his arms while they reconnected, remembered the vows they had shared so many years ago.

He broke the kiss, staring into her eyes. "We can make this work, Zoe. I want to try."

Just as she opened her mouth to reply, her phone pinged. She blinked before slowly moving away to pick it up. She read the message, placed the phone on the table and averted her eyes.

"Problem?"

"No. It's, um, Tim. He wanted to know if I'm free for coffee."

Why did it seem as if they were moving forward, only to have another setback thrown into the mix?

It took every ounce of strength he possessed not to express his frustration. He took Zoe's mug back. "I'd say you are."

"Mitch—"

"I can stay here with Leo."

She slowly rose, pushing in the chair. "I at least owe Tim the courtesy of telling him where we stand."

"Which is?"

"That you and I are working on co-parenting. Which won't leave time for dating."

The pent-up air in him escaped like a pin-prick piercing a balloon.

"And the other? Making our marriage work?"

"You're right. I have to make a decision. The only way to do that is for us to spend time together. Fix the trouble or decide to go our separate ways."

He nodded.

"You promise to thoroughly consider the future? You owe me that much."

Relief swept through him. "I can do that."

She sent him a small smile. "Then no more babysitters for the babysitter. Let's move forward." Grabbing her phone, Zoe swept out of the room. Mitch leaned against the table, a flicker of hope flaring inside him. Zoe was giving them a chance.

He went back to the counter to pick up his mug, a shadow looming over his joy. He hadn't lied when he'd agreed to consider the future. In fact, the future was all he thought about. Problem was, it was all tied up with the past, and he could only hope that what he discovered about the accident didn't ruin the positive truce he and Zoe had reached today.

CHAPTER TWELVE

IT TOOK MITCH almost a week to track down Jack Parsons. He'd called contacts from his time in Jordan, reached out to fellow journalists and got in touch with the rescue organization working in the area of the accident. Now that he had a number, he stared at the digits written on the piece of paper staring up at him from his desk. Yes, he wanted the truth. But the tingling at the back of his neck warned him he might not like what he uncovered.

Just as he reached for his cell, the studio landline rang. Sandy, the assistant he'd inherited when taking over for Mr. Haynes, answered on the second ring. She'd worked here going on ten years. He guessed her age to be midforties, with short brown hair, a petite frame and boundless energy. She was efficient, he'd give her that. Taken him under her wing to walk him through the studio appointments, account books and anything pertaining to running the business.

Since starting a week ago, the studio routine was becoming easier every day, which surprised him. He'd told Zoe he'd give it a try, and so far, he enjoyed the work. His clients were excited to be here, a long cry from the wildness or popularity he'd recorded the last few years and the tragedy more recently. He'd needed a break from such jaw-dropping or heart-wrenching scenarios, a fact made clear when he turned the key in the lock and walked into the quiet space each morning. Instead of being restless for new adventures, he experienced peace. He chatted with clients and discussed their everyday lives. He would never regret the years spent documenting international events and famous people around the globe, but right now, home felt good.

And it would get better if he stopped procrastinating and made the call.

He poked his head out of his office door. "Sandy, hold any calls. I need about fifteen minutes personal time."

"You got it, boss," came her jaunty reply.

He closed the door and stared at the paper again. Took a deep breath and punched in the numbers.

After five rings, Mitch was ready to leave a

message or hang up. Suddenly, a harried voice sounded on the other end.

"Jack Parsons."

Mitch nearly sagged with relief.

"Jack. Mitch Simmons here."

A brief pause, then, "Mitch?" Another pause, then surprise. "Good to hear your voice, man."

"It's been a while."

"After we got separated the last time we were together, I'd heard you, ah…died."

"Thankfully, that's not the case."

"What happened?"

"Long story. Short version is I was laid up in a hospital for a long time and finally made it back home."

"You're in the States?"

"I am. How about you? Did you get hurt in the crash?"

"No, man. I mean, I had some cuts and bruises, but nothing major."

"That's good to hear. My memory is sketchy, but I remember driving to a refugee camp when all of a sudden a truck was on our tail. Ran us off the road."

"We were being followed."

"Do you know why?"

"It was a crazy day. I'm not sure."

"Rebels?"

"Can't answer that."

Mitch rubbed his hand across the back of his neck. "I heard shots. I called to you, but when you didn't answer, I thought you'd been taken out."

"No. I got lucky. No holes in this body."

Mitch sank down in his chair, relieved. He still couldn't remember what happened to Jack, no matter how many times he called up the flashback. "There was a guy with the gun. Who was he?"

"You really can't remember?"

"He clocked me with the butt of the pistol. Knocked me out cold."

"I didn't know what happened to you in all the confusion."

"I suffered a head wound. Now I only have bits and pieces of the accident. I just recently recalled you being there."

"Hey, I'm sorry. I managed to get away."

"From a guy with a gun? How did that happen?"

"Good luck?"

"Had to be more than that. It looked like there might have been others in the truck."

Jack hesitated. "I never saw anyone else. While the guy was talking to you, I jumped out of the truck bed and took off. Made it to a stand of trees where I hid until he left. Slowly made my way back to camp."

And left him there to die? "You didn't check on me?"

"I was afraid to take a chance. Sent help your way when I made it to safety."

That would explain how Mitch had gotten to the hospital, but it didn't explain why Jack's explanation seemed off.

"Can you tell me anything else?"

"No. Went back to the States not long after. Been in Miami since. You know, my home base."

Mitch's antennae went up. Miami? Why did that city seem familiar?

"You work there, right?"

Jack chuckled. "That must have been quite a blow to the head if you don't remember."

"Yeah." That prickly feeling came over him again. What was he missing? "Any chance you'll be up near Tampa in the near future? I'd like to get together and see if I can piece together the events surrounding the accident."

"Let me check my calendar."

Mitch heard noises in the background, then Jack spoke again. "I'll be in St. Pete in two weeks. Does that work?"

"Sure. Got a time that's good for you?"

"Ah… How about three on that Thursday. I'll come up to…Cypress Pointe, wasn't it?"

"Yes, but I can meet you halfway." It would be worth the drive to get answers. Maybe gain insight into the few memories he did have about the day of the accident.

"Sounds like you went through an ordeal, Mitch. I'll come your way."

"Thanks." Mitch penciled in the appointment on his calendar. "There's a coffee shop, Cuppa Joe, right on Main Street."

"It'll be good to see you."

"I'll see you at three."

"Right. And Mitch?"

"Yeah."

"Good to hear your voice, man."

Saying goodbye, Mitch ended the call. A low-grade ache took up residence in his temples. A sign he was stressed. But why? And why had Miami set off an internal warning?

He closed his eyes, trying to remember the company Jack worked for. Allied? No. Something with the word *associates*? No. Brothers? It was there—so close he could almost see it in his mind.

The block was too strong. Instead of forcing a result, which he'd learned didn't work and only made his head ache worse, he eased off. Something was there in his subconscious and it would come to him. In time.

A knock sounded on the door, yanking him from his thoughts.

"Mitch. Your eleven o'clock appointment is here."

Right. Back to work. He opened the door. "I'm ready."

Sandy shot him a grin filled with mischief. "You're gonna love this one."

He walked, his steps a bit halted as he mastered the pain, to the portrait area. One look at a young, frazzled mom holding a red-eyed toddler and he knew he was going to earn his money's worth.

"Hey, little buddy," he said, approaching the toddler. "Ready to have fun?"

"His name is Matty," his mother said.

"Great name. Did you pick out the backdrop you wanted?"

"Yes. Sandy showed me the choices."

"I'm changing it out now, Mitch," Sandy called from the background display against the far wall.

"Props?"

"If we can get Matty to sit, I'd like some

shots on that stool. Then, I don't know, have him playing with toys?"

"Got it." Mitch grabbed a stuffed animal and waved it before the child. "Why don't you hold Mr. Dinosaur while I get ready?"

The boy took the animal, engrossed with it while Mitch adjusted the light stand and umbrella and made sure he had the right sized lens attached to his camera before setting it on the tripod until he was ready to shoot. He pulled the colorful low-to-the-ground stool closer to the backdrop. The mother placed Matty on top, straightened his shirt and backed away.

"Okay, Matty. Here we go."

Mitch reached for the camera and started snapping, but Matty kept his head down.

"Buddy, look at me."

The child looked up, saw the camera in Mitch's hands and his face puckered up. Oh, no. This wasn't good. He recognized the quivering lip, had seen it on Leo's face enough times to know they were in trouble.

As if right on cue, Matty belted out a loud cry and reached for his mother.

"I'm sorry," the mother said as she rushed to Matty.

Okay, the stool wasn't going to work. Mitch looked around the area for inspiration and smiled when he found a toy that might do the trick.

"Matty, want to play with this train?"

The toddler stopped crying but looked leery.

"Why not have him sit right on the mat?" Mitch suggested to the mom while Sandy slipped the stool away. He hunkered down beside the child. "See how the train makes a noise?" He demonstrated by pressing the yellow button on the blue engine. The boy giggled and reached for the train. Mitch fist bumped Matty, who let out a delighted chuckle.

"Now we've got it," Mitch said as he went back to the camera and started snapping shots.

"What noise does the train make?" Mitch asked.

Matty made sounds nothing like the toy, but everyone laughed and encouraged the toddler to pose. He went along, giving Mitch enough time to snap some good pictures, with Matty running the gamut from shy and unhappy to outgoing and the star of the show.

How did Mr. Haynes do this day in and day out?

After twenty minutes of trying new poses and bribing Matty to sit still, the session ended.

"Check with Sandy on when to expect the proofs," Mitch told the harried mother.

The mom picked up her son. "Thanks again. Matty's a handful."

He thought about Leo and smiled. "He's a boy."

The bell over the front door chimed, announcing customers. Mitch glanced over his shoulder to see his parents standing in the doorway, tentative smiles on their faces.

He groaned.

Sandy leaned over and said in a low voice. "It's going to be a long morning."

"Hi." Mitch hobbled toward his parents. "What're you guys doing here?"

His mother hooked her hand into the crook of his father's elbow. "We were going to lunch and thought we'd stop in and see the studio. Zoe told us your plans to take over."

He bit the inside of his cheek.

"How about giving us the grand tour?" his father suggested.

"You're sure?"

His father smiled. "Absolutely."

"Then we can go have lunch together," his mother interjected. "If you're free, that is."

He viewed the hopeful faces of his parents, stopping the immediate excuses he'd already come up with to get out of spending time with his father. They both seemed genuine and for once, he decided to give spending time with him a try. "Sounds great."

And with their undivided attention, Mitch began to explain the workings of the portrait studio.

THE NEXT DAY, Zoe slipped in through the back door of the studio just after noon, carrying an oversized takeout bag from the Pointe Cafe, following the hallway leading to Mitch's office.

They'd spent more time together since the kiss in her kitchen. Tim hadn't liked her decision to stop seeing each other, but what could he do? She was still married and wanted to see if she and Mitch could recapture the goose-bump excitement of first love. Mitch had been living up to his declaration of making their relationship work. Seeing his enthusiasm, she'd decided to stop trying to control the outcome and just let things be. It helped that she didn't show up at the studio to see if Mitch needed anything or that she left Mitch and Leo alone so they could continue to bond. So far, so good.

"Knock, knock," she called out before entering.

Mitch was seated at his desk, surprise crossing his face when he looked up. "My memory is still a bit fuzzy. Did we have plans?"

She held up the to-go bag. "Nope. Just an impromptu lunch." She glanced at the photos scattered across his desktop. "Where can I set this down?"

"Give me a sec to straighten up here."

"New project?"

"Just finishing one for Mr. Haynes. He didn't have a chance to put together a package from the last wedding he photographed so I volunteered for the job."

"Is putting albums together in your job description?" she teased. Quite a change from global photojournalist.

Once he'd collected all the photos, he placed them on top of a nearby filing cabinet. "Sandy does, after I make the final decisions. She likes putting the fussy finishing touches on the albums, and since the clients seem happy with the end result, I let her do her thing."

"It's coming together then, you having someone to work with?"

"No complaints. Sandy was with Mr. Haynes for so long she knows the ins and outs of running the studio. And since I never ran the business side of my own career, thanks to many others, including Maria holding the reins down here, I appreciate her knowledge in that area. She's great at dealing with people and the day-to-day stuff. And she never tells me how to conduct a shoot, what lighting is best or which equipment to use. Ours is a symbiotic relationship."

"I get it," Zoe said as she placed the bag on the now-empty desktop. "She doesn't pry."

"Exactly." He turned from the filing cabinet and peeked into the bag. "Looks good. I could use a break."

"Long morning?"

"Two sittings."

She placed her purse on one of the empty chairs and started unpacking the bag. "Fill me in."

"A very particular bride-to-be and a retired couple."

"Sounds like fun."

"It was. And speaking of retirees, my parents stopped by yesterday."

Zoe stopped in the process of removing two wrapped sandwiches. "How did that go?"

Mitch reached in for the drinks and chips, setting the empty bag aside. "Okay. My dad was acting…weird."

"In what way?"

"Interested in the studio. Wanted a tour.

Talking up my career when before he thought it was a waste of time. I expected him to be totally negative since I was hurt because of my job, but he didn't bring it up. Not once. Then we went out to lunch."

"Your father cares, Mitch. He was a wreck when we thought we'd lost you."

"But he's being...nice."

Zoe bit her lower lip to keep from laughing. "What?"

She unwrapped her turkey sandwich. "You and your dad have never seen eye to eye, but now you have something in common."

"Really? And that is?"

"Fatherhood."

Mitch stopped before taking a bite of his ham-and-cheese, and leaned back in his chair. "If anything happened to Leo, it would kill me."

"Maybe if you look at it that way, you'll understand your dad's change of heart. Imagine how horrible he felt, never getting a second chance to make things right."

"I suppose I hadn't thought of it like that."

"Until recently, you never thought like a dad."

"Certainly puts a different perspective on life."

"Think you and your dad can…coexist?"

"I'll try," Mitch said after swallowing. He glanced at the bread in his hand. "This is really good."

"Your appetite is returning?"

"And my balance. The doctors were right. Once I gave therapy my all, I've gotten positive results."

"I'm happy for you, Mitch."

"So am I."

As they gazed at each other over the desk, Zoe couldn't deny the tingle of excitement. Especially with that certain twinkle in her husband's eyes. She couldn't put a definite name on her feelings. Yes, she loved Mitch. She always would. They had a past and they shared a child. But had the pain of the past healed enough for her to fall in love all over again? Because that had to be the next step in order for them to move on.

Lately it had been like the early days when they'd started dating; holding hands, sneaking kisses, talking on the phone late at night. He was still living with Wyatt, but she was toying with the idea of asking him to move to Samantha's house. They still had a ways to go, but she wanted the three of them to be a real family. Could she put away her fears and just go for it?

Edgy and a tiny bit nervous, she jumped up, pretending interest in the many years of Mr. Haynes's pictures lining the office wall. She began a circuit of the room, stopping at one in particular, letting out a peal of laughter.

"You okay?"

She turned to face him. "Come look at this."

Mitch rounded the desk to join her. As he moved closer, his tangy cologne captured her senses as she pointed to a picture on the wall. He stared at her profile for a second, then focused on the picture.

"That's you and Bethany, right?"

"We must have just turned thirteen." Two girls, dressed in old-time long dresses and bonnets, mugged for the camera. "The town held a Heritage Day Picnic and we dressed up like children of the original pioneers of Cypress Pointe."

Mitch peered closer.

"Are you holding a musket?"

"It was a replica and I didn't say we were historically correct."

"Yeah, because Cypress Pointe had to run off marauders in its past?"

"It was a fun day." She sent him a glance

out of the corner of her eye. "This took place just before you moved to town."

"And I missed you all dressed up, ready to defend our fair town?"

"You probably would have taken one look at that costume and run."

"More likely talked you into letting me shoot your gun."

"You always were a sweet-talker."

Mitch moved closer, took her by the shoulders to face him. "Still am."

He leaned down, his lips warm as they closed over hers. With a sigh, she wrapped her arms around his neck while his arms circled her waist. After a few moments, he broke off the kiss and smiled at her.

"Just like old times."

"Except these are new times."

Mitch backed up, but still held her in the circle of his arms. "Speaking of new, I almost forgot to tell you. I got a call from *Suncoast Spectacular*. You know, the Tampa area magazine for tourists that features local hidden treasures. They asked if I'd be interested in working for them."

"Word of your return got around fast." She tilted her head. "This something you'd consider doing?"

He shrugged. "Not my usual gig, but it could be fun. They asked me to head up to Horseshoe Beach for some outdoor shots. What do you think? Want to tag along?"

At his request, her stomach dipped. "I'm not sure if I can get time away from the office. Town council meets pretty soon, I have to prepare for that. And then there's the—"

"I get it, Zoe. Forget I asked."

He was trying. Shouldn't she? "When you have a date let me know and I'll rearrange my schedule."

"I will." He sent her a grateful smile. "And since we're talking about dates, care to accompany me to Wyatt and Jenna's wedding this weekend?"

"I'm officiating."

"I'm the photographer."

She hesitated. Were they rushing things? Going public too quickly?

"Okay, a working date," he offered. "What do you say?"

"I say it sounds like a plan, but I do need to get back to work."

They moved over to the desk to finish their lunch. Afterward, they collected the sandwich wrappings and dropped the trash into the to-go bag. As Zoe grabbed a napkin, a piece of paper fluttered to the floor.

Bending to pick it up, she read a name and number. "Who's Jack Parsons?" she asked when she stood again.

"A guy I know."

"Mysterious," Zoe teased, even though her stomach twisted at Mitch's uneasy expression.

He blew out a breath. "He was with me at the accident."

"You remembered?" she whispered.

"Not everything. I had a flashback the other day and I saw Jack's face. Recalled his name."

Zoe looked at the paper in her hand and back again. "You're going to call him?"

"I already did. This morning."

"Oh… I…" She swallowed the disappointment. And fear. "Were you going to tell me?"

"Not until I had some answers."

"Did you think I'd try to stop you?"

"Zoe, things are going good between us. There was no point getting our hopes up when Jack may not know what happened."

Their hopes? Honestly, she would have been happy leaving well enough alone, but knew Mitch would never stop his search for the truth.

"But you said you spoke to him."

"He didn't have much to say, but he'll be in

town in two weeks. I'm going to meet with him. Maybe if we see each other, talk more, events will fall into place."

Slowly, she placed the paper back on Mitch's desk.

"Do you want me there?"

"Not this time. It'll be better if it's just Jack and me, two guys sharing information."

Or maybe he didn't want his normally bossy wife in the picture, calling the shots and messing up his chance to finally discover what really happened?

She grabbed her purse and draped the strap over her shoulder. "I'll talk to you later."

"You're not upset?"

Mitch was an adult, one who had traveled the world. She had to trust him. "No. It makes sense. You need to talk to this person and you don't need someone hanging around, making it seem like a social visit when you want answers."

"I'm glad you understand."

She stopped before him. "But I do expect answers."

He pecked her cheek.

"I promise."

Even though he said the words, Zoe couldn't fight the dread building inside her. Finding out what had happened, filling in the lapses in his memory, was important to his recovery and, if she were totally honest, to their marriage. But why did she think the truth would bring new problems to their fragile relationship? Was she looking for a way to sabotage the steps they were taking toward their future? Did the fact that he hadn't confided in her mean he could walk away again?

She stepped into the sunny Cypress Pointe afternoon, trying to shake off the cold chills that refused to let go.

CHAPTER THIRTEEN

PUSHING HER WORRIES to the back of her mind, Zoe pasted on a smile when she picked Mitch up the following Saturday for Wyatt and Jenna's wedding. Time had flown by since the announcement a month ago.

"Jenna was pretty adamant about a backyard wedding," she said, pulling into the driveway a few hours before the ceremony. "Think it'll be a problem for picture taking?"

"I doubt it." He winked at her. "Just let the professional do his magic."

The intimate exchange made her chest tight, from both attraction and concern. She was definitely falling for Mitch again. Her heart had softened, even though her head called her a fool.

He looked great today, dressed in black slacks, a white button-down shirt and a sports coat. She'd chosen a cranberry-colored short dress with a deep vee in the front, a slim gold belt at the waist, the hem skimming her bare knees, along with strappy gold sandals to finish off the look.

"Hey. You okay?"

Zoe put the car in Park. "Sorry. Just thinking ahead."

"That's what everyone loves about you. You're always prepared."

She sent him a sideways glance. It was fine and dandy that everyone loved her, but did Mitch? Should she ask? You'd think after ten years of marriage she'd know the answer, but in their case, it was the exact opposite. They had more questions now than in the good old days.

She reached into the back seat for her wedding-script binder, her fingers brushing against Leo's car seat.

There's more at stake now.

She did not need that bossy voice, sounding suspiciously like her own, reminding her of her current state of affairs.

"C'mon, slowpoke."

Zoe took hold of the binder and joined Mitch, his camera bag slung over his shoulder, as he walked up the sidewalk to Jenna's rental house. His stride was much more steady than when he'd first arrived home. Had it really been over six weeks? His hair had grown out, covering the telltale scars from the accident. He'd gained weight and his skin had returned to its normal tanned color. She knew he still suffered headaches occasionally. When the bad ones came upon him, he laid low, returning when he was feeling better. She'd gone with him to the doctor appointments in the beginning, but even now he had his schedule under control. Which meant he didn't need her as much. The idea stung.

Her thoughts were making her crazy. She knew all she had to do was sit down with Mitch so they could talk about their options. Stay together? Divorce? Leave the status quo? And still, she put it off. Why? Maybe if she figured that out, she could take a positive step forward.

Pull it together.

Time to get into the joyous wedding spirit.

"Any idea where the happy couple is going to live after the wedding?" she asked, focusing on other people's lives.

"Wyatt is moving in here until they find a new house. Jenna's lease renewal is coming up and Wyatt's cottage is way too small for the entire family."

A family that consisted of the bride, the groom and Jenna's two adopted daughters.

"The girls are as excited as Jenna," Zoe said as they reached the door and she pressed the bell. Taking a step back, she surveyed the front yard. "It's a beautiful day for the ceremony."

The bright morning sun rose into a clear blue sky. The temperature promised to rise later in the day, but for the noon wedding, a constant breeze would keep the humidity at bay. There had been talk of rain, but thankfully, it was holding off for a few more hours. Moving into the Florida summer, afternoon showers would become commonplace, but on this early mid-July day, they couldn't complain.

The door opened to reveal one of the twins. Bridget, she thought.

"Welcome," said the little girl of eleven, her brunette hair already styled in an intricate updo.

"So serious," Mitch teased.

"I'm practicing. It's my job to greet the guests." The young girl's eyes narrowed. "Why are you here so early?"

Mitch held up his camera bag. "I need to start taking pictures."

Zoe angled her thumb in his direction. "I'm his ride."

The door opened wider as Bridget ushered

them in. "I'll tell Jenna you're here for pictures," she announced and ran off.

"Where's Wyatt?" Zoe asked as she closed the door.

"Had errands to run."

Brisk footsteps echoed down the hallway. "Good, you're here. We can get started," Nealy said in her no-nonsense tone. "Mitch, Jenna isn't quite ready for her prewedding shots. Why not get the lay of the backyard? Dane is out there making sure the tent is set up correctly."

"Got it." He leaned over to give Zoe a quick kiss, then disappeared through the kitchen.

Nealy's brow rose. "Guess you guys kissed and made up?"

"I'm trying to be more in the moment and not borrow trouble."

"Glad to hear it." She hooked Zoe's arm through hers. "Now come help me with the bride."

Nealy dragged her to Jenna's bedroom. When she opened the door, Jenna twirled from in front of a full-length mirror. "I'm not ready for this."

"You've been ready since you met Wyatt," Nealy disagreed.

Despite Jenna's nerves, she was a vision.

A long creamy white off-the-shoulder dress hugged her petite frame. With a short pixie-style cut, her hair required only the fresh gardenia lying on the dresser, its sweet scent lingering in the room.

Beside the flower lay a beautiful bouquet made with small barely-budding white roses scattered within coral and aqua-colored seashells, the handle wrapped with white satin. There were also two smaller bouquets, a collection of rounded shells held in place with lace, which Zoe assumed were for the girls. By the looks of it, Jenna had taken a tropical Florida wedding to heart.

"I know I should be excited, but this is so…"

"Permanent?" Nealy suggested.

Jenna waved a hand. "I don't have a problem with permanent. After growing up in foster care, I'm all for roots and family."

"Then what is the problem?" Zoe asked as she set her belongings on the bed.

Jenna blew out a breath. "Is it normal to be nervous?"

"I wouldn't know," Nealy snorted. "When Dane and I eloped, I was too young and excited to be nervous. Then Dane filed for the annulment and we broke up, so…"

Jenna sent a beseeching glance at Zoe.

"I suppose. My wedding day went by in a blur. If I was nervous, I can't recall." She took a seat on the edge of the bed, pulling the wedding binder to her chest. "You and Wyatt wrote your own vows and I gotta tell you, there isn't going to be a dry eye in the house once you recite them to each other. You two have a very special relationship. Don't doubt or second-guess it now."

"Yeah," Nealy said as she lifted the delicate flower. "That's Zoe's job."

The comment smarted, even if it was the truth. "Someone has to be in charge today. You wisely chose me, so I'm telling you, you have nothing to be nervous about."

Jenna placed a hand over her belly. "I'm really happy you're both here."

There was a knock on the door, followed by Mitch's deep voice. "Is the bride ready for pictures?"

"Now?" Jenna twirled to view her reflection in the mirror. "Do I look okay? Should I let him in?"

Nealy went into event-planner mode, calming the bride. Rising from the bed, Zoe patted her friend's arm and went to open the door.

"Be patient," she told Mitch on the way out, trying to ignore the butterflies in her stomach.

Why was she suddenly nervous around him? It wasn't like she was the one getting married. Maybe it had to do with the way Mitch's dark eyes sparkled, or the secret smile he sent her.

Pushing away this new response to her husband, she tried to brush past him.

"Don't worry," he said, leaning close to her ear. Telltale goose bumps raced over her skin. She swore Mitch smiled wider, even though she tried to hide her response.

"I…um…should check out where I'm supposed to be later," she stammered. "I'll see you in a little while."

With that, she hurried down the hallway. Why on earth was she suddenly acting like a giddy teen rather than a woman who'd been married for ten years? Okay, she most definitely was falling for Mitch all over again. Could that be why his long stares and secret smiles made her heart race? And his kisses? Oh, man. "This is silly," she muttered under her breath.

In the kitchen, she sidestepped the employees from Jenna's catering business, who were busily preparing lunch. The savory scents wafting from the uncovered containers made her stomach rumble, despite having eaten breakfast. A young man wheeled a box into the room; champagne, she imagined. The team had things under control, so she slipped out of their way, ready to journey out back to see where she would stand when she officiated the ceremony.

Once outside, all thoughts of nerves and crushes on her husband left her mind as she viewed the backyard, which had been transformed into a wedding wonderland. "Incredible," she said, walking from the patio to one of the two large decorated tents.

Several rows of chairs were set up at the far end, covered in white cloth. Beside each aisle seat, a slim white post with a hook held a mason jar tied with a white tulle ribbon and a sprig of baby's breath. Tiny shells and a handful of sand lining the bottom of the jar were visible through the clear glass.

A small arch had been set up with enough room for the bride and groom to gather under as they repeated their vows. Matching tulle draped the structure to soften the look.

Long tables covered in white linens with brightly colored centerpieces, consisting of shells, flowers and candles, had been set up on the periphery. After the ceremony, the chairs would be moved to the tables and lunch would be served. From here, the freshly lit candles mingled with the earthy scent of the yard. Tall moveable fans were placed in the four corners, ready to be used once the temperature started rising. The staff would work from the kitchen and the porch, leaving plenty of room for guests, who would enter by the side gate, to mingle in the yard.

Before long, people started to arrive as Zoe went over her script one last time. She looked over the small crowd, mainly family and close friends. Max and Lilli arrived, still clearly in the honeymoon phase, followed by Wyatt's family. Wyatt hovered near the back door, waiting until it was time to take his place by Zoe and watch his bride walk down the aisle.

A satisfied smile curved her lips as the guests took their seats. She saw her mother enter the backyard, dressed in a flowing, gauzy dress, her eyes alight as she spoke to someone over her shoulder. Zoe frowned. Had her mother come with someone? She hadn't mentioned it when they'd discussed the upcoming wedding. Her question was answered when the police chief appeared, taking Samantha by the elbow to lead her to their seats.

Her mother and Bob Gardener? When had they become an item? And why didn't she know about it?

"Zoe."

"Huh?"

"Zoe? We're ready."

She snapped out of her shock to face Wyatt. "Right. Sorry. Your wedding."

"That's why we're all here," Wyatt chuckled.

Straightening her shoulders, she flipped on her professional persona. "Of course. You're ready?"

"I have been for months."

She grinned. "Then this should be a breeze."

As Wyatt turned to face the door, soft music flowed from corner speakers. The sliding door opened to reveal the twins in matching style dresses, one yellow, the other green. Bridget still had her serious face on, but Abby grinned at the guests as they proceeded down the white-runner aisle.

The music turned to the wedding march. Everyone rose. Zoe felt Wyatt tense beside her until Jenna stepped out, stunning in white accented by the colored shells of the bouquet.

Zoe snuck a glance at the groom, blinking back tears at the total rapture on his face. This was why she officiated weddings, to see the joy on the couples' faces. This was how all couples should feel, how she felt the day she'd married Mitch. Like the world was yours and together you were unstoppable. She turned to the crowd, meeting Mitch's intent gaze. Could he be thinking the same thing? Oh, she wanted him to.

Wyatt stepped forward to meet his bride and together they turned to face Zoe, who started the ceremony. Once they exchanged their vows, tissues came from purses and pockets to wipe away happy tears.

"I now pronounce you husband and wife," Zoe told the couple.

With a whoop, Wyatt scooped Jenna into an embrace, lifting her off the ground as he kissed her. The crowd clapped as they walked hand-in-hand down the runner, stopping at the far end for another kiss. All the while, Mitch stayed discreetly out of view, snapping pictures of his best friend marrying the woman he loved.

The mood shifted from hushed to high energy as the beat of the music picked up and everyone mingled or offered their congratulations to the couple. Zoe closed her binder. Another ceremony in the books.

"You did a beautiful job," her mother said as she joined Zoe before she could join the revelers.

Taking a breath, she asked, "Are you here with Bob?"

Samantha's cheeks went a vivid shade of red. "Yes."

"Are you two dating?"

"We have been for a while."

"How long is a while?"

"Six months."

Zoe blinked in disbelief.

Her mother smoothed a hand over her loose skirt. "I've been meaning to tell you, but I wasn't sure how you'd react."

"Why would I react? If you're happy, then I'm happy for you."

Her mother frowned. "But…"

"I don't understand why you'd keep it a secret. From me, of all people."

"The past year has been good for us. I didn't want to make things awkward, but Bob and I recently decided to make it official."

"Awkward?" Zoe frowned. She thought they'd moved out of the awkward stage where her mother did things on a whim without telling Zoe. Acted like the child instead of the parent. Or at the very least, she'd decided to finally act like a family. "That explains why Bob would stop by at odd hours to 'help you' get ready for a show. You were dating him right under my nose."

"You make it sound sordid. Everyone loves the chief."

"Including you?"

"I think so."

She thought so? "You'd better be sure. This isn't like when I was growing up and you dabbled in relationships. He's clearly besotted with you."

"I would never hurt him." Her mother stepped back. "And this isn't your concern. You have your own relationship problems to deal with."

Just like her mother to throw the onus of the argument back at her.

"We aren't talking about my marriage."

"Maybe we should. That is, if you even have one. Mitch has been back almost two months now. Are you ever going to tell him where you two stand?"

She'd been working on it. *Getting better*, she thought. But her mom was right—Mitch deserved an answer. But he'd hear her decision before Samantha did.

"This isn't the place to discuss family problems."

"I agree. And I'm not sorry I kept this from you."

Samantha twirled and marched off to her boyfriend. Her boyfriend? Zoe shuddered. Did that sound weird or what?

"You okay?" Mitch asked, camera in hand as he sidled up to her.

"My mother has a boyfriend, which she failed to tell me about."

Mitch cringed, guilt crossing his features.

"You knew?"

"The chief swore me to secrecy."

"How many other people knew?"

He shrugged.

"Great. Just great," she muttered and headed to the other side of the yard for a cold drink. Just when she thought she was getting a handle on one area of her life, another went haywire.

"You're upset," Mitch said as he joined Zoe. He hated the hurt in her eyes. Had put it there himself too many times in the past.

"Why wouldn't I be? This is huge and my mother kept me out of the loop, as usual."

"She didn't mean to hurt you."

"Then why not tell me?" Zoe's face became downcast. "I thought things had changed. Mom was so much help when I moved in, then after

Leo was born. I felt like we finally had that mother-daughter relationship I'd always longed for." She shook her head. "It was a fantasy."

He doubted Zoe would agree, but he had to make her see she was wrong. "From the outside, it looks like you do have that bond."

"What do you mean?"

How to put it in words? He decided to just say it. "I've had the opportunity to watch you two since I've been home. At first, I was surprised at how easily you and Samantha get along now, so unlike when we were kids. How many times did we meet at the beach and you'd cry over another argument with your mom? Or vent when she forgot one of your events?"

"Leo probably had a lot to do with the change."

"I'm not so sure." He lowered the camera, letting the strap around his neck carry the weight. "She doesn't say it, but I believe she's proud of you, Zoe. With everything on your plate the last few years, you've shouldered it and kept going."

"I had to."

"Sure, but not everyone handles the stresses in life well. You became a mother, town mayor, even a widow for a short while, all because life threw you curves and yet you survived."

She tilted her head. "Why are you telling me this?"

"To suggest that you should give your mother a break. She's gotten more settled in her art career. In life. Seems you both have." He paused to let the truth sink it. "Maybe she sees you can take care of yourself and it's okay for her to have her own life. To lean on someone else now."

"She's always had her own life," Zoe whispered, glanced into the crowd as if seeking out her mother.

"Not as much as you'd think."

Zoe's head jerked at this.

"I'm not denying she put a lot of responsibility on you. She depended on you when you were a kid because she didn't have a partner. It was always the two of you. Now, you have a child, a job. A husband." He sent her a pointed look. "I'll bet she feels out of the loop."

Zoe's face softened as the truth dawned on her. "I hadn't thought of it that way."

"Life doesn't always turn out like we plan, Zoe."

A grudging smile crossed her lips. "How'd you get so philosophical?"

"Almost dying puts life in a different perspective. That, and being a parent."

"True." She took a flute of champagne from a nearby table and handed it to him, then took one for herself. "Toast?"

"To what?"

"Finally figuring out what being an adult means."

They touched glasses with a clink and drank.

He wanted to stay here and talk to his wife. Pretend the rest of the world didn't need them. Maybe later he'd suggest they get a quiet drink together. "I should get back to taking photos."

She stopped him from leaving by placing a hand on his sleeve. He looked down at her slender fingers, the one with the slim gold band on the fourth finger, and back to her.

"Thanks."

"For what?"

"Talking some sense into me. Being so good with Leo." She swallowed. "Being alive."

"Not like I had much control over that, but I'm glad I'm alive, too."

They stood looking at each other when Nealy interrupted their moment.

"Mitch, we need pictures of the bride and her friends before lunch starts." She looked at Zoe. "That includes you."

Mitch bowed. "After you."

Zoe giggled and joined the other women, Mitch snapped picture after picture, enjoying the sparkle in his wife's eyes. She'd had so much to handle on her own since he'd been gone and that was on him. If she let him, he would make it up to her. His patience might be running thin, but he owed her time to make up her mind. Running the studio was fine right now, and the freelance job would keep him in Cypress Pointe. It would keep Zoe happy.

Maybe, in time, they could venture out to other locations, the three of them, where he could show her that she didn't always have to play it safe. That they were stronger together, something they'd missed the first time around.

He'd meant it when he said nearly dying had changed him. Each day was a gift. His health was improving. And even if returning to the physical state before the accident might not be in the cards, at least he was surrounded by his family, able to commit himself to a job he loved.

In time, he'd get answers about the accident and the past would be firmly behind him. He'd be able to place all his attention on his family.

Playing it safe had never been his strong suit, but as he watched his wife laugh with her friends, he decided she was worth making adjustments for as long as they stayed together. Now all he had to do was wait on her.

"See you've taken to wedding photography," the police chief said as he strolled up beside Mitch.

"Piece of cake. Wyatt and Jenna are easy subjects, especially since they can't pry themselves away from each other. Makes my assignment simple."

Bob chuckled. "They do make a good-lookin' couple. Wyatt needed to find himself a measure of happiness."

The men went quiet. Wyatt deserved a second chance. It reminded Mitch that he and Zoe did, too.

"How about you and Samantha?" Mitch asked, checking the settings on his camera. The light under the tent had begun to fade. Were rain clouds rolling in?

Bob took a hardy swallow of the bubbly in the delicate glass that looked like a fragile hostage in his beefy hands. "Zoe figured us out."

"She told me."

"She isn't happy."

"Did you really think she wouldn't be upset that you guys hid the truth?"

"Tried to tell Samantha otherwise." Bob

shook his head. "That woman has a stubborn streak a mile long."

Mitch chuckled. "True. But Zoe's not a kid anymore. She deserves to be spoken to plainly."

"That whole mother-daughter dynamic doesn't work well for those two."

"I guess Zoe was hoping that had changed."

Bob's gaze scanned the tent, grimaced when he spied his ladylove. "I'd hate to be the thing that comes between them."

Mitch slapped him on the back. "Don't worry. I talked to Zoe. Tried to get her to see your side."

"And?"

The hopeful expression on the normally stern man's face would have been uncomfortable if Mitch didn't understand how the guy felt. "They'll be fine."

Bob let out a shaky breath. "This datin' thing is harder than I remember."

Mitch twisted a dial on the back of the camera. "Some milestones in life never change."

"Speakin' of datin', how's it going on your end?"

"We're moving closer to middle ground."

"That's good, right?"

"Pretty sure. At least, I feel like we've talked

things through. Heading toward a good chance at working out our issues."

Bob glanced across the room and frowned. "I know datin' is a younger man's game, but maybe you two talk too much. Go out and have fun."

After looping the camera strap around his neck, Mitch glanced at the older man. "Are you giving me advice?"

"Go take that girl for a walk on the beach. Hear it's romantic."

"Who told you that?"

The chief sent him a grin. "Samantha. Been out there at sunset a couple times." He winked. "Scores major points."

Mitch laughed. "I'll see what I can do."

As the chief strolled away, Mitch's mind started turning. They lived in a beach town. Gorgeous sunsets that translated into sharing romantic moments, if a guy were to take advantage of the opportunity in his own backyard. He weaved through the guests to find Wyatt, who was alone for the first time since saying "I do."

"Nice ceremony." He decided to rib his friend. "You really wrote those vows?"

"Yep. Did a pretty good job, if I do say so myself."

"Heard plenty of women sigh afterward."

Wyatt grinned. "That was my intention. Of course, Jenna's sigh was what I was going for."

"Speaking of making women sigh, I have a request."

"Shoot."

"Mind if I grab a bottle of sparkly and two glasses? I'd like to take Zoe down to the beach later for a stroll."

"Sure, since you insist on not charging me for your time today."

"You're my best friend."

"And in the spirit of friendship, let me say you're making a good call here."

They shook hands.

The rest of the afternoon flew by and before Mitch knew it, he was packing up his gear. Most of the guests had departed and the event crew had moved in to start clearing up. Zoe was chatting with friends when he made his way to her.

"Ready to take off?"

She glanced up at him, her smile bright. "Let me get my purse."

Minutes later, they were pulling out of the driveway.

"Do you mind if we stop by the beach?" Mitch asked.

Zoe glanced up at the gray sky. "It looks like it's going to rain."

The weather might be problematic, but Mitch was determined to see this through. "Humor me."

She sent him a curious glance. "Okay. What did you have in mind?"

"You'll find out soon."

As Zoe parked, dark clouds were gathering over the water. Most of the beachgoers had scrambled to their cars to head home. Still, the old electric sensation of excitement sizzled through Mitch's veins.

"Are you sure about this?" Zoe bit her lower lip as she scanned the horizon.

"It's time you and I had an adventure," he said, opening the door before common sense stopped him. He wasn't a guy to hold back just because a little rain might interfere with his mission.

He fished the bottle and glasses from the back seat and held them up. "You and I are celebrating."

"We are?" She laughed, her hair tousled by the wind as she exited the car.

"I'm alive. We're together. That's all I could ask for." He rounded the vehicle and took her hand, leading her to the sand. "Lose the shoes and let's have fun."

Despite the heavy humidity and promise of a storm, his heart lightened at Zoe's laugh. They might not be kids any longer, but they could still enjoy a special moment together.

The waves were choppy and white tipped, the scent of rain and sand tickling his senses. Stopping just before the surf, he opened the bottle, the cork zinging into the sky with abandon. Zoe held the glasses while he filled each one. Setting the bottle down, he held up his glass, the wind baring down on his upraised arm.

"This wasn't exactly how I pictured this, but here's to us. To finding each other again."

They clinked glasses and drank. The surf eddied around their ankles. Zoe cried out and nearly lost her balance until Mitch steadied her. They stood close, gazes locked, the wind and threat of rain growing stronger around them. He moved in for a kiss, as electrifying as the static in the air. He missed this. Missed them.

Before he had a chance to deepen the kiss, a loud crack of thunder had Zoe jumping away. As if on cue, fat raindrops hurled down on them.

Mitch grabbed the bottle and they ran through

the downpour, laughing the entire way. Once in the safely of the car, shivering and wet, Zoe reached in the back seat for a towel.

"You always carry towels with you?" How like her to be prepared for the worst while he ran straight into the storm.

"It's Florida in the summertime. We're bound to get caught in the rain one time or another."

He flashed her a smile. "But it was fun."

She picked up the wet weight of the skirt and let it fall. "If you call getting drenched fun."

"C'mon. It was an adventure. Like we used to share."

Zoe ran the towel over her face. Droplets of water ran from her hair to her slender neck.

"We should do this more often now that I'm home."

Her brows rose. "What are you talking about?"

He angled himself in the seat to face her better. "I have the beach photo shoot scheduled for Monday. Come along."

"Mitch, I have a job. Responsibilities."

"Ditch them for a few hours. You said you'd rearrange your calendar."

"You're right, I did. And I will."

She tilted her head toward the heavy rain.

"Getting caught in the rain kick-started you, didn't it?"

At the change in her voice, he grew wary and reined in the exhilaration still feeding his racing heart. "I'm happy to be back on course. Look, the shoot is just a few hours. You'll be there in case I need help."

Her eyes narrowed.

He wiped the water from his face, his high spirits sinking at her dubious expression. "I'm still getting headaches." That was true.

Her lips twitched. "You've convinced me," she said. Sticking the key in the ignition, she fired up the engine. Tossing the damp towel at him, she backed out of the parking space.

The drive home was quiet. His elevated mood plunging as the storm passed as quickly as it had kicked up. Sun streamed through the cloud cover.

Today, he'd felt more like himself than he had in months. His old self, muted by the effects of the accident, had been revived by the power of the storm. But he had to question, would the jaunt to capture beach scenes be enough to satisfy his inner adventurer? He'd vowed to make things right with Zoe. To give her, and Cypress Pointe, a chance. But would staying put really satisfy him? He wanted to do the right thing, but the freedom he'd just experienced on the beach opened up his eyes to the truth. He ran on risk and adrenaline. The very things Zoe shied away from.

He'd just have to try harder. Find ways to make his career more exciting here. He'd do it for Zoe.

CHAPTER FOURTEEN

MONDAY MORNING, ZOE found herself sitting in her office instead of out at the beach location with Mitch. He was supposed to come by the house yesterday but called off the visit, claiming a ferocious headache had sidelined him. Although she couldn't see him through the phone line, his voice had sounded muddy, masking the pain.

She'd wanted to soothe him somehow, but he'd told her to stay home, as he was lying low for the day. Then, early this morning, he'd called to say he'd canceled the photo shoot. At her urging, he promised to call his doctor and go to the clinic if necessary. No point in being foolhardy, she'd told him, which only got her a responding grunt.

He probably wouldn't call the doctor.

Stubborn man.

It shouldn't bother her, it was his hard head after all, but she was concerned and wanted to take care of him. That part of their relationship hadn't changed: the need to care.

She'd come to terms that this was the way she was wired. But her family? Friends? She knew they thought she was borderline extreme. Deep down, she agreed. Problem was she never made any changes. Why didn't she make changes?

Because it's easier to ignore what makes you tick than to fix it. Easier to make excuses than face your fears.

Ironic, coming from the woman who wanted to make everything better.

Since her husband refused her help, she'd come to the office instead, to a morning full of calls to return, fires to put out and decisions to make. The reality of it all was enough to give *her* a headache.

She rose from the desk and moved to the window. Her office gave her a second floor view of Main Street and just a hairbreadth sight of the beach. Her gaze caught and held on to the small piece of sparkling water visible to her.

Today, the sun shone bright, but her mind replayed the Saturday afternoon romp in the rain with Mitch. She didn't want to admit it to herself, but the race to the car had been fun, the

vibrant current coursing between them an aph-
rodisiac. She'd wanted to keep kissing him in
the storm, reinforcing the underlying certainty
that she'd gone and lost her heart to him again,
no matter how cautious she was determined to
be. Mitch, holding her hand, laughing as carefree as when they'd been in high school, had
awakened a long dormant part of herself, the
curious take-a-chance young girl she'd lost at
the bank the day she'd been held at gunpoint.
The cautious girl who'd walked away from the
experience and never looked back, despite the
flicker of exuberance she'd kept buried, and ignored, deep down inside. Why else would she
have ever fallen for a guy like Mitch if there
wasn't still a living ember of risk waiting to be
fanned to life?

Since she was being totally honest with herself, she comprehended what struck her most
while dashing through the rain was the look
in Mitch's eyes when they finally found shelter in her car.

Freedom.

There was no denying Mitch Simmons was
addicted to freedom.

This was the first glimpse she'd had since
he'd returned home, the first whisper of the
old Mitch. It scared her as much as it electri-

fied her. Which made her shiver in her shoes because she had to ask herself, where was the old Zoe? The one who didn't take chances or controlled every minute of every day? The wife who'd been the one to put limits on their marriage?

Gone. Wrenched from her and tossed into the turbulent storm-fueled depths of the Gulf waters. Along with all her fears and trepidations?

No. If anything, seeing the real Mitch brought her back to her original fear that he'd leave her again. Leave behind the woman who wanted to run through the rain, but didn't want to do it alone. Didn't want to raise her child, like she had her mother, all by herself.

If she gave her heart to Mitch again, if he broke it a second time, she wouldn't recover.

Shaking off her melancholy, she turned her gaze to Main Street. Townsfolk hurried about, running errands, rushing to work. She noticed Police Chief Gardener talking to a young man. Reassuring a tourist, maybe? Why not? That was part of the man's job. Making people feel secure.

Not stealing away their mothers.

"Stop with the pity party," she admonished herself at the thought of her mother with a serious boyfriend and returned to her desk. Samantha had made it clear she and the chief were going to continue seeing each other.

"We're in love and you can't stop us," Samantha had said with trembling surety when they'd finally hashed it out, which only made Zoe stand her ground more. Once again, she'd been thrust into the mother role. Once again, she needed to take control of the situation.

"Why would I try?" she'd retorted. "You're an adult."

"I am and that's why I'm ninety-five percent sure we're staying together."

"How does the chief feel about those odds?"

"Eighty percent sure we'll get married."

Zoe had finally broken down and laughed. It had eased the mood in the room. Her mother was just as unsure about life as ever. Once they talked it out, apologized and shed a few tears, they'd ended up watching *While You Were Sleeping*, their favorite rom-com, and eating popcorn. One of the many good memories she'd had with her mother since Leo was born. Maybe the last, if Samantha married the chief and Zoe had to find a new place to live.

The intercom buzzed. She pressed the red button on the phone console. "Yes?"

"There's a call for you. Says he's with the military."

"I'll take it." Zoe pressed the blinking button. "Zoe Simmons. How may I help you?"

"Mrs. Simmons, I'm Major Evans with the US Army. I'm actually trying to contact your husband, Mitch. Would you please pass on his current contact information to me?"

Uneasiness shivered over her like ghostly fingers. "May I ask what this is about?"

"I'm afraid I can only discuss it with your husband. It is important I find him."

Zoe didn't have much interaction with the military, her only example being Mitch's father, which didn't help her much. But she'd dealt with enough constituents to recognize the steel in the man's voice. If he didn't want to tell her what the call was about, he wouldn't. Even if she pressured him or refused to cooperate, he'd find another way to locate Mitch. She was usually good at getting what she wanted, when it came to the town. This was about her husband.

"Are you sure I can't help you?"

"Positive."

At least she had this man's name, phone number and the knowledge he was looking for Mitch, just in case of what, she wasn't sure.

She rattled off Wyatt's address and cell phone number.

"I must warn you, Major. My husband is under the weather today so I can't guarantee he'll speak to you."

"I'll take care of it," he assured her.

He signed off, leaving her with questions. Was Mitch in trouble? Was this about the accident? With her 10:00 a.m. meeting looming, she put the questions on hold and spent a heated hour with the zoning committee trying to agree on the new restoration of an old building down by the marina verses just razing it. The motion ended up being tabled until another time. Government bureaucracy at its best.

She worked through lunch and was just getting ready to read an updated city financial report when her intercom buzzed again.

"Yes?"

"It's your mother. Sounds important."

Samantha had Leo all day today. He'd been sleepy and unusually fussy when she'd left, which was odd since he'd just woken up, but her mother had assured her she'd keep an eye on him.

She pressed the console button. "Mom?"

"Zoe, Leo is burning up. I called the pediatrician and he said to bring him right over."

"Why didn't you call me sooner?"

"I thought he'd be fine. I'm sorry. I'm getting him into his car seat as we speak."

Zoe had risen and was searching for her purse. "I'll meet you there."

"Should I call Bob? Arrange a police escort?"

Her mother's outrageous question stopped Zoe for a second. "No. Just go. Drive carefully," she nearly shouted as an afterthought.

Ten minutes later she pulled up to the pediatrician's building. Her mother had arrived already because she could hear Leo crying from the other side of the parking lot. Running, she passed the chief—had her mother really called him?—to snatch up her baby. Leo calmed for a moment when Zoe held him, then he tugged on his ear and let out a loud wail. She ran inside, leaving her mom and the chief behind, hurrying to the doctor's office.

She was told to take a seat, even though Leo was having none of it. She cooed, paced, sang a song and finally rocked him to a drowsy state, to only then be called back to a cold examining room to have the fussing start all over again. He refused to let the nurse take his temperature, even though Zoe could tell by his heated skin that it must be high. When the doctor came in, Leo took one look at the man and howled. Thankfully, the doctor's ease with crabby children and frazzled parents had mother and son calm in minutes.

"It's an ear infection," Dr. Birney diagnosed. "Let's start him on an antibiotic here and I'll give you a prescription for home."

"This isn't the first time we've been here for the same problem. Why does he keep getting infections?" she asked.

"Chronic earaches come from a buildup of fluid. Because Leo seems to be in here more often than I'd like, I'm thinking the buildup initially doesn't bother him until it gets painful. His fever seemed high today, not the usual low-grade we expect under the circumstances. We may have to consider putting tubes in his ears until he grows out of this stage. We don't want the fluid to cause any future hearing problems."

"Future hearing problems?" Her chest grew painfully tight. "No, I don't want that."

"Let's get him feeling better and then discuss the options."

"But shouldn't we—"

"Not today, Zoe. Let's get his fever down and go from there."

The doctor typed into the computer while Zoe rocked Leo, blinking back tears. At least the emergency hadn't been more dire. Ear infections, they could handle. The nurse came in with a small cup filled with bubblegum-pink liquid and had Leo swallowing it before he knew what had happened. He puckered up his face, fisted his hands, then sagged against Zoe, finally out of steam.

"He'll feel better soon," the nurse assured Zoe.

"The prescriptions will be up front," the doctor said as he moved away from the keyboard. "I'll see him in a few days."

She nodded. "Thanks, Doctor."

He opened the door, only to have Mitch come barreling in at the same time, his face pale and drawn.

"Is Leo okay?"

The doctor stopped his forward momentum. "He'll be fine." He held out his hand. "Mitch? I'm Dr. Birney. Heard a lot about you."

"Great. Um, and Leo?"

"Just telling your wife he'll be fine. I'll give you a few minutes to get the little guy ready to go home."

The doctor closed the door behind him. Mitch hurried over, taking Leo's small hand in his. "What happened?"

"Ear infection." She glanced at him. "I'm so sorry I didn't have a chance to contact you. My mother called me at work and I raced over. How did you find out?"

"The chief. He came by Wyatt's to give me a lift over."

"Please don't tell me he turned on the emergency lights when he drove you here."

Mitch shook his head. "What? No."

Leo's heavy lids drooped until he totally nodded off.

"Tough visit?" Mitch asked in a low tone.

"Always scary when he's crying and I'm trying to soothe him."

She held Leo out for Mitch to take him. "Let's check out and go home."

Leading the way, Zoe took care of the insurance information, collected the paper prescriptions and made another appointment. Leo slept the entire drive home and hadn't moved when Mitch carried him inside and placed him in his crib.

"He's so still."

"The screaming wore him out."

Mitch jerked his head to look at Zoe.

"Okay, it wasn't that bad, but he must have been fighting the infection for a few days."

"You didn't notice?"

Her spine straightened at his accusation. "He wasn't acting sick until today. I hadn't a clue until Mom called me."

"Sorry. Didn't mean to imply you weren't paying attention. Seeing him in the exam room took me aback."

"I get it. First baby sickness for you."

"Yeah. I don't like it."

Zoe rested her head on his shoulder. "Never gets easy."

They stood staring at their son in the quiet room. The adrenaline started to wear off and Zoe's muscles went limp, but she shook off the effects. "I need to get Leo's prescriptions."

"Go ahead. I'll stay here."

She ran the errand, stopping for takeout along the way. When she got home, she went to her room and changed into shorts and a T-shirt. Poked her head in Leo's room to find Mitch in the same position she'd left him in, leaning over the crib. She then went to the kitchen to start a pot of coffee. Leo may be resting now, but she knew from experience he'd be fussy after a few hours of sleep.

Minutes later, Mitch joined her. "He's still sleeping."

"It's good for him." She took in his worried gaze. "We need to recharge our batteries while he's resting. We may be in for a long night." She held up a bag of burgers. "Best I could do last minute."

He took a seat and they divvied up the food.

Zoe unwrapped her burger, releasing the succulent scent. "In all the excitement, I didn't ask, how are you feeling?"

"The headache was easing off when Bob came by." He rubbed his temple. "Came back with a vengeance once I saw Leo."

"Stress triggers the pain?"

"Seems that way."

"Do you need to take anything?"

"My meds are at Wyatt's and besides, I don't want anything putting me to sleep. Not until Leo is better."

Zoe took a bite of the burger and regarded Mitch. He was pale, like he'd been when he'd first come home. It bothered her, especially when he'd been full of life just a few days before at the beach.

"Sure you can handle this?"

"He's my son, Zoe."

"I just don't want you making yourself sick, too."

He lowered the burger he'd been about to bite into. "I'm not the sick one. But I'd give anything to change places with him so he didn't have to suffer."

"Spoken like a true parent."

As much as she wanted to, she decided not to pester him about his role as a parent or patient. To make sure she didn't slip, she sipped her iced tea.

"You told Leo's doctor about me?" Mitch asked, breaking the silence.

"I had to. For the medical history and all."

His lip quirked in the corner. "It wasn't because you missed me?"

"No. Now that we all know you're just fine." She shifted in her seat. "We do have something to discuss."

One brow rose.

"The doctor suggested inserting tubes in Leo's ears. To keep him from getting so many infections."

"It's that bad?"

"Frequent." She went on to explain the problem and how to solve it. "We need to decide. Together."

He nodded. "It is for his benefit?"

"I've done the research. Yes."

Reaching out, he placed his hand over hers. "Then we should have it done."

Zoe let out a breath she hadn't realized she was holding. We. One simple word that removed the weight she'd had to carry on her shoulders alone since the day Leo was born. "Okay. We'll get the details at the next doctor's visit."

He tilted his head toward the living room. "Mind if I camp out on the couch tonight?"

There was no way she was sending him away. Even less of a chance of him leaving.

"I suggest you get some sleep before Leo's next dose of meds. He'll let us know when it's time."

"Thanks, Zoe."

She swallowed the lump in her throat. "Anytime, Mitch."

In a matter of a few days, Leo was pretty much back to his usual self. It still amazed Mitch how quickly kids got back on their feet. Leo's goofy grin and cool skin went a long way in easing Mitch's headache. Enough to reschedule the photo shoot at Horseshoe Beach to this muggy Thursday afternoon.

While Leo had been sick, Jack Parsons

called to inform Mitch he had a conflict in his schedule and wouldn't be near Cypress Pointe until the following month. So worried about Leo, Mitch had told him they'd catch up later, his only concern at that moment being the welfare of his son.

Now, standing on the beach, the sun high, the temperature balmy, a sense of foreboding swamped him. Getting answers to his past had moved to the top of his list in importance. After Leo's medical scare, it became crystal clear that he needed a clean slate before he could ever be a family man. Needed to know what went down that day before pledging his life to his wife and son, because the more he remembered, the more he realized the accident overseas wasn't random. No, it had been thought out and executed in a way he'd only seen the military pull off. Which created a whole different level of anxiety.

"Hey, what about the rise over here with the cluster of sea oats?" Zoe called out from a few feet away. Her dark hair lifted in the breeze, along with the scent of vanilla she favored. She tucked the lose strands behind her ear, her face in profile, taking his breath away.

Spending the last few days nursing their son back to health had been huge. He'd watched

Zoe, in awe of her abilities. She'd been born to take care of others, a point of contention between them just a few years ago, but seeing her soothe their son was like nothing they'd ever shared before. When she'd had to run into the office, she'd left Mitch alone with Leo, sure now that he could handle any calamity thrown at him without worry or needing to call in reinforcements. Her trust went a long way in easing his concerns. They'd weathered this emergency together, bonding them like nothing in their marriage had done before.

Once Leo was on the road to recovery, Zoe had agreed to accompany him to Horseshoe Beach for his location shoot.

"You're sure, being the busy mayor and all?" he'd asked. "You don't like leaving Cypress Pointe."

She'd smiled gently at him. "You canceled everything to help take care of Leo. I can repay the favor by going to the beach with you." Her eyes went dark. "I need to do this, Mitch."

Her answer was far from simple, so he hadn't argued, happy to have her along.

Gazing at her as she trudged through the sand, dressed in a yellow T-shirt and denim shorts, he had to admit, the spot she'd selected was a good place to start.

"Good eye," he told her.

"Between you and my mother, I've picked up a few artistic abilities of my own."

He handed her his gear bag after removing the camera. "Mind holding on to this?"

She looped the strap over her shoulder. "It's what an assistant does, right?"

"Not sure. I've always handled photo shoots on my own."

"Guess there's a first time for everything."

"For you, too," he said, changing out the lens. "You're usually in control."

She shrugged. "Which gets old after a while."

He tried not to gape at her.

"What?"

"You love being in control."

"Do I?"

He frowned. "I thought you did."

"Me, too, but expectations have gotten a bit blurry lately." She waved off her explanation. "Today, I'm going to enjoy being the assistant and let you call the shots."

"Okay, then. Let's do this."

He spent the next hour taking photos from different perspectives. Different angles. The small inlet, shaped like a horseshoe, created a myriad of artistic choices. Taking Zoe's suggestions on what might be interesting, it occurred to him that this was the most fun he'd had on a job in a long time.

A family passed by, laughing and darting about on the sand, father and son racing each other for lengths at a time. Could this be what it would be like when Leo got older? Spending the day together, playing with his son? Not off to parts unknown, taking pictures of other people's children?

His best work had always been taking candid shots of people from all walks of life in different situations, whether playing in a park or surviving in a war zone. Mitch possessed the uncanny ability of revealing the depth of the human spirit. While it had filled his soul before, now Zoe and Leo filled that space.

"Come on," Mitch said once the family splashed into the water. Back to work. "I want to get a few shots of the abandoned snack shack now that the shadows are getting longer," he said, pointing to the old structure.

Zoe hooked her arm through his as they strolled toward the old shack. Once, Horseshoe Beach had been a local hot spot. But the surrounding town had fallen on hard times and tourists now made arrangements to visit thriving beach towns, like Cypress Pointe. They were silent for a while before Zoe said, "I saw you people watching."

"And?"

"People are the most powerful forces in your pictures."

He'd learned that back in the beginning. With the click of his lens, he could forever capture the range of human emotion, from tragedy to joy. The more intrigued he was, the more powerful his images became.

"I'm surprised one of the big magazines hasn't called to offer you an assignment."

"Who says they haven't?"

Zoe shielded her eyes against the sun with her hand. "You didn't say anything."

"That's because I turned them down."

"Why?"

"Life has been much more interesting in Cypress Pointe. I also need more time to heal if I'm going to take a big job seriously."

"Then why take this local job?"

He couldn't explain, just knew he wasn't ready to go back to that world, so he'd kept a low profile. "This suits me right now."

"Do you miss it? Taking photographs around the world?"

A loaded question due to their past. "Not as much as I would have thought."

He hadn't dwelled on it much, busy now with the studio sittings and other scheduled events. Lately, whenever he thought about it, he didn't miss the challenge of chronicling a global event. Yes, the people had always intrigued him, but the traveling had just been a way to keep running from their marital problems. Since coming home to his wife and son, traveling didn't appeal. But the people still did. Putting the focus on people as subjects enabled him to catch lasting moments in time. And he could do that here in Cypress Pointe and the surrounding areas just as well as any place else in the world.

"I enjoy the studio," he confessed. "I thought I would hate being cooped up in a small space, but I was wrong. There are plenty of characters to keep me interested. I'm never bored."

"But?"

"There are no buts. I like photographing weddings and families." He gave her a sideways glance. "Like hanging out with my wife."

They came upon the old faded structure, boarded up, aged by the elements and time. He took multiple shots, intrigued by the shack. The light hit the wood perfectly and brought the old place to life, at least in his mind's eye.

"Hey, can you get me the longer lens?" he

called to Zoe, still focused on the changing light and how it affected the process.

He snapped a few more times before hearing Zoe say, "What's this?"

Glancing over his shoulder, he saw Zoe walking toward him, holding a small object in her hand. Once in the shade of the building, she held it out. The picture of her he'd taken at the fund-raiser.

"I've been carrying this around with me for a while now," he said sheepishly.

Her brow wrinkled. "I don't recall you taking any pictures of me."

"You didn't know."

She studied the print. "The food bank fund-raiser?"

"You love your job and it shows," he said, as if that alone explained his motivation.

When she looked at him, tears glistened in her eyes.

"Did I do something wrong?"

She sniffled. "You never showed this to me."

"It was a spontaneous moment. I'd focused on you from across the room and the look on your face captivated me, so I had to take the shot. There was this…reflective expression on your face. I couldn't resist."

Zoe stared at the print in her hand. "I can't recall what I was thinking about."

"It was during the fund-raiser, so maybe what a good job you'd done?"

They stood in the shadow of the snack shack for a long moment before she handed the photo back to him.

"You keep it," he told her.

"No. I like that you carry it around with you."

His chest squeezed. Why hadn't he ever thought to carry a picture of her when he traveled the world? To keep her close to his heart? Because it hadn't been important. Until he almost lost her. Now he had another chance.

"I'm thinking that working for this small press and the studio should keep me occupied. What do you think?"

"You're asking me?" Her face relayed her surprise. "You've never done that before."

"Well, we have this partnership thing going now. It's working pretty well."

"If that's what you want, Mitch, I'm all for it." A slow smile spread across her lips, lighting up her face tinged pink from the sun. "And speaking of all in, we're going to dedicate the new playground this weekend. Up to being the official photographer for the day?"

"Sure, if I get to spend it with you and Leo."

"Then consider yourself hired."

"Great." He reached for the gear bag and stowed away his camera. "What do you say we go get a cold drink? I'm hot and thirsty. Heard the Sand Dune is still open."

"That dive?"

"It was good enough for us back when we were in school. Why not go visit one of our old stomping grounds?"

She shrugged, a twinkle of merriment in her eyes. "Why not?"

CHAPTER FIFTEEN

DARK CLOUDS SCUTTLED across the sky as Zoe and Mitch pulled up to the Sand Dune. She peered at the run-down building at the north end of the beach. It had been a long time since she'd stopped here. "Looks the same to me."

"How many times do you think we holed up here when we were kids?" he asked.

"Too many to count." She glanced at him. "Sure you don't want to go someplace more... updated?"

He opened the door. "We're here. Let's check it out."

As much as she'd rather gone somewhere else, she couldn't deny the nostalgia as they climbed the uneven steps to the worn wooden porch leading to an equally worn-out dining room. Mitch held the screen door open for her as she walked inside. The scent of sugary confections taunted her taste buds, and the chatter of young voices bombarded her with memories.

Dating. Long hot days spent at the beach.

Root beer floats. The idea of them getting married was first brought up here. Scanning the place quickly, she decided maybe spending an idle hour with Mitch wouldn't be horrible.

The school year hadn't started up yet, evidenced by the number of kids hanging out. Mitch found an empty high-top table in the corner and they sat, taking in the surroundings. Her gaze stopped at the wizened man behind the counter, doling out words of wisdom to the kids seated there.

"Mr. Wilson still works here?"

Mitch glanced over, a smile lighting his handsome face. "Looks like it. Being around these teens must keep him young." He turned back to her. "The usual?"

"Might as well since we're walking down memory lane."

He went across the room, striking up a conversation with the elderly business owner. How many times had he stood in just that position, elbows resting on the counter, leaning in to place all his attention on every word the man spoke? Only, now his shoulders were wider and his face carried lines of experience, a different look from the boy she'd fallen in love with.

Zoe noticed Mitch rub the side of his leg.

Bony fingers of guilt unnerved her. Had she put too many demands on Mitch? Would he wake up one day, see what he'd given up and resent her all over again?

She hoped not.

Minutes later, he returned with a double-portion banana split, scoops of vanilla and chocolate ice cream already melting around the creamy fruit slices. He pointed to the two red cherries on top. "We don't have to fight over them."

"Wow. You went all out."

"That's what you do when you want to impress the girl."

Flutters kicked up in her stomach. The kind that came when Mitch focused on her. Made her believe everything would be all right, just like he'd assured her back in high school.

She took the spoon he'd handed her and dug into the gooey calorie-laden treat. "So, you want to impress me?"

"You haven't figured that out yet?"

"Maybe I'm afraid what's happening between us is too good to be true."

He shook his head. "Always expecting the worst."

Was she? Probably. After the bank robbery, caution was stamped on her heart. Even though

Mitch had tried to coax out the risk-taker she'd been before the shooting, she'd held back. Allowed herself to cower when she should have been brave. Her impromptu idea had nearly gotten her and Bethany killed.

It was easy to get things done for the good of the town, but her personal life? Not so much. Especially since Leo had arrived. She'd probably grown more hypervigilant than ever. But was it also an excuse? By making Cypress Pointe a strong and thriving place, was she selfishly insulating herself and Leo?

Until Mitch had come home and reminded her that there was more to life than caution and control. Just like he'd done when he'd skateboarded into her life all those years ago.

Pushing aside the morose thoughts, Zoe spooned up a portion of ice cream and fruit, a burst of tastes and textures exploding in her mouth. "Mmm. I'd forgotten how good Mr. Wilson's desserts are."

"Don't tell me you don't splurge once in a while?"

She scooped another spoonful. "Not normally."

"Trying to keep your girlish figure?"

Rolling her eyes, she pointed her spoon at him. "You're out of control."

He winked. "You like it."

Yes. She did. Way too much. From the compliments, to the long looks, to his place in Leo's life, yeah, she liked it all. So why didn't she tell him? Take the leap and give Mitch the answer he wanted?

They ate in silence, polishing off the dessert in no time. Zoe grabbed a napkin to wipe the ice cream from her lips. Her fingers trembled as Mitch watched with stark emotion in his dark eyes. Was it her imagination or had the temperature in the room risen ten degrees?

She wadded the napkin in a tight fist, trying to come up with a way to sever the blazing connection before they both overheated. "Any regrets about being back?"

He shook his head. "Leo's the best. And after everything that went down, I think I needed a break. You can only see so much, run so far, so fast. You get to the point where you doubt anything you do is good enough."

"As much as I didn't like all your traveling, you know I was never against your work."

"I do. I also came to understand that after a while, chasing stories was my way of dealing with the miscarriages."

In the act of lowering her napkin, her hand stilled in the air. "What? You never said anything. I mean… I knew you were hurting, but…"

"I knew how much you wanted a baby. You spent a lot of time grieving and I didn't want to pile on with my own pain."

"If I'd known… I was angry because you weren't there for me."

"At the time, I felt there wasn't anything I could do to help you. You were sad and hurting…and I… Nothing I did relieved you of your pain."

Had she made it so difficult for him that he'd had to leave rather than grieve together? "I'm so sorry," she whispered, mortified at how her actions had affected him.

Mitch reached across the table to take her hand in his. Squeezed tight. "In retrospect, neither of us handled the losses well. I made my own share of mistakes."

Still stunned at his revelation, she remained silent.

"You want to know one of the last things I remember just before the crash?"

She nodded, her throat too tight to speak.

"I'd decided that was my last story for a while. I was coming back to fight for you. For us."

Her eyes went wide. Stung with hot tears.

"I can't quite recall what, exactly, cemented the decision, but when I was in the overturned truck, I kept thinking I'd never make it back to you, never get a chance to make things right, and it broke my heart."

"And all that time, I thought you were dead," she said in a hoarse voice. "Thinking you loved your job more than me."

"I'm not your mother, Zoe."

The truth cut deep. Mom had always put her art first. Then Mitch. They both said they loved her, but they'd put their passions ahead of her needs and it had stung with unfathomable pain.

"Yeah," Mitch continued. "For a while I let my career be number one and look at what it cost us. You thought you were a widow and I lost a year of my son's life."

"How did we ever let the rift in our marriage get so out of hand?"

"It's hard to remember now." He loosened his hold but still kept her hand in his. "So in answer to the question you've been asking since I came home, I don't know what my career will look like. I may want to travel, if it's for a worthy story. Or I may want to stay put in Cypress Pointe."

"On the one hand, I'm relieved. Having you

home is nice." Her smile faded. "But on the other? Your work reached a lot of people. Your impact shouldn't be forgotten or pushed aside."

"I'll figure it all out." He emptied the bowl, finishing the last swirls of cream and brown syrup. "You do the same thing, you know, only on a different scale."

"Do what?"

"Point out changes that should be made, like the food bank, for instance. Or the new playground at the park. Hard work with big rewards."

She blinked. "I hadn't thought of it that way."

"Every time you come up with a new way to make Cypress Pointe a better place to live, you're touching lives."

Her chest went tight. She was proud of what she'd accomplished, even if it was born from fear.

"I was going to surprise you," Mitch said, "But I can't wait."

"Surprise me with what?"

"The new playground you spearheaded? *Suncoast Spectacular* wants a layout. Even though you asked me to tag along, I was already scheduled to shoot on Saturday."

"Really? I'm thrilled. It was more of a personal project, because of Leo, but I'm happy the magazine exposure will draw more people to the park."

"I'm glad we're making it a family day."

"Leo can see what his daddy does."

"Along with his mom, the mayor."

Their gazes met as shadows darkened over the room. Outside, the wind had picked up and the humidity in the air grew thick.

"Looks like the daily rain blowing in," Mitch observed.

Zoe slid off the stool. "We should get home."

The clouds had increased as they stepped outside. In the distance, thunder rolled. As they drove back toward town, the wipers swished across the window to clear off the steady rain.

"Do you want to come over for dinner?" Zoe asked.

"I think that banana split was dinner." Mitch chuckled. "But no, I need to go by the studio. Look at today's shots. Finish a special project I started."

She pulled onto Main Street, double-parking in front of the studio to drop him off.

"Thanks for today," she said, suddenly conscious of the shift in the atmosphere that had nothing to do with the rain and thunder. Mitch slipped a hand behind her neck, his fingers tangling with her hair, and gently tugged her in his direction. Their lips met. So natural. So real. Like the years of being at odds had melted in the blink of an eye.

The moment stretched out as the kiss deepened. Just as she leaned closer, a car horn blared behind them. Mitch broke contact, his gaze piercing hers. She shivered, trying to breathe evenly, waiting for more.

"I guess you should move."

"Move where?"

He shot her a lazy grin that had her heart galloping harder.

The horn blared again.

"I'll talk to you later."

Disappointed, she nodded. Then he was gone.

Driving back to the house, Zoe replayed their conversation at the Sand Dune. She'd never known how Mitch had dealt with the miscarriages. In her own pain, she hadn't thought to ask. It bothered her that she could have been so clueless of her own husband's suffering. She'd been so quick to blame him for their marriage falling apart but hadn't been able to accept her role in the damage. Today had been quite a wakeup call.

She blinked back tears of regret and by the

time she'd pulled into the driveway, she had made a decision.

Once in the house, she headed straight for the bedroom, running into her mother who was collecting Leo's toys.

"How was your day?" she asked, trucks and stuffed dinosaurs in her arms.

"Mitch got some great pictures."

"You can tell me about it over dinner."

"Give me a couple minutes, Mom."

She hurried on before she could change her mind about her mission.

Closing the door behind her, she opened the top drawer of her dresser and pulled out the envelope with the unsigned divorce decree. Taking a breath, she removed the papers and sat on the bed. Stared at them for a moment, waiting for the usual anger to wash over her. When it didn't come, she ripped the papers in half. Again. Then again.

A peace that had eluded her for a long time settled over her shoulders. She collected the pieces of paper and deposited them on the dresser top before joining her mother. Next time she saw Mitch, she'd give him her decision, to get back together and be a family.

Samantha looked at her with curiosity as she entered the kitchen. "Is everything okay?"

The scent of simmering tomato sauce made Zoe's belly rumble.

"It is now," she said, taking a place at the dinner table, hungry despite the banana split she'd eaten just an hour earlier.

THE NEXT MORNING, the bell positioned above the door to the studio clanged, announcing a customer. Mitch, immersed with the special project that had become very personal, started when he heard a male voice say, "Hello?" Remembering that Sandy had left to run an errand, he walked up front to find a man dressed in an army uniform, perusing the work area.

"Can I help you?"

The man stuck out his hand. "Major Evans. I left a message on your cell."

"That's right. Sorry, I meant to call you back, but my son was sick and in the excitement, I forgot."

"It's okay." He glanced around. 'Is there someplace we can talk? In private?"

Mitch didn't like the gravity of the man's tone. "Sure. Let's go to my office."

A sense of high alert was impossible to ignore. He offered the Major a seat and closed the door.

"What's this all about?" he asked, taking his seat behind the desk.

"The accident in Jordan. I have some questions."

"Why would the army be interested in my accident?"

The Major's steady gaze met his. "We believe you might have information that will help us tie up a case we're working on."

"I'm still fuzzy about the events that day, but I'll help any way I can."

The Major opened the file he'd carried in with him. "You were in Jordan working on a story at a refugee camp, correct?"

"Yes. I'd been in the area for a while and this time I was helping a boy find his father."

The Major nodded. "You were working with a man named Jack Parsons?"

"That's right."

"And you've been in contact with him?"

"Yes. Once I remembered more of the accident, I figured out he was also there. I finally tracked him down a few weeks ago. We were to meet but he canceled last minute."

"That meeting won't be happening."

Surprised, he asked, "Why not? I was hoping he could help me jog loose some details about why we were attacked."

"I'm afraid you contacting Parsons has opened a door."

Mitch frowned. "What kind of door?"

"One that has alerted them that you aren't dead."

Them? "Why would my telling Parsons I'm alive be a problem?"

The Major paused before saying, "Do you recall the name of the company he worked for?"

Mitch rubbed his temples. He could feel the start of a headache. "No."

"Does Allied Brothers Defense ring a bell?"

Mitch closed his eyes. Ran the name around in his mind. And like a dam cracking open to allow water crashing through, events unfolded before him.

Walking with Hassan, trying to come up with a plan to find his father. Seeing Jack in the distance. Waving. Jack, a look of surprise crossing his face, turning to the other guy after handing him an envelope. Mitch stopping in his tracks to see the other man open the envelope, take out what looked suspiciously like money and stuffing it back inside. The other guy running off. Jack, head down, moving quickly in the opposite direction.

The next day, rebels attacked an outdoor

market in a nearby town. A town where Allied Brothers, a private contractor firm, had just pulled out, leaving the townspeople unprotected and at the mercy of a violent takeover.

A raw groan escaped Mitch's throat.

"You remember?"

He nodded and relayed the details of the incident.

"Allied Brothers have been on our radar for a while. We have intel that the company pays local rebels to attack areas the company vacates after reporting it is safe. The rebels hit hard, Allied goes back in, this time upping their fees where we've already employed them to safeguard. Until now, we couldn't pin anything on them. After an investigation, we discovered your eyewitness account could help us nail them."

Stunned at what he'd just heard, Mitch shot a pensive look the Major's way. "I remember talking to Jack after I saw him. He came up with a bogus story about buying goodwill with the locals. I guess I didn't want to know what was going on. I acted like I believed him."

"It wasn't until we found the boy you were helping that we discovered the truth. He also saw the exchange."

Alarm skittered through him. "Is Hassan okay?"

"Yes. We have him in protective custody."

"And his father?"

The major shook his head.

Mitch blew out a breath. "So what happened the day of the accident?"

"From our reports, Parsons figured out his mistake. Joined your group last minute to keep an eye on you. His buddies followed in a truck. Staged an attack."

"Yeah. I got that part." He rubbed his head, the fading scars sensitive to the touch. "Once the truck flipped, a guy knocked me unconscious."

"Can you picture him?"

Over the screaming headache now firmly entrenched in his skull, Mitch recalled the scene. Until now, he'd only been able to make out a hand holding the gun that had clocked him. The more he forced his mind to think, the less he could make out. "I'm sorry. I'm not sure I actually saw his face."

The Major took a photo from the file and slid it across the desk to Mitch. A man in his forties, black hair, dark sunglasses, wearing fatigues, the desert in the background. Mitch lifted the picture. As he studied the face, a shiver went through him when he noticed the scar dissecting the man's cheek.

"Who is he?"

"Chad Duncan. CEO of Allied Brothers Defense and the subject of a joint task force investigation."

Mitch stared at the photo, but instead of any recognition, his head pounded harder, causing double vision.

"Are you okay, Mr. Simmons?"

Mitch lowered the picture and rubbed his eyes. "Headache."

"I understand you experienced a brain injury."

"Yes. Trying to force memories makes the pain intensify."

The Major nodded. "I'm going to leave this picture with you. Maybe, in time, you'll remember more."

"Where do we go from here?" Mitch asked, fighting the fatigue that came with battling the headache.

"We keep investigating."

"I want to help."

"Are you certain?"

"Of course. This guy, or people from his company anyway, tried to kill me."

"Parsons has gone underground, but Duncan is back in the States."

That explained Parsons's canceling their meeting after Mitch had revealed the only card he held to his advantage. His supposed death.

"You can help us by bringing the company down, Mr. Simmons. Your positive ID would make the case stronger once we arrest him but at the same time, I can't guarantee how Duncan will react."

Mitch closed his eyes. By calling Parsons, had he unwittingly set a trap in motion? Or had Parsons's surprise been a ruse? Now that Mitch thought about it, Parsons hadn't seemed that shocked when he'd heard Mitch's voice over the phone. If he and his boss suspected Mitch was alive, that would explain the feeling of "being watched" he'd experienced when he'd been traveling. Could this mean danger had followed him home?

No. Not now, when he was finally getting his family back.

"What about my wife and son?"

"I don't believe they are in danger. Duncan's not interested in them."

He opened his eyes. "Can you offer protection?"

"If needed. We have eyes on Duncan. He's

in Miami. We don't want to pick him up until we're sure our case will hold up in court. I'll let you know if he moves."

Made sense, even if it didn't make Mitch feel better.

"In the meantime, I've also spoken to the police chief. He is aware of the situation."

This was so much worse than he'd ever suspected.

"I suggest you lie low. Try to remember if you actually saw Duncan's face and can testify." The Major rose and gathered up his file. "I'll be staying in town for a few more days. You have my cell number. Call me anytime."

Mitch walked him to the door, his legs numb. How on earth was he going to explain this to Zoe?

They shook hands again. The Major exited the studio and to his dismay, Zoe walked in seconds later.

"Who was that?" she asked, gifting Mitch with a quick kiss. "You're not thinking about enlisting, are you?"

She chuckled at her own joke while Mitch tried to figure out how to explain the current situation.

When she glimpsed his serious demeanor, her smile slipped. "Hey. What's wrong?"

"We should go to my office."

Her expression turned serious. "I don't think I like the sound of this."

He ushered her along, his mind racing while pain drummed a steady tattoo against his skull. He didn't have any pain pills handy, but even those wouldn't bring relief after he told Zoe the truth.

"Take a seat. I need to tell you something."

"That's the man who called my office, isn't it?"

"He called you?"

She ran a shaky hand over her chin. "I forgot all about it when Leo got sick."

Mitch pulled his chair from behind the desk next to Zoe's. "He had some news about the accident."

"I don't understand. Was he there?"

He sank into the seat and faced her. Told her about the investigation, what he saw and how they needed his help to identify the man making illegal deals while working as a contractor for the US Army.

Her hands fisted in her lap. "Do you remember everything?"

"Most of it, but not the guy they're looking for." He picked up the photo. "The Major hoped seeing this would jog my memory."

Zoe glanced at it, looking uneasy. "And did it?"

"I'm afraid not."

"What happens next?"

"I want to help their investigation."

She jumped up. "And put yourself in danger again?"

"I have to do something, Zoe."

"Even if it affects your family?"

"It already affects us," he said quietly.

The color swept from her face. "What do you mean?"

"I'm a target, Zoe."

"Did the Major tell you so?"

"Not in so many words, but look at the facts. That accident? It was staged on purpose to silence me. Along with everyone else, if they thought I'd died, their secret was safe. The Major came here not only to warn me but to update me on the investigation."

Zoe slumped back into the chair. "Can't they protect you?"

"They have eyes on Duncan. And until I can positively confirm his identity, I'm only of use for part of the investigation."

"But you told the Major you wanted to help?"

"I do. By remembering this guy."

"How?"

"I don't know. Talk to my doctors. Maybe hypnosis. Anything."

"What happens in the meantime?"

"I'll keep you and Leo safe."

She rose and began to pace the small room. "How can you when you're the one who brought danger here to Cypress Pointe? Right to our doorstep."

"I'm sorry about that. But I have to help catch this guy. I have to see it through."

Stopping, she jammed her hands on her hips. "I'm canceling the playground ribbon-cutting ceremony."

"What? No." He stood. "This guy isn't going to risk showing up where there are lots of people around."

"You can't guarantee that won't happen."

"No. Not any more than I can predict any other calamity that might take place in the future. Neither can you."

Her eyes narrowed. "So what do you suggest?"

"We go about business as usual. The Major contacted Bob and he's aware of the situation."

"Great. My mother's boyfriend is involved in the danger, too." She shook her head. "I don't like this."

"Neither do I, but we'll go to the park. Celebrate another good accomplishment for the town. After, we can take off. Lie low for a while."

"Will that really change anything? This guy will just keep looking for you."

"Maybe, but in the end, the good guys will stop him."

"You hope."

"I saw the determination on the Major's face. Heard the facts. It'll happen." He reached out to take her hand, but she jerked it away. "We'll figure this out, Zoe."

"No." She stomped to the door, but had parting words before she walked out. "As long as you're in danger, you need to stay away from Leo and me."

CHAPTER SIXTEEN

ZOE STARED OUT her bedroom window at the gloomy gray sky. The forecast called for a fifty percent chance of rain.

"Perfect day for a ribbon cutting," she muttered under her breath.

The dreary weather only added to the menacing undercurrent that had taken up residence ever since Mitch's revelation. His memory had, for the most part, returned, in a most spectacular way. If she'd had to come up with a scenario of what happened to him, the truth would not have come close by a mile. The accident? Tragic, but people were in accidents every day. An accident because he'd witnessed something he shouldn't have? More like a movie plot than real life.

How could this have happened? Their world turned upside down by a chance encounter that had taken place on the opposite side of the world.

She still couldn't believe it.

"Zoe?"

She jumped at her mother's voice, placing a shaky hand over her chest as she turned.

"Ready to go?"

Puffing out a breath, she took one last glance in the mirror to check her cream-colored blouse and navy slacks, fluffed her hair, then picked up her purse from the bed as she went out of the room. "Is Leo ready?"

"Chomping at the bit. Literally. That teething ring has seen better days."

She stepped into her son's room to find him in the playpen, carrying on a conversation with his stuffed lion. Indecision gripped her. Should she stay home? Keep her child safe? Canceling last minute had been an option, but after discussing the pros and cons with the police chief, they'd decided to go ahead. There was no proof danger lurked outside her door. She couldn't stay inside forever.

"I'll be home later this afternoon," her mother chattered as she tidied up the room. "The art show will probably be a bust due to the threat of rain, but I promised to attend. Bob put up the booth last night so I'll be protected."

Protected.

Never before had reality hit her in the face as keenly.

Promised.

As the town leader, she'd always been good to her word.

Two words wholly at odds with her mission today. Couldn't hold up one if she didn't make good on the other.

When she talked to Mitch, he assured her they would be fine. She had to accept that, even though she wanted nothing more than to stay home, draw the curtains and keep her son safe in her arms.

"Okay, kiddo. Let's go."

Leo bounced around, giggling as she tried to pick him up. "Hold tight," she said as she rested him on her hip, smoothing his flyaway hair.

"What's gotten him all wound up today?" her mother asked.

"He knows we're going out. That's enough."

Samantha swooped in for a big kiss. "Have fun, little man. Grandma will see you later." She glanced at Zoe. "I'm not sure what's up with you, but enjoy yourself today."

She hadn't told her mother about Mitch's revelation, and apparently neither had the police chief. No point in having another worried person living in this house. "I'll try."

Procrastinating as long as possible, Zoe finally got Leo in the car seat and off they went. As she traversed the town, her mind stayed busy. She'd been worried about reconciling with Mitch because she was afraid he would leave, when instead he was determined to stay put and defend his life. His family. She admired the man he'd become, but how did she fight her own fears? Get through her own nightmares when he'd literally brought danger right to her?

It's not like he did this on purpose, her inner voice argued. No, but the results were still the same. They would all be looking over their shoulders until this stranger, this man who wanted Mitch out of the way, was apprehended. She couldn't fault Mitch for wanting to help catch the guy, but his actions reinforced all the fears she'd lived with since the bank robbery. Since the day she and her friend walked into danger, blithely thinking an adventure could never hurt them. She'd learned a hard lesson then, one that had formed who she was today.

And it had all come back courtesy of the husband she had fallen in love with again.

Pulling into the parking lot, Zoe was surprised to find a large crowd gathered in the park near the playground despite the cloud cover. Leo laughed and bounced when she settled him on her hip. She made her way through the throng, saying hello to various attendees as she headed in the direction of the blue-colored ribbon with the printed words *Grand Opening* in gold across the span of cloth. She found the chief waiting for her.

"Thanks for coming," she said as Leo reached out for the older man. To her surprise, Bob didn't scoop up Leo like he normally would. Instead, he seemed…focused. On what?

"No problem," he replied. "I felt you needed me here."

"Well, it is just a ribbon cutting," she said, adding a note of humor to her voice. "We've done this many times."

When he didn't assure her his presence was no big deal, her internal alarm clanged big time. "Is there something going on I don't know about?"

"Change of plans." His gaze met hers. "You should talk to Mitch."

That explained the cop face.

The ideal strategy was not to interact with Mitch until the current situation was resolved. Then they needed a serious sit-down.

Scanning the crowd, she glimpsed Mitch, dressed in a casual polo shirt and jeans, camera in hand, taking pictures. "I really don't have time. The ceremony is starting soon."

The chief sent her a scorching look. "Talk to him."

LOWERING THE CAMERA, Mitch's gaze swept the crowd. No one suspicious. Still, he remained on guard, especially when he saw Zoe head his way, Leo on her hip.

She wasn't happy. He could read it in her body language from twenty feet away.

"The chief said you needed to speak to me," she said, coming to a stop before him.

He swallowed. This wasn't going to be easy.

"The Major's people in Miami lost sight of Duncan. Early this morning, he was spotted in Tampa."

Her mouth gaped. "You think he's coming here? Today?"

Mitch nodded. "He must have realized his game is up and wants to take care of loose ends."

"Meaning you?"

"Most likely."

He watched her control her composure. "Why didn't you call me?"

"I only found out a little while ago. By that time, it was too late to cancel the ceremony. It was last minute, we couldn't figure out how to get the word spread in time. The chief is going to be stationed by you, so cut the ribbon, make the speech and leave. He also came up with a plan to divert the crowd, so play along."

She glanced down at Leo. "I… What…"

"Max and Lilli are going to take Leo. Just a couple of friends holding the baby while you make your speech. While you're busy, they're going to move to the police station for safety."

She tightened her hold on their son. "And you?"

"The Major has his men surrounding the park. I'll be fine." He kissed Leo's head and touched her hand with his. "Go," he said, his voice low and intense.

Setting her nerves on edge.

RETURNING TO THE area set up for the ceremony, Zoe had to force herself to get a handle on her emotions. They were using her ceremony to catch a bad guy? What surreal world had she woken up to this morning?

Max and Lilli waited for her, Max carrying on a low conversation with the chief. Lilli's face was solemn when Zoe joined them.

"Are you okay with this?" her friend asked.

"Like I have much choice?"

"But you do. You can choose to take Leo and walk away." Lilli patted her shoulder. "No one would blame you."

"Except the people who are trying to catch this guy."

"It's up to you."

Zoe bit her lower lip. She was no hero. She was a mom and the mayor, faced with a tough decision. Stay or go?

Yet she couldn't make herself leave.

She scanned the crowd, folks she'd known all her life, talking, laughing, waiting to hear what she had to say. Townspeople who had voted for her, stood beside her in her darkest days. Would they turn and run if presented with the same dilemma? No. They'd rally together. She was sure of it.

Despite her misgivings, despite being sure she was foolish for sticking around, she had her answer. She'd stay and fight.

Turning to her friends, she reluctantly handed Leo off to Max.

"He'll be fine," Max assured her in his steady voice, even though passing her son to him was like ripping her heart out. She knew it was for the best, just like she knew this elaborate ruse to catch Duncan was going to make her family safe in the long run. As long as things went as planned.

"We have your back, Zoe," Lilli said, a big smile planted on her face for show; Zoe could read the nervousness in her posture.

If her friends would willingly get involved, risk themselves to help her family, she could hold up her end.

She blinked back tears as Max stepped away with Leo and Lilli and the chief took his place beside her, speaking in her ear. "Just as a precaution, I have all my officers dressed in civilian clothes stationed around the playground. When I learned about the possibility of a problem here this morning, I called the owners of Swindler's Ice Cream. They offered to hand out free ice cream as a way to draw the folks away from here. As soon as you're finished speaking, tell the crowd to go to the far end of the park and I'll have my team redirect anyone who might want to linger around the play area."

"But what if they don't want ice cream?"

"Nealy is on the other side of the park, as well. Tell people in order to keep confusion to a minimum, they need a ticket to get on the playground. Nealy will stall them."

"You act like you know for sure this guy is in town."

"I don't, but we can't be too careful."

"Thanks, Chief. I'm glad you're on our side."

He nodded, then spoke in his lapel mic in a low voice.

Taking a breath, Zoe then greeted the crowd, flourishing the scissors to get their attention. All while her heart threatened to beat right out of her chest.

"Today we celebrate another milestone for the town," she said, her voice shaky at first, then picking up strength. "The thing I love about Cypress Pointe is how we come together. Like a great big family. That's why I ran for mayor, to make my town a safe and productive place to live."

She nodded over her shoulder at the new playground equipment behind her. "You all rallied together, holding fund-raisers and taking up collections, to make a beautiful place for the future generation to play and be kids for the short time before they grow up. We did that. You and me." She held up the ceremonial ribbon cutting scissors. "Here's to Cypress Pointe."

The crowd clapped and cheered as the cloth fluttered to the ground.

"Now, before we christen the playground, I want everyone to go to the far end of the park. We're giving away free ice cream before the park officially opens. Nealy is handing out tickets so we won't have major confusion once we move back to the play area."

At the mention of ice cream, the crowd was more than willing to trade swings and slides in order to fill their bellies first. Children, with their moms and dads right behind them, hurried to the tables set up in the distance. At this rate, it would take Zoe a few minutes to get to the police station. Townsfolk stopped her, thanking her for her dedication to the town, when all she could think about was gathering Leo in her arms and racing off, until she remembered her vow to fight. Still, no one was keeping her from getting to her son.

As she began to cross the grassy section of the park, mostly cleared out as the crowd had moved away from the playground, she noticed a man by himself, loitering near an empty bench. He was tall, with a ball cap pulled low over his eyes and polarized sunglasses hiding his eyes—odd, since the clouds obscured any sunshine. He glanced her way and Zoe froze, noticing the edge of a scar on his cheek.

Duncan? He sure looked like the man in the picture Mitch had shown her.

When she followed the path of his gaze, her stomach dropped. It led directly to her husband, who was walking in the opposite direction away from the children and their parents.

Digging her cell phone from her pocket, she dialed Mitch. No response. Drat. Why wasn't he answering?

Uncertainty rooted her to the spot. She searched for the chief, but he was preoccupied and too far way to be waved down.

She'd just made the decision to follow the plan and retrieve Leo when Duncan moved. Walking at a determined pace, his shoulders stiff, he turned his head left and right to check out his surroundings, and alerted Zoe that he was up to no good.

Suddenly, a thought went through her brain. *Mitch is the bait.* No wonder he'd agreed to stay in full sight. He *wanted* Duncan to come after him. His family was in danger and he'd found a way to save them.

Oh, Mitch.

Her chest tightened. He was doing this, knowing full well how much Zoe worked to keep away any threat of danger. This had nothing to do with risky behavior. Nothing to do with adrenaline or the thrill of getting a story. No. This was a man putting his life on the line for those he loved. Right at this moment, scared as she was, she couldn't have loved Mitch more than she already did.

Never mind the plan, now it was time to do her part.

With determination, she power walked toward Mitch. He dropped his camera into the gear bag and walked farther away from the crowd. She heard the chief call her name but ignored him, instead heading toward her husband, straight into danger. Closer now, she saw Duncan approach Mitch, pull an object from his pocket and aim it at her husband.

Bright dots flashed before her eyes. She stopped dead in her tracks.

In her memory, a gunshot rang out. The scar on her inner arm ached just as it had the day a bullet ripped through her flesh. She thought she might be sick. Did she really think she could make a difference?

The haze of the past cleared and second thoughts about intervening made her hesitate, until she noticed Mitch look her way. His eyes widened, causing Duncan to look around. She had her opening.

"Mitch," she called out, waving in his direction.

Duncan's focus remained on her. Mitch took that split-second opportunity and lunged at the man ready to harm him in order to save his own skin. Mitch's momentum caught the other man by surprise and they ended up toppling to the ground.

Barely able to breathe, Zoe ran their way. Before she could reach Mitch, a swarm of undercover cops surrounded them, yelling for the gun to be dropped. Duncan fought, but soon armed men pulled Mitch off him as they took possession of the weapon and dragged Duncan away.

It happened so quickly, Zoe marveled that she hadn't missed the entire takedown. But she had seen it. And her husband now stood, gazing at her.

Zoe ran to Mitch, throwing her arms around his neck. He hugged her back as she tried to slow her racing pulse and brush aside the residual fear. "We're safe," she kept repeating to herself.

Mitch pulled back to gaze down at her face. His jaw tightened imperceptibly.

"You did this on purpose," she accused.

A brief shadow covered his eyes. "I had to," he said, his voice raw.

"You could have left town. Taken the danger to parts unknown."

"I could have. But this seemed a more expedient way to take care of the problem."

"Mitch, I… It doesn't seem enough but, thank you."

"You have to know I'd do anything for you, Zoe."

He'd proven it, in spades.

"Once I tell the authorities everything I know, I'll be back, Zoe. Then you need to make your decision about us, once and for all."

He walked away, meeting the Major and falling into a heated discussion.

Your decision.

She'd thought she'd made it when she'd torn up the divorce papers. When she'd lost the fight to keep from loving Mitch again. When she was forced to face her own past and decide which was more important: overcoming fear or running away.

A tear trickled down her cheek. Did she know anything at all?

MITCH PRESSED THE DOORBELL, forcing down the nerves playing havoc in his stomach. Smoothed his button-down shirt and straightened the box he was holding. Ignored his shaky hands.

Zoe would give him her decision today. Either they were going to live together like a family or he'd leave, because the pain of losing her and being separated from Leo would be too much.

The door flew open. Zoe's brows rose.

"Sorry I didn't call first."

She ran a hand over her tousled hair, looking gorgeous in a T-shirt, shorts and bare feet. "Actually, I've been expecting you."

He held out the wrapped box. "For you."

Her lips pursed. Moments passed before she reached out. "What's this?"

"Open it."

A giggle came from just inside the door, then his son crawled into view.

"Come in," Zoe invited.

Mitch entered, picking up Leo as he went. The baby laughed and hugged him tight.

Zoe perched on the armrest of the couch, her fingers running over the paper.

"It's something I made for you."

Curiosity in her eyes, she tore at the paper, opened the box. Inside, nestled in sparkly tissue paper, sat a book, the words *Our Wedding Album* in cursive script across the front. Lifting the album, the box slipped from her lap to the floor. Mitch set Leo down and he scampered right to his new toy.

He watched as Zoe opened the first page. Knew the inscription from memory: *To my wife. I'll always love you, Zoe.*

She flipped one page, then the next and the next, each a memorial to their life together; featuring pictures from when they were teens, their wedding day, to more recent shots including Leo.

"When did you do all this?" she asked, looking up from the last page.

"I've been working on it for a while at the studio. Wanted to give it to you when I asked you to renew our vows."

Her eyes went wide. "Renew our vows?"

"Either way, whatever your decision is," he said, "I wanted you to have it."

She clutched the album to her chest. "Oh, Mitch."

"Look, I get it. What happened at the ribbon-cutting ceremony must have crossed a line for you. There's no coming back from that."

"But there is." Leo tugged at her ankle. She laid the album on the cushion and leaned down to pick up their son. "I've spent too many sleepless nights, spent too many endless hours thinking, and I've come to this conclusion."

Her eyes watered. "You had no control over events in Jordan or at the park. I haven't made life easy for you since you came home, shoot, even before then. I let my unresolved fears color my reactions. I know you'd never ever do anything to intentionally put us in harm's way."

"But I did and I take responsibility for it all."

She met his gaze, eyes shimmering. "I love you, Mitch. Always have, always will. You're my husband and the father of our son and deserve more than I've given you."

He took a step back. Afraid there was a "but" coming. Could almost see the invisible wall forming between them. Knew the last brick had fallen into place when Zoe stayed glued to the couch instead of walking into his embrace.

"Dada," Leo giggled, his arms outstretched.

Unsure, he stayed put until Zoe made her intentions clear.

"You can't leave. Leo needs you." She stood. "I need you."

Relief, swift and hard, overtook him. "Are you sure?"

She sent him a beaming smile. "Never been so sure in my life. You stood in harm's way to protect us. I could have run but instead intervened when you were almost shot. In a weird way, what happened in the park put things into a new perspective for me. Made me see I can't insulate our world. Bad things happen in life, but so do beautiful things. We worked together, Mitch. In a way that counted the most."

Her sentiment touched him, but she hadn't said if they were going to stay together. He needed to hear the words. "What is your answer, Zoe?"

She paused. Grinned. "I want more than anything for us to be a family. Maybe you need to temper some of your fearlessness and I need to work on being brave, but we'll figure the rest out as we go. For now, I'll be happy to watch the two men I love most discover the world around them while I tag along."

He crossed the room in two long strides, hugging Zoe and Leo tightly until Leo squawked. He pulled back and met her gaze.

"You're really sure?"

"Yes."

He kissed her hard and felt her love seep down to his toes. When Leo fussed again, Mitch loosened his hold, but his arms remained circled around his family.

"Coming back to you, finding out about Leo, I learned that I didn't need to run around the world for excitement or meaning. Raising

Leo with you, right here in Cypress Pointe, will be all the adventure I need."

She smoothed the hair on Leo's head. "And when you do need to go off to exotic locales for a job, we'll be right by your side."

Mitch kissed her again, love and gratitude welling inside him. Being at home would surpass traveling alone. On that dusty road back in Jordan, he'd had his eureka moment; he'd wanted a family all along, never dreaming how much until he'd almost lost them.

When he finally broke the kiss, Zoe said, "There's one thing that bugs me, though."

Mitch tilted his head, his expression in check as he waited.

"I can't believe Leo called you Dada first. He's never said Mama."

Barking out a laugh, Mitch hugged her again. "He will," came his positive reply. "There's plenty of room in the Simmons family, and in that photo album, to treasure all the memories we're going to share. Together."

EPILOGUE

SIX MONTHS LATER, Zoe stood at the edge of the wooden deck in the backyard of their new house. She and Mitch had just renewed their vows, surrounded by family and friends. They'd come a long way, she and Mitch, and she couldn't deny her love for her husband. After much discussion, they'd come to the mutual agreement to keep Mitch's base here in Cypress Pointe, holding a family meeting to vote whether or not he would take any of the offers for photo layouts located in faraway places.

The holidays had been eventful, this being the first Christmas Mitch had spent with Leo. There were way too many presents, Zoe had scolded, but she'd understood Mitch was making up for lost time. He'd surprised her by writing a check to the refugee organization assisting Hassan's village. Father and son had finally been reunited, thanks to the international coverage Mitch had garnered through different news agencies.

The New Year had brought new changes. Lilli and Max announced they were expecting. Nealy and Dane had just come back from Las Vegas where they'd gotten remarried. Jenna and Wyatt had bought a new house, and Jenna had confided in Zoe that they were hoping to have baby news soon.

Other friends, musicians Cassie Branford and Luke Hastings, held a private performance in honor of the festivities. Cassie's newly released album was wildly successful. If Zoe didn't miss her guess, she'd wager those two would be walking down the aisle soon.

She noticed Kady standing alone. Zoe sauntered in her direction. "Thanks for the beautiful flower arrangements. As usual, you came through "

"My pleasure," Kady said after a quick hug. "The Lavish Lily is busier than I could have ever hoped. My plan to be the number one florist for weddings in the area is taking off and working with Dylan's mother, a total professional, has increased business, too."

Zoe had no doubts. Kady had a way of coming up with exactly the right flower choices for her brides.

"Where's Dylan?"

Kady pointed to her boyfriend, who was pacing the yard. "He just got a call from one of his brothers. By the look on his face, it can't be good."

Dylan, a DEA agent, along with three other Matthew brothers all in law enforcement, lowered the phone.

"From what Dylan has told me, his youngest brother is working an undercover operation. I hope there weren't any problems."

Zoe nudged her friend. "Go."

Kady left to talk to him.

Zoe's mother and the police chief sat at the patio table with Mitch's parents, feeding Leo. Her son giggled and played with his food, despite his new grandfather's attempt to get him to eat.

Two arms circled her waist from behind. Mitch's cologne announced his arrival, even before his words.

"Happy, wife?"

She leaned back against his hard chest, savoring being cradled in her husband's embrace. Mitch still suffered infrequent headaches, but that seemed to be the last of the lingering effects of the brain injury. He was alive and home, which was all she could have asked for.

"Happy to have everyone I love in the world here today."

"And if you could do it all over?"

All the pain and hard times had been difficult, but had made them both stronger. In her mind, they deserved every bit of happiness they could carve out of life.

"I'd do away with the drama that got us to this point, but I'd never wish us apart again."

Mitch kissed her neck. "Good answer."

She turned in his arms, oblivious to the guests around them. "I'm proud to be your wife, Mitch. Here, or any place else on this planet."

He brushed his lips over hers for a long, satisfying kiss.

"And I'm proud to be your husband," he said when they surfaced. "As it turns out, Cypress Pointe is an awesome place to live. Especially since you're here."

Yes, Cypress Pointe was exactly her dream destination come true. For now, and always. And she was sure she could safely say that sentiment resounded with all the special people gathered here today.

* * * * *

Get 2 Free Books,
Plus 2 Free Gifts—
just for trying the Reader Service!

Love Inspired

Get 2 Free Books,
Plus 2 Free Gifts —
just for trying the *Reader Service!*

YES! Please send me 2 FREE Love Inspired® Suspense novels and my 2 FREE mystery gifts (gifts are worth about $10 retail). After receiving them, if I don't wish to receive any more books, I can return the shipping statement marked "cancel." If I don't cancel, I will receive 4 brand-new novels every month and be billed just $5.24 each for the regular-print edition or $5.74 each for the larger-print edition in the U.S., or $5.74 each for the regular-print edition or $6.24 each for the larger-print edition in Canada. That's a savings of at least 13% off the cover price. It's quite a bargain! Shipping and handling is just 50¢ per book in the U.S. and 75¢ per book in Canada*. I understand that accepting the 2 free books and gifts places me under no obligation to buy anything. I can always return a shipment and cancel at any time. The free books and gifts are mine to keep no matter what I decide.

Please check one: ☐ Love Inspired Suspense Regular-Print   ☐ Love Inspired Suspense Larger-Print
                    (153/353 IDN GMWT)   (107/307 IDN GMWT)

Name _____ (PLEASE PRINT)

Address _____ Apt. #

City _____ State/Prov. _____ Zip/Postal Code

Signature (if under 18, a parent or guardian must sign)

Mail to the **Reader Service:**
IN U.S.A.: P.O. Box 1341, Buffalo, NY 14240-8531
IN CANADA: P.O. Box 603, Fort Erie, Ontario L2A 5X3

Want to try two free books from another line?
Call 1-800-873-8635 or visit www.ReaderService.com.

* Terms and prices subject to change without notice. Prices do not include applicable taxes. Sales tax applicable in N.Y. Canadian residents will be charged applicable taxes. Offer not valid in Quebec. This offer is limited to one order per household. Books received may not be as shown. Not valid for current subscribers to Love Inspired Suspense books. All orders subject to approval. Credit or debit balances in a customer's account(s) may be offset by any other outstanding balance owed by or to the customer. Please allow 4 to 6 weeks for delivery. Offer available while quantities last.

Your Privacy—The Reader Service is committed to protecting your privacy. Our Privacy Policy is available online at www.ReaderService.com or upon request from the Reader Service.

We make a portion of our mailing list available to reputable third parties that offer products we believe may interest you. If you prefer that we not exchange your name with third parties, or if you wish to clarify or modify your communication preferences, please visit us at www.ReaderService.com/consumerschoice or write to us at Reader Service Preference Service, P.O. Box 9062, Buffalo, NY 14240-9062. Include your complete name and address.

LIS17R3

Get 2 Free Books,
Plus 2 Free Gifts -
just for trying the Reader Service!